This job with the drover just might save him,
if it doesn't kill him first.

THE DROVERS

BOOK 1: PREY

JOHN D. BROWN

BLACK
SWORD
BOOKS

The Drovers, Book 1: *Prey*

Published by Blacksword Enterprises, LLC

Illustration copyright © 2019 Dixon Leavitt

Series logo design copyright © 2019 Shawn T. King

Map copyright © 2019 Spenser Farnes

ISBN 13: 978-1-940427-18-8 (ebook)

ISBN 13: 978-1-940427-19-5 (paperback)

First edition: October, 2019

❀ Created with Vellum

GET EXCLUSIVE CONTENT!

Join John's newsletter to stay up-to-date with new releases and receive exclusive bonus content.

www.johndbrown.com

To the young men of Laketown.

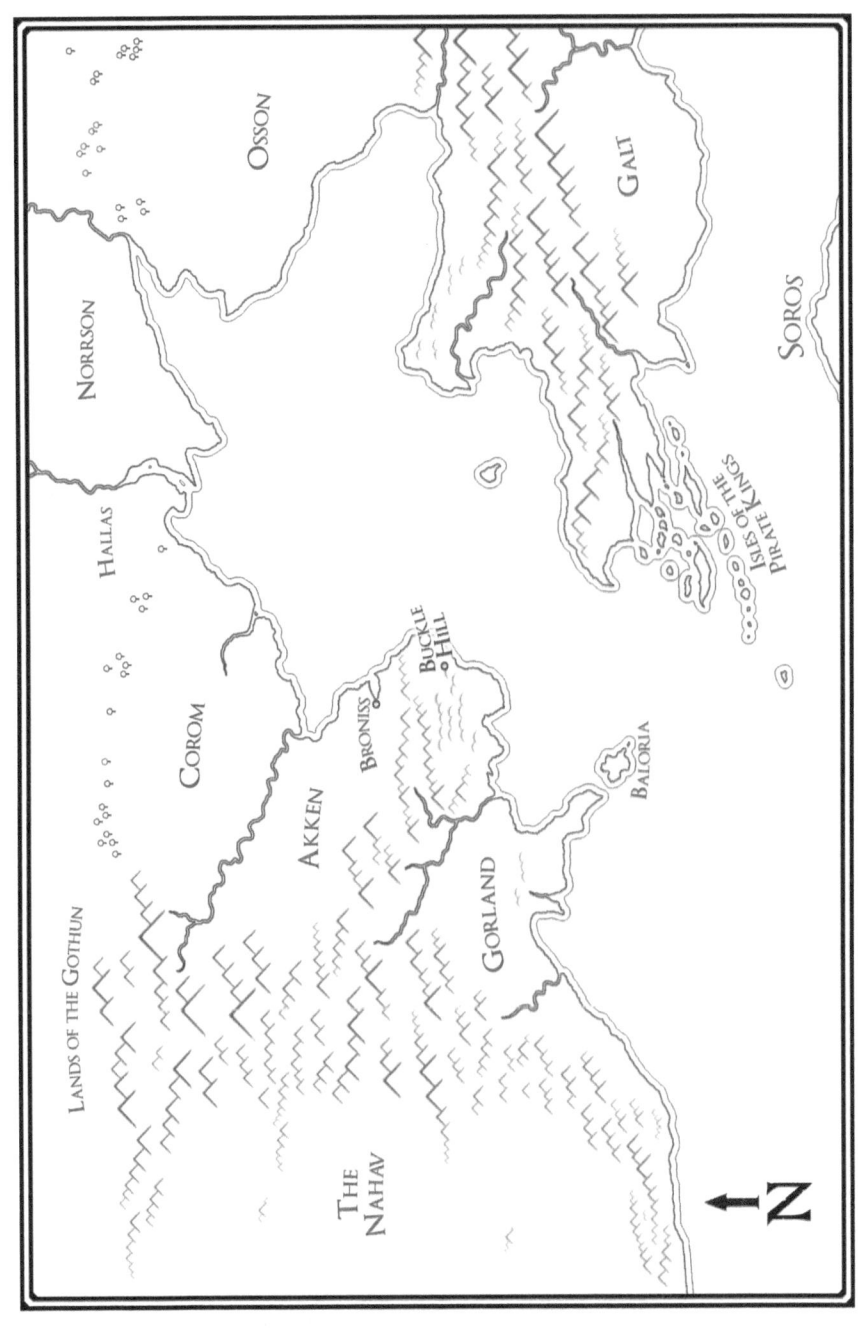

PROLOGUE

Borros figured the men would try to kill him and Lagash today.

If he were in their shoes, he would have waited until they reached Kog's Pass. But this lot was eager and impatient and thought they saw an opportunity.

He sat on his short-legged stool by the morning campfire with his breakfast of dried dates, hard bread, and watered vinegar. He was stroking Peer and Digger, his two dogs that the men most assuredly had poisoned.

Peer was the older of the two. Gray with ears and a snout that ran to black. He was smart. But obviously not smart enough to avoid whatever he'd been given. Digger was younger, a brown and white that Borros had gotten from a mountain shepherd. He was normally full of energy, but he could barely lift his head now. The two dogs just lay there, weakly keening with each breath.

They were excellent herding dogs. Excellent guards.

Excellent companions.

He stroked Peer again. The dog whimpered.

Anger boiled in Borros, but he refused to show it, for if the men suspected he knew, they would immediately attack.

Sunrise wasn't far off. The clouds were starting to turn pink in the east. Around him in the vale, the two hundred and twenty head of cattle he was driving to Broniss were dipping their heads into the dew-wet grass and getting their morning fill. And with him, at the campsite, were the four murderous men.

The skinny one was still sleeping a few paces away from the fire. The bald one was lying in his bedroll, hands behind his head, looking up at the dwindling stars in the sky. The third, the big hairy one, was sitting on a large rock picking breakfast out of his teeth with a horn toothpick. The fourth, Drogan, their leader, the one who liked to outline his eyes in kohl, was sitting on another short-legged stool across the fire from Borros, watching the flames.

He should never have hired them. But a week into this drive, his original crew had all become deathly ill, and he'd told himself he couldn't wait the week it might take for them to heal. Which was true. War with Osson was imminent, and the mage queen needed beef to feed her troops. Borros had contracted with one of the queen's agents and promised a delivery date, and you did not miss a delivery date to the mage queen. Furthermore, a portion of these cattle was put into his trust by an old widow and a few other of his neighbors. He'd convinced them it would be safe, and he wasn't going to short shrift them.

So he'd left his original crew to recover and hired Skinny and Baldy. A day farther along the trail, Skinny had said he knew of two others who could help. That's when Drogan and the big hairy one had joined them. It's also when Borros had begun to have misgivings.

Borros looked at Drogan and Hairy. They were definitely not going to wait. They were going to strike today. He could feel it. It was the dogs, of course, but it was more than that. He could sense it in the way they carried themselves. And the fact that they were avoiding each other's eyes. Not completely, but enough for him to know something was afoot. Furthermore, the tip of a scabbard was poking out of the hairy one's bedroll. A scabbard the man did not have the day before.

Drogan said, "I'm sure they'll get better. They're good dogs."

"Yes," said Borros. "Excellent hounds."

"We'll certainly miss their help, but the bright side is that it appears the rain has let up." He motioned at the sky. "Looks to me like it'll be a day full of sunshine. A pleasant walk to our next stop at the village of Buckle Hill."

Borros pushed down his rage and grinned. "It's going to be a corker," he agreed with great enthusiasm.

Drogan's eyebrows lifted with surprise at the energy in Borros's voice. "There's a happy man despite his setbacks."

"Indeed," said Borros, and his plan for dispatching these worthless turds began to take shape.

Drogan smiled his crooked-toothed, kohl-eyed smile, then shared the briefest of smug and knowing glances with Hairy.

"What was that?" Asked Borros.

"Just haven't seen you this chipper before," said Drogan.

"Right," said the hairy one.

Borros glanced at the dark trees where Lagash, his companion on this trip, had gone to do his business, but the man was still nowhere to be seen. Great birds, how long could it take for a man to relieve himself?

He wanted Lagash with him, but it didn't matter. Borros was done waiting. He, not these four louts, was going to choose the time and place for this fight. And right here and now seemed like very good ground for a fight. Besides, he wasn't going to be fighting all four of them anyway.

Like most such gangs of men, there was one who was their best fighter. And there was one who was probably not too far behind him. The fighter might be the leader. Or he might be the right-hand man. Either way, if you started at the bottom with the weakest, you would have to fight all of them. But Borros wasn't going to start at the bottom. He was going to start with Drogan. And when he fell, the rest would hesitate. That's when he'd take down Hairy. And then, with their deadliest men down, all thought of fighting would depart the other two.

Borros drained the last of the watered vinegar out of his wooden cup, made a loud sound of satisfaction, and set the cup aside. It began now.

He pointed at the tip of the leather scabbard poking out of Hairy's bedroll. "That's new," he said happily.

Drogan looked at the scabbard tip, then up at Hairy, and narrowed his eyes in the smallest bit of condemnation and worry.

"New?" Hairy asked, trying to feign ignorance.

"That sword," Borros said and pointed again.

Hairy looked down. "Oh, that," he said. "No, I've had that for almost a year."

"You didn't mention it when I asked what weapons you had for the job."

"Well, I," he stammered.

"I'm sure he did," Drogan said.

"I'm happy you have it," Borros said. "Surprised is all. I suppose that means you've done a bit of sword work then?"

"A bit," Hairy said.

"You mind if I have a look?"

Hairy glanced at Drogan for direction.

"Let the man see it," Drogan said, relieved. "It's a beauty."

"Right," Hairy said. Then he reached down, picked up the scabbarded sword and held it out to Borros.

Borros took it. The scabbard was covered over with leather the color of doeskin. White linen tassels hung at intervals along its length. And along the side, contrasting nicely with the light doeskin, was a dark woodland scene featuring two hunting dogs chasing some deer.

"Very nice," Borros said, not believing at all that this was Hairy's sword.

Drogan said, "He won it in Kava last year."

Borros grabbed the hilt, partially withdrew the sword, and immediately recognized the ornate design on the flat of the blade. It was a Norrson design of loops and curls. Until last night, this had been hanging above the mantle of the old farmer's house in the village six miles back. Back there a yellow ribbon had been tied around it, marking it as a memorial to a warrior slain in battle. The ribbon was gone. Probably now somewhere in Hairy's possession.

"That must have been some wager," said Borros.

"A drunken gentleman," Hairy said.

"Which teaches you not to drink," Borros said. "Or not to keep strange company when you do."

Borros held the blade up to the morning light and made a big show of examining it. "Look at this," he said and pointed at the figure of a running wolf incised into the blade. "A Himesbor blade to boot. Unless it's one of those fakes from Gorland or Trimu."

4

"I hear they're just as good," Hairy said.

"They're not," said Borros. "The only fakes worth their steel come from Cassamon."

"Well," said Drogan, "only a master would know."

Borros ran his thumb across the blade. It was sharp. He held the sword out, felt the balance, the comfortable grip. Noticed the brightness of the blade, which had been excellently maintained. As anything kept above the mantle and lovingly cared for would be.

Some distance away, Lagash of the Everlasting Toilet, emerged from the dark trees, and Borros took that as his cue. He stood with the sword, stepped back a bit, then walked through the form of the ox slowly, cutting down, following it around, then turning, acting as if he were trying the blade out. And he was. He wanted to have a good feel for it. It wasn't a Himesbor. He'd wielded those before, and such blades almost came alive in the hand. This blade was good, but it wasn't a Himesbor, which meant the mark of the running wolf was a fake.

He lunged, felt the old pain in his knee flare up, and finished the form.

"Looking like a champion, Master Drover," Drogan said.

Hairy wasn't as happy as his leader. He stood there eyeing Borros with suspicion.

Borros cut the air again in a smooth arc. "With such a blade," he said, "you can smite off hands." He shuffled a step closer to Drogan. "You can smite off legs," he said and brought a cut down close to Drogan's thigh.

"Whoa," Drogan said and leaned back.

Borros shuffled forward again, and then he put his full strength and speed into it. He whirled, grabbed the hilt and the blade in a two-handed grip for stabbing, and thrust the point directly at Drogan's face, stopping a hair's breadth from the man's nose.

"Shanks!" Drogan cursed and crabbed back.

"With such a blade," Borros said, "you can skewer a skull. I've seen it."

"What are you doing?" Drogan demanded.

"I wanted to like you," Borros said, keeping the blade pointed at Drogan. "I wanted to pay you. A good business transaction has such a satisfying feel to it."

"What are you talking about?" Drogan said.

"Give us back the sword," Hairy said in warning. Behind him, their bald companion kicked the skinny one to wake him up.

Borros said, "But then I had to fall in league with four thieves."

Drogan said nothing.

Borros continued, "Hairy there didn't get this last year in Kava."

"I did," Hairy said.

"You stole it. You went back last night. Instead of watching the cattle, you went back to the village and stole it from the wall above the mantle in the alewife's house."

"We did no such thing," Hairy said.

"You greasy dolt," Borros said. "How many times have I traveled this road? You think I never stopped at that alewife's house myself and took a mug through her window and saw the sword inside?"

Drogan's eyes shifted. He knew he'd been caught. It was plain on his face. But it appeared he was going to play it out until he could see a way to get the upper hand.

"Did you kill him?" Borros asked.

They didn't answer.

"This sword was given to his son who fought in the Dark War. A son who died fighting three Og."

He waited to see if any of them had the slightest bit of remorse.

"Three Og," said Hairy dismissively. "Nobody but an anointed would take on three Og. He probably deserted his post and pilfered this on his way out."

"Did you kill him?" Borros asked. "The old man?"

"We were there and out again in a blink," Drogan said. Then he took on a conciliatory tone. "What's the old geezer going to do with it anyway?"

"He didn't have to do anything with it."

"He'll get over it," Drogan said. "Meanwhile, we'll put it to good use. It's going to fetch a fine price in Broniss." He opened his arms generously. "Now that you know, we'll split the money with you. Each of us an equal portion."

"I can't abide thieves," Borros said, sword in hand. "I can abide liars even less."

"Okay," Drogan said and held his hands wide in submission. "You're right. I told the boys it wasn't a good idea. If it offends you so much, we can take it back."

"Yes, it's going back," Borros said. He knew the owner. A good man. A hard-working stable hand who'd barely managed to scratch out his existence after his lord had brought younger men in to do his job. A man whose only solace in the death of his son was the honor he had won. The honor memorialized by this sword.

"It's going back in style," Borros said, "and you're going back with it." And then something that had been puzzling him about these men fell into place. There had been something about some of their offhand comments that had struck him as odd. Jobs they'd been on. Places they'd been. But it all now came clear.

"You're part of that rotted band of louts, aren't you," Borros said. "Led by that big man. The one who likes to call himself The Bull. What's his name? Offa?"

Hairy and Skinny glanced at each other, and Borros knew he'd guessed right. He should have known. He shouldn't have trusted their references. He said, "If I'm not mistaken, there's a reward on your heads."

Drogan's kohl-eyed expression went from submission to calculation and disdain, for he obviously thought Borros was an easy and stupid target. Drogan shook his head in amusement. "He wants us to go back boys. He wants a little reward coin."

Behind Drogan, Skinny stood and grabbed his spear. The bald one pulled a long knife.

"What do you think?" Drogan asked. "Shall we go back?"

Hairy picked up his axe. "Yeah, we should go back, for the old man's daughter. She'd fetch a decent price at the market. And could give us a bit of entertainment along the way."

Drogan said, "Now that's something to think about. But not just yet." He stepped back from Borros, giving the others more room to fight.

"We were going to break it to you a little later today," Drogan said, "but since you've pressed the issue, we'll do it now. The four of us, we're going to take these cattle. That's going to happen whether you like it or not. But we don't have to kill you and your dark-skinned Sorosian friend. Put down the sword, and we'll spare you. Keep it, and the crows will be pecking your eyes out before noon."

"How generous," Borros said.

"We're not brutal Osson rot," Drogan said. "Just men looking for an opportunity. And you happen to have been it. Now put down the sword."

Borros could kill them. But then he'd have to bury them. And bury them deep, or they'd be dug up by some animal, and the crows and vultures would hover, or someone's dog would come to investigate and bring home a hand or femur, and then the lord of these lands would start a hunt for the murderers, and there would be a search, and the lord's court and lawyers. Days of time, maybe weeks. Weeks that Borros didn't have. He had cattle to get to the queen. He needed to move down the road and get to the village of Buckle Hill today.

Lagash finally arrived. "What kind of fun have we got going on here?" he asked.

"Took you long enough," Borros said.

Lagash picked up the wooden spade leaning against the wagon. The men behind Drogan fanned out to attack.

Borros wanted to run these four pustules through, for Digger and Peer. They deserved nothing less.

But he wouldn't. Better to let someone else deal with them, Borros thought. The villagers would be awake by now. And if the old man or woman hadn't noticed the missing sword already, they soon would. And the drovers that had just come through would be on the top of the list of suspects.

A band of villagers was probably on the road right now, coming after them. They could be here within the hour. If they were on horses, they'd be here much sooner. So he and Lagash would need to subdue these men without killing them. Although that didn't mean he couldn't bloody them a bit.

"Come," Drogan said. "There are four of us. You'll lose some cattle, but at least you'll walk away with your life."

"Such a lie," Borros said. "It wasn't even a good one. You could have at least promised me a dancing pony."

Drogan shrugged.

Borros smiled. "They used to call me The Mangler."

"Very nice," said Drogan.

With his free hand, Borros reached down to the pile of firewood and picked up a fat stick.

"They used to call me The Body Cleaver."

"Watch out," Hairy said in mock alarm, "he's got himself a stick."

Skinny chuckled and readied his spear.

"They used to call me Death."

"Right," said Drogan, and then he motioned at his men. "Please be good fellows and take care of Death, will you?"

Borros didn't wait for the good fellows to come at him. He'd always thought attack was better than defense, and so he hurled the fat stick at Drogan's face.

Drogan flinched, trying to duck the missile and, in doing so, presented a splendid target. Borros figured a nice stab in the leg would do the trick and lunged.

1

ROBBERS

Five months earlier, Ferran, a youth from the village of Buckle Hill, was pushing his wheelbarrow along an empty stretch of road. His wheelbarrow was loaded with a half-filled barrel of barley. His purse was loaded with coin. He'd just finished humming a rousing verse of *"The Race of Captain Red"* when three men wearing grain sacks over their heads stepped out of the trees ahead of him. The sacks had slits cut for eyes. Two of the men carried sticks that looked capital for beating someone black and blue. The other held a long knife.

Itch, Ferran's dog, stopped. He was a hard-muscled, short-haired, multi-colored mongrel with a big black patch around one eye. He growled, then barked at the men.

This deserted stretch of road was about nine miles into Ferran's fifteen-mile journey to Cor's village. His arms and back were aching because it was a long way to go with a wheelbarrow, especially for a young man his size, but he didn't mind the ache.

Today was a lovely day. In fact, he'd been singing most of the way because he was going to buy a set of used cheese vessels from a widow in Cor to replace the ones someone had stolen from his family. And those vessels were going to save him from being sold into bondage to pay their debts to the lord.

Ferran looked at the men and stopped, his alarm rising, but he didn't lower the wheelbarrow because he couldn't quite believe what he was seeing. It had been years since the last person was robbed on this road. In fact, he didn't know anyone who had been robbed here. This was not a road for robbing. It was a road for grannies and goose girls and lads with wheelbarrows.

"Put it down," the man with the knife said. "You'll be handing all of that over now."

"My barrel with its two cups of barley?" Ferran asked. "Are you sure you've got the right person?"

"Shut your trap and call off your dog," the man said. "And I don't want to hear any begging or wheedling. We want the barley *and* the coin."

Ferran realized this was no joke--he was actually being robbed. Fear shot through him. And then a surge of determination. He wasn't going to lose this barley, which was far more than two cups. Not to these louts or anyone else. He couldn't. He needed all of it plus the coins he carried in the hidden pouch tied around his waist to buy the vessels.

And that was another thing. The man hadn't said to hand over "any coin" but "the coin," as if he knew Ferran was carrying money. How had this brigand known he had any coins? Ferran was an urchin with a wheelbarrow, dressed in low-class, patched-up rags. Nobody would expect him to be carrying coin.

He knew if he were in other circumstances, the smart thing to do would be to run, immediately, and simply let these men take the barley. But he couldn't do that because the widow had said if he didn't show today with the full payment, she would sell her vessels to another who had expressed interest and was willing to pay more.

And he couldn't simply purchase a set elsewhere because he and his mother had already searched high and low. These were the only vessels in the district anyone was willing to sell that were cheap enough for him and his mother to buy.

He set the wheelbarrow down and arched his back to as if to relieve some pain and moved his hand to his belt where his sling was. "How can I call my dog off if my trap is shut?"

"This one's got a mouth," the taller one said.

"Come on, boy," the knife man said. "Be quick."

Itch was playing his role well, barking and snarling, attracting the men's attention.

Ferran sighed. "Okay," he said in mock defeat. "Just don't hurt me," and then he secretly pulled open the mouth of the pouch at his waist where he kept a handful of sling stones. Three of the stones were smaller, about the size of robin's eggs, excellent for sending mad dogs on their way. Two were larger, the size of hen's eggs, excellent for sending greasy, pig-stinking robbers packing. Or send them to their graves if you scored a smart shot to the head.

"Don't even think about it," the knife man warned.

"What? Are you talking about this?" Ferran asked, grabbing a stone and whipping out his sling.

"Get him!" the man growled.

The two taller ones charged. One went after Itch with his stick. The other rushed Ferran.

Ferran stepped back from the wheelbarrow to get some room, slipped the stone into his sling, and swung it back. He was going to sling the stone right into the man's sack face. But just as he brough the sling up and around, a fourth man rushed Ferran from behind and tackled him, slamming him into the dirt.

Ferran's head bounced off the ground. The stone and sling flew wide. He tried to scramble away, but the attacker punched him in the side of the head, then again, then a third time.

Ferran's ears starting ringing. The world turned a bit tipsy, but he kicked and tried to scramble up.

And then another one of the men was there. He raised his booted foot and stomped Ferran in the ribs.

There was a sharp crack. A pain sliced through Ferran, and he found he couldn't breathe.

The other man struck Ferran in the face. Another crack and more pain. Ferran saw white. Someone kicked him hard in the back, and Ferran flinched and curled in to protect himself.

Somewhere Itch was snarling and barking with rage, and then he let out a yelp.

Ferran tried to get up, but one of the men grabbed his feet and then his trousers, yanking them clean off. The other man yanked Ferran's tunic over his head, leaving him there in his small clothes.

"There it is," one of them said and drew his knife. "Hold him."

"No!" Ferran said and struggled.

But one of them struck him again, then knelt heavily on Ferran's shoulders and throat to keep him down while the other cut the cord around Ferran's waist and took the coin pouch.

"Stop," Ferran said. That was his family's salvation, slipping away like sand.

"Shut up," the fourth man said, but then Ferran realized the fourth man, from his size, wasn't a full-grown man like the others. He was a young man, probably in his later teens, someone maybe only two or three years older than Ferran.

"Tie him up," their leader said.

One of them grabbed his wrists and wrenched them behind his back. Another tied his ankles, then yanked them up behind his back as well and used the same rope to tie wrists to ankles. Then they pulled everything tight, leaving him hog-tied.

The one who had gone after Itch strode over holding his arm like it had been injured, his face still covered by the slit-eye mask. He walked up to Ferran and kicked him in the gut.

Pain shot through Ferran again.

"That one's for your dog," the man snarled. Then he stomped on the side of Ferran's head. "And that one's for you."

"All right," the leader said and waved him off.

"Rotted dog," the man said and kicked at Ferran's groin. The blow was hard, but he missed Ferran's manlies and hit his upper thigh instead.

Ferran grunted in pain.

"Go!" the leader ordered and shoved the man aside. And then the leader squatted down next to Ferran's face and looked at him with the brutal eye slits of the sack on his head. "You're lucky it was only a dog bite," he said, the smell of the man's sausage breath coming through the sack. "If that stone of yours had struck, well, I wouldn't have been able to hold them back. And you wouldn't be walking away from here. So thank your ancestors that you were slow in addition to being stupid."

Ferran heard the crack of breaking wood, and he glanced toward the sound. One of the big men was breaking the wheelbarrow. The two others joined in, jumping and stomping.

The blood from Ferran's broken nose was running back into his throat, so he turned his head down to let it run the other way. The thin stream of red blood pooled in the dry dirt.

"You tell anyone what happened here," the leader said, "and we'll find you. We know where you live. Remember that." Then he stood.

There were a few more crunches of the wheelbarrow, and then all fell silent. The silence stretched long, and Ferran began to wonder if they had reconsidered and were preparing to finish him off. He turned to see what they were doing, and found they were gone. He craned his neck to look up and down the road, but only the pieces of his smashed wheelbarrow remained.

The breeze gusted the leaves in the sunlit trees and over his bare stomach and legs. Some flies came to investigate him and the blood about him. One landed on his face.

He couldn't believe this had just happened.

Multiple places on his back, side, and face throbbed in pain. Blood was still dripping out of his nose and pooling in the dirt. He groaned.

Itch came over and licked his face.

"Yeah," Ferran said. "That was lovely. I want to do that at least once a year." Then he groaned again. More than ribs were broken inside.

Itch whined. Ferran looked over Itch's mottled gray coat, but didn't find any wounds.

"Looks like it's time we get a big ugly mastiff that can rip off arms and legs," Ferran said. "Would you like a buddy?"

Itch licked his face again.

Ferran tried to twist his feet and arms free, but the lashings were tight. He arched his back farther, his broken ribs stabbing him with a sharp pain, and bent his feet up more until he could touch the lashings around his ankles. He felt around and, at last, brushed the end of one of the ropes.

"It might be too late for our mastiff," Ferran said. "But the headman of the village of Cor has bloodhounds. We can track those whoresons."

He struggled with the rope, trying to loosen it, but had to stop for the pain.

"Or maybe I'll just lie here until some wild boar finds me and decides a bit of human flesh would taste good for dinner."

Itch just sat there, panting.

"I should have taught you how to unpick knots."

Itch whined.

And Ferran struggled again, failed, and tried yet again.

It took him about an hour to finally free himself. He then took stock of his condition, gingerly probing his wounds. He was badly beaten, but he found he could stand. More importantly, he could walk. He'd started early that morning, so it was not yet midday. And that meant there was plenty of time to track those whoreson, pig-stinking, scum, especially if the headman used horses.

He looked around, spotted his tunic and trousers tossed in some bushes. He hobbled over and learned that bending down made his side hurt like there was a little man inside him with a knife. So he knelt to pick his clothes up and grimaced as he put them on. The men had torn his clothes in a few places, which only meant he'd be adding more mends and patches to the multitude of patches that were already there.

He looked at the broken wheelbarrow. There was no way his family could afford a new one, but it looked like most of the pieces were recoverable. If he could get them home, he could have the carpenter help him put it back together. So despite the pain, he gathered up all the pieces and laid them at the side of the road. He'd get them on the way back.

And then he wondered why the men hadn't just wheeled the barrel of barley away. Why break a perfectly good means of transport?

Because they already had some other way to carry it, he thought. Horses. Or they'd split it, and each of them had lugged his portion away in a sack.

Ferran shook his head. It didn't matter how they got away. What he needed to do was get to the village of Cor, which was six miles down the road. He looked for his leather water bottle, but they'd taken it, so he set off, having to limp a bit because walking with a normal and free gait prompted that little man with his knife to start poking.

2

THE WIDOW

Ferran arrived at the village a few hours later only to find the headsman was out at some field half a mile away. A boy was sent to fetch him, and Ferran waited. While he did, a good woman of the village tended his nose and bruises and wrapped him with an old but clean cloth where the robbers had cracked his ribs. She gave Itch water and a small bone to gnaw on that he cracked and ate in short order.

The headsman came an hour later and heard Ferran's story. Then he rode off with three other men and his dogs. But Ferran didn't wait for them to come back. He needed to secure the cheese vessels and hoped to convince the widow to rent them, and so he thanked the good wife and walked to the house of the widow he'd originally intended to meet.

He found her with her adult daughter in the shade of her garden mending clothing.

"A good day to you," Ferran said. "I'm the son of Lutrell from Buckle Hill."

The widow smiled kindly. "Ah, come for the cheese vessels. Good, good, good. But what happened to you?" she said and motioned at his face. "Did you take a tumble in the rocks?"

Ferran told his tale. As he did, the widow clucked and shook her head in sympathy. But the daughter narrowed her eyes at him sourly.

When he finished, the widow said, "The headman has kept that road safe for years. How unlucky for you that today was the day when brigands should appear. In our own woods!"

"Well, I sincerely hope he catches these."

"He has excellent hounds," the widow said. "I have no doubt he'll track them down."

Ferran glanced at the daughter, found no sympathy there, and focused back on the widow. "I know you needed full payment today, but if by chance he doesn't find them today or recover all that was stolen, do you think we might be able to come to an agreement where my mother and I might—"

The daughter cut him off. "We are terribly sorry for your situation," she said, "but she cannot give the vessels to you with a promise of payment."

"I was hoping we might rent them."

"No," the daughter said firmly. "I'm sorry."

"My daughter's husband," the widow began. "There was an argument."

"Mother," the daughter said in warning.

"There's blood money that needs to be paid," the widow said, cutting to the chase.

The daughter sighed in frustration.

Blood money was the payment set by law that one person must pay to next of kin when one person maimed or killed another.

Suddenly Ferran pieced it together. The daughter's husband was probably being held in some prison. And if he couldn't come up with the blood money, he'd be sold for it. And if he'd killed someone, even that might not be enough, and they'd come and take the payment from his wife and even this widow, for she was next of kin.

"I see," Ferran said. "How much would you need?"

The widow looked at him with sympathetic eyes. "I'm sure the headman will return with all that was lost." She patted the bench next to her. "Sit with us. Let us wait."

She began her mending again. Ferran knew the stitch and offered to help. She gave him a pair of yellow trousers and needles. When he finished, he handed it to her.

She held it up to examine his work. "Look at this," she said and held it for her daughter to see. "A very tidy stitch indeed."

Her daughter agreed without much emotion.

"My mother taught me," Ferran said.

"What does your father do?" the daughter asked.

"He farmed and helped the smith."

"You say that as if he is no longer with you."

"He disappeared on a patrol of the western mountains three years ago."

"Oh my," the widow said. "Was he killed?"

Ferran shrugged. "Disappeared." Many had speculated. They'd sent him out to scout ahead, and he'd simply disappeared. Some wondered if he'd fallen from some height or been attacked by a bear. Others wondered if he'd maybe been taken by some bands of Gorlanders to be sold as a slave. Others figured he'd simply abandoned his obligations, but only those full of spite voiced such views. Da would never do that.

"And so you've stepped up into his place," the widow said.

"I've tried." And he had, but it hadn't been enough. Without Da, they hadn't been able to pay their full annual rent. The old lord had been lenient, but the lands had passed to a new lord, and this new one demanded all his rents and intended to make an example of those who failed in their obligations. They now owned two years' worth of rent. And the lord's agent had said that if they didn't pay when it was due at the end of this year's harvest, he would sell one of the family into bondage to pay it off.

"You've had a run of ill luck," she said.

"We've had a run of thieves," Ferran said. "First our cheese vessels and now this."

"They were stolen?" the daughter asked.

"Earlier this month we awoke to find the door to the cheese shed standing wide open and all the cheese-making vessels gone."

"And no ideas who did it?"

"We followed the trail all the way to the road, but that's where it confused the dogs."

"Do you think it's this same band of brigands?" the widow asked.

"I don't know," Ferran said, but now wondered if that was true.

"Brigands," the widow said and shook her head in disgust.

Ferran nodded. And his only hope now was that the headman had caught them.

It wasn't long after that when the headman returned.

"We followed their trail for a mile to the river," he said. "We searched up and down the banks of both sides, but the men must have had a canoe and escaped on the water. And you didn't see their faces?"

"No," Ferran said.

"Then there's no catching them now," the headman said. "They're probably miles downriver. And since you don't know what they look like, there's no use sending a message to the various river towns and villages. Too many men come and go every day."

Ferran's shoulders slumped.

"I'm sorry, son. You probably should not have been traveling alone."

"No," Ferran said. But who could have known that stretch of road would cause problems? Then Ferran corrected himself. He should have known. A lone boy makes a perfect target. He should have taken every precaution with his family's one hope. He'd been a fool.

"Thank you," Ferran said.

When the headman left, Ferran sighed and stood.

"I wish I could help," the widow said.

"My mother and I thank you for your willingness," Ferran said.

"I'm sorry," the daughter said firmly.

Ferran looked up at the sun. He had fifteen miles back to his home. He figured it was going to take him at least six hours.

"They stole my water bag," Ferran said. "Do you perhaps have one I might borrow?"

"Yes," the widow said and rose.

"Mother," the daughter said.

But the widow ignored her and went into her house. She came back a few minutes later with a small, but full, goatskin water bag. "Take this," she said and held it out to Ferran.

Ferran took the bag. "Thank you. I promise I'll return it."

"And take this." She held out a chunk of bread that had been slathered thickly with butter.

Ferran accepted it gratefully.

The widow patted Itch on the head, and then Ferran bid them both a good day. He and Itch left the pleasant garden with its early spring flowers and growing vegetables and walked out onto the road home. Dread filled Ferran. How was he going to break this news to his mother and sister?

3

HELLUM

A s he journeyed back home, Ferran considered what to do about their plight. One hundred and twenty pennies is what they owed. Two years' worth of rent.

If they had a milk cow, they could have sold it to help pay the debt. But their cow had died a year and a half ago. And now, on top of all the debt they already had, they needed to pay the money his mother had borrowed from friends to purchase the widow's vessels.

When the cheese vessels had been stolen, Farmer Hellum, one of the farmers with a large holding, had offered to help. But Mother had politely refused, and Ferran had been happy about that. He didn't like the man. Farmer Hellum was married, yet he was always coming round, leering at Ferran's mother and touching her.

No good could come from being beholden to such a man. And so Ferran had proposed a better idea—why not purchase a set of used vessels? They might not be as good as the ones that had been stolen, but they would still get the job done.

His mother had agreed. They'd found the widow. The set cost more than Ferran had imagined, but they'd scraped and scratched and gathered the required funds, taking the last coppers that his mother kept in the box they hid in the rafters, plus all of the grain left in their barrel, plus some money and barley a few friends in the village lent them.

Ferran shook his head. This morning he'd set out, ready to bring home a bright future. He was bringing home their ruin instead.

———

He limped along the road. Afternoon turned to evening. The sun set and the stars came out. And Ferran trudged along in the dark. A few miles outside the village he saw two people coming along the road toward him with a lantern. When they were a few dozen yards away, Ferran recognized their walk—it was his mother and sister.

"Mother!" he called.

"Ferran?" she called back. "Is that you?"

Itch barked.

"It's Itch," Lily said.

"Oh," Mother said in a worried tone and hurried forward.

When she neared and her lantern light lit him, she cried out in relief and then shock.

"What's happened?"

Ferran told her the story. When he finished, she closed her eyes knowing all was lost. And then she hugged him gently around the shoulders. "We'll figure something out. There has to be a way."

"I'll hire out day and night," Ferran said.

"You need to rest," she said. "Broken ribs take time."

"It's early spring. We can earn it." Although he had no idea how.

On the way home, they passed by a small group of folks still outside the ale-wife house, drinking and chatting around a little fire.

"You found him," one said.

"Thank the ancestors," Mother replied.

"I thought he went for cheesemaking vessels," another said.

And Ferran had to repeat the story. The villagers made sympathetic groans and shook their heads, but with every word, Ferran felt worse and worse. His mother had entrusted him with their future, and he'd returned with nothing. And the villagers would talk about how he had been foolish to go alone.

They made their way home and took to their beds. But he didn't sleep well. When he'd finally grew tired enough to ignore the dull ache of his ribs, he dreamed of those men stomping and kicking him, and that woke him. So he lay there in the dark with the low embers glowing in the hearth and his mother and sister sleeping on their beds.

He dozed and had a nightmare about the lord's agent coming to demand the money and woke again. He dreamed and woke a number of times. It was during one of those times of wakefulness, when he was trying to think of what else he might have done to escape, that he remembered seeing a peculiar tattoo in the triangle of flesh between the thumb and index finger of the knife man. A little loop and two dots. He'd never seen it before and wondered how many men had such a thing and what it meant. And then he'd nodded off again to sleep.

The next day he rose in more pain than the day before. His mother made him a willow tea and told him to rest at least one day. And then she gathered up her fine comb, the blue dress Father had given her, and the yellow ribbons that went with it--the last items of any beauty she owned. She folded them neatly and then carried them out of the house. A few hours later, she came back without her cherished things.

When he asked where they were, she smiled and said she'd sold them, paid her friends back the money and barley they'd lent her, and then purchased food to last two weeks.

Ferran looked to the side, devastated, knowing how she would sometimes take that dress out of her clothes chest. She would hold it up to herself and talk about Father.

"It's okay," she said. "When was I ever going to wear that dress again?"

That evening as the sun was dipping in the sky, Farmer Hellum showed up and talked to Mother outside the door.

"It's so unfortunate," he said to her. "It looks like your scheme to restore your cheese enterprise has failed."

"We'll make do."

"You know I could make it easier for you," he said and put a hand on her arm. "Surely now you see the wisdom of accepting my help."

Mother removed his hand. "We don't need your help."

"Don't say things you'll regret," he said, all oil and charm. He stepped closer. He stroked her cheek with the back of his hand, then dropped his hand to stroke her arm. "Turn away now, and you'll just come begging later."

"I'll come nowhere near you," she said and pushed him firmly away.

"You will," he said. "Hardship will make you generous with your affections. But you could avoid all that suffering, and the suffering of your children."

Ferran's anger kindled. Hellum needed to keep his hands to himself. He had a wife! But that moneyed maggot thought he could push his way around because he was rich enough to own slaves and rent parcels of land out to other farmers. Ferran rose from his bed. "We don't care about your lands and horses here," he said and looked for a stick to threaten the man with.

Hellum looked through the doorway at him. "Careful boy."

"Fetch Itch," Mother said to Ferran, fire in her voice.

Ferran whistled and called, knowing that Itch was out with his little sister somewhere and was not likely to hear. Then he spotted his father's old walking stick and figured that would work well enough to cow the likes of Hellum.

Mother leveled her voice at Hellum and said, "You will leave our property at once, or I will loose my dog upon you. I have told you time and again. Your offer is not anything I am interested in."

Hellum smiled at her. "I hear the lord's agent has taken to putting debts like yours up for sale. Any interested buyer can pay him something less than what is owed. The agent is happy to take the reduced amount because it relieves him of the burden of having to collect. Maybe I'll purchase your debt, and then you will owe me."

"You will not."

"Either way, you will come begging. And I'll be waiting. You don't want to have to sell one of your children. Just a little generosity is all I ask." He stroked her cheek again.

She turned it away.

He pulled her chin back so that she looked at him.

"A little gratitude is all I ask," he said. "Is such coin so difficult to come by?"

Mother said nothing, just glared.

"I bid you a good evening, Widow Lutrell. And you," he said, looking in at Ferran. And then he doffed his rich man's hat, turned, and walked away.

They watched him go, and when he was out on the path leading past the house, Mother turned, her face ashen.

"He couldn't buy the debt, could he?" Ferran asked.

"I think he could. This new lord cares only that his lands make him rich."

"We'd end up being in debt to Hellum?" Ferran asked in dismay.

"Yes," she said.

Ferran couldn't imagine it. Hellum would call on the headman and force them to work on his lands and in his house. And he would make his leering demands on Mother. Every day would be a repeat of what had just happened outside the door.

"That piece of filth," Ferran said.

His mother sighed.

"We'll earn it, Mother."

She nodded, clearly not believing it.

"We'll earn it," he said more forcefully. And if they didn't, he'd have to sell himself and pay the debt so there was nothing for Hellum to buy.

They made their food last four weeks. After that, they ate their last old chicken. And when he was gone, they foraged for anything worth eating. And they worked.

It took eight weeks for Ferran's ribs to heal, but he hired himself out the day after his mother sold her things. He took any job he could find and worked through the pain. He cleared weeds, plucked insects off of the plants in gardens, mucked out stalls, killed rats, fetched water for the miners at the tin mine a few miles away, repaired fences, dug a cesspit, spread manure, ran messages, chopped wood, and more. Much more.

Eight weeks turned to twelve, which turned to sixteen. Hunger began to stalk them day and night, and then it was late summer. And still, they didn't have enough. Not for the debt. Not even for themselves.

4

RAT SNAKE

It was mid-morning, and Farren was returning from checking with the smith and the miller to see if they had any work, which they hadn't. He passed the fork in the trail that ran between the Grouser's field and Hem's pasture, and that's when he saw the snake.

It was a fat, brown rat snake. Almost four feet long. It was holding its head up from the dirt, watching the barley on the other side of the path as if investigating the possibility of a mouse.

Ferran stopped and couldn't help the grin that spread from ear to ear, for that right there was four feet of dinner.

Yesterday, he'd eaten nothing. The day before that it had been one little egg. Two days before that, he and his mother and sister had shared a chunk of hard bread and a soup made with two lice-ridden sparrows and a limp, wild onion. The bread was so old they'd had to scrape off a sizeable portion of it to remove the mold. It was so hard he'd almost broken teeth trying to eat it.

So his mother had dipped the little chunk of bread into the soup first, taken a nibble, and passed it to his sister, who'd dipped, nibbled, then passed it to Ferran. Around they'd gone, trying to make it last. But it hadn't lasted for more than a couple of turns, and the three of them had ended up hungrier than when they'd first started.

The days before that hadn't been any better. It had been weeks since the three of them had eaten decently. Weeks with his ribs becoming more and more prominent. Weeks since he'd gone anywhere without hunger grabbing him every minute with its bony fingers.

But a four-foot rat snake would change that! At least for one day.

He could taste the flesh already.

Ferran licked his lips, drew his sling from his belt, and slowly unwound it.

The breeze rolled gently through the barley in long waves. The snake held steady. It was only twelve feet away. An easy shot, right to the head.

He slipped his hand into the stone sack at his waist.

"Cheese Turd!" someone bellowed.

Ferran glanced in the direction of the voice and saw Caswal the Cruel and his idiot thug Lome coming down the trail. They were carrying long-poled bird nets. Both of them were taller than Ferran, and Lome was much stronger and liked to do the beating. He'd given Ferran a black eye a week ago that still hadn't totally faded. Ferran ignored them.

"Hey!" Caswal shouted angrily.

Why did those two blights upon humanity have to show up here at this very moment? Ferran swore there was some evil spirit out there who had taken a disliking to him.

"Don't turn your back on me! You'll get off my road, you stinking goat lover."

They were still a ways off, so Ferran turned fully to the snake and grabbed a nice round stone.

"I'm talking to you, turd brain," Caswal said.

Ferran slipped the stone into the sling's pouch, then shifted his weight for a quick whirl and throw.

And suddenly a large clod of dirt struck Ferran in the back of the head, jolting him with a sharp pain. The clod broke into pieces, dirt falling down the neck of his shirt. A speck of grit got into his eye and made him wince. He blinked and cleared his eye, only to see his dinner slithering off the path and into the barley.

No! he thought and whirled his sling, but the stone had fallen out.

The snake was disappearing into the barley, and he dashed forward to grab it by the tail, but by the time he reached the spot, the snake was well into the field. He scanned the barley, looking for any sign of movement, but the barley did not move in a way that would indicate the slithering of a snake. Ferran pushed aside some of the stalks of grain and scanned the ground below, hoping the snake hadn't disappeared into a hole. He waded out a step into the grain, trying to scare the snake into moving. "Hey!" he shouted and walked another step. "Hey!" He didn't care if he got bit.

But the barley stalks didn't move.

"Hey!" Ferran shouted and took another step.

"What are you doing?" Caswal cried. "Get out of there!"

Ferran needed food. His mother needed food. His little sister was starting to look like a skeleton with big eyes.

"I said get out of there!" Caswal snarled.

Ferran glanced back just in time to see Caswal swinging his pole at Ferran's head.

Ferran ducked, and the pole whooshed above him.

Caswal swung at him again, and Ferran danced to the side.

"You're smashing our grain," Caswal said.

Ferran gave the barley one more glance, but the snake was gone. His heart sank, and hunger's bony hand clutched him tighter.

"Come out of there right now. You're going to pay for that!"

Ferran wished he could make them pay for his lost dinner. "Your hog-farting grain is fine."

"Now," Caswal demanded.

The safest route away from these two would be straight through the field, but Ferran knew he couldn't run that way. He would break the stalks. And with the harvest only a week or two away, it would cause damage. And Caswal's father would come demanding satisfaction, and neither he nor his mother or little sister had the money to pay. So Ferran picked his way out of the field at an angle from Caswal, but Lome got ahead of him and met him on the path.

"What were you doing?" Lome asked and shoved him at Caswal.

Ferran stumbled toward the other boy.

"None of your business."

"It is when you go onto my property," said Caswal.

"Especially when you can't pay for the mess you make," said Lome.

"It's not your property," Ferran pointed out, which was technically true. Caswal's father was leasing it.

"The grain is ours," Caswal said, then jabbed the end of his pole into Ferran's side. The side he knew had been injured.

The jab hurt, and Ferran gritted his teeth in pain and sidled away from Caswal, only to have Lome jab him in the back with his pole.

"Ow," Ferran cried out. "Stop that."

Caswal asked, "So who is it going to be: you or your sister?"

"For what?" Ferran asked, stepping back so he could see both boys.

"To pay your debts. My father says your mother is not going to get another extension from the lord's agent. Which means she's going to have to bond one of you out. Unless she decides to dance the bed for Farmer Hellum."

By the king's stinking feet, Ferran hated Caswal. "You'll be dancing his bed before she does," Ferran said.

"Then one of you will be sold, and the other is going to have to work off your debt here."

"We don't owe you anything."

Lome leered. "I think his sister could do us a great service."

His sister wasn't going to do them any service. Nor was Ferran. And then Ferran saw his escape.

"He never learns," Caswal said.

"Another painted eye might help," Lome offered.

"A matching pair," Caswal said. "I think that would improve his looks greatly."

Ferran took a step away from both of them, reached into his pouch, and grabbed a sling stone.

"You throw that," said Lome, "and I'll pound you like a cabbage."

Caswal jabbed the butt of his pole at Ferran's face, but Ferran dodged aside. Then he cocked his arm and threw the stone at Lome's head with all the force he could muster.

Lome ducked, bringing his arm up to shield his face and giving Ferran the opening he needed.

Ferran darted past.

Lome tried to slug him, but it was a bad angle, and he only succeeded in bopping Ferran in the back.

"Get him!" Caswal growled.

The two boys took off after him, but Ferran was faster, and he soon outdistanced them both. And then he sped over the rise and out of their view.

They stopped at the top of the rise and slung stones at him, but there was a rock wall along this stretch of the path and a few trees, both of which made any shot difficult. The stones they slung struck close, one zipping by so closely behind Ferran's head the hairs on his neck stood up, but none struck him. And by the time he was mostly visible again, he was out of their range.

It was a good thing too because he was tired and panting. It used to be he could run almost endlessly, but lately, the distances had been getting shorter and shorter.

He looked back at the field, wanting that snake, and cursed his luck. And then he cursed Caswal because the truth was that Caswal was right —Ferran would be sold. Despite everything they'd done, they were not making enough headway against the debt.

But maybe the carpenter had some work. Ferran had been walking that way when he saw the snake. The carpenter was repairing a roof for one of the wealthier farmers who had a wooden roof with a couple of tricky crannies. A man had already fallen off the roof and broken his leg. It made others wary, but that was Ferran's opportunity because he'd be happy to scramble up to all the dangerous places. Surely it was worth something.

Of course, such work wouldn't bring in much. And in the back of his mind, Ferran knew they were putting off the inevitable. They had scraped together only about one-third of what they needed to pay. The lord's agent was coming in three weeks, and no amount of odd jobs for the miller or carpenter would make up the slack. They would come up short, and Ferran would be forced to offer himself to be sold. His sister would fetch a better price, but he wouldn't allow it. He knew the stories of what happened to young bond girls. And it was his fault they were in such a bad state of affairs anyway.

Once he was sold, the idea was to labor for the buyer until he paid his debt, but he'd overheard the men speaking and knew that's not what happened. Because the debt holder would charge him for lodging and food and clothing and for sneezing and breathing and pooping in the outhouse and take all of that out of his pay. Some masters deducted so many different costs that the debt stretched on for years. Sometimes it was never paid. Some few lucky ones did get out, but very often this was a path that led to slavery.

He rounded a corner, thinking how nice it would be to find a lost gold piece at the edge of the path, thinking of what a different situation they would have been in had he actually gotten the cheese vessels and not let himself be robbed, and saw little Ors running up the trail. Ors was the youngest son of a family with two pigs Ferran had often imagined himself eating.

The boy spotted him and shouted excitedly, "Spread the word!"

Ferran stopped.

"Spread the word! A drover's come to town. He's looking to hire a crew. He's down at the ale-wife's place and will explain the job in an hour."

"He paid you to announce?" Ferran asked.

"Aye," Little Ors said. "He promised a full birdseye. He sent three of us out."

A birdseye was the smallest of copper coins. It was the size of a normal small copper but with a hole punched through the middle. Eight of them was a good wage for a full day's work. "Three of you? Each for a birdseye?"

"Yes."

"Does he need another?"

"I doubt it. But you can try."

Ferran perked up. A birdseye. That was something. He thanked Ors and began to jog down the path. And then he realized what Ors had said: this drover was looking for a crew.

Why couldn't Ferran hire himself out to work on that crew?

True, he was merely a stripling and one of the smaller ones in the village at that, but he was lively. And fast, even if he did tire more quickly these days. And there wasn't anyone better with a sling. A youth like himself could herd cattle as easily as a full-grown man.

He quickly added up what he might earn for a week's work if the drover was paying a normal laborer's wage. He added up what he would earn if the drover needed him for two weeks, and his hopes rose. It wouldn't be enough to pay the full debt, but it would get close. Maybe that would be enough to convince the lord's agent they were worth waiting for. Enough for him to grant them another six months or year to pay the rest.

His spirits soared, and he began to run faster, his bare feet eating up the road.

5

STRANGER

Ferran turned onto the main road through the village and ran up to the ale-wife's house. Her large ale window was open, and a man stood outside of it drinking from a wooden mug. He was a strongly built man with wide shoulders who looked like he could still throw many a challenger in a wrestle. However, he wasn't young. He was balding and had a dark beard that was starting to show streaks of gray. His face was weathered and had a scar on one cheek.

Many strangers stopped at the ale-wife's window, but Ferran knew this was the drover because he wore a cap with a royal, scarlet drover's badge on it.

The ale-wife was leaning on the window sill. Old man Harm was sitting on an old chair and leaning up against the house.

The big drover laughed at something the ale-wife said, and Ferran noted he still had most of his teeth. A big man from hardy stock then. With boots.

And suddenly Ferran wondered if the job required boots. He had nothing but a few fleas he could call his own. Shoes were out of the question, much less boots. And then he thought about the state of his clothes, mended and patched until there was hardly a whole piece of cloth left. They were rags. Clean and mended, but rags.

Ferran put the thought aside. The drover wasn't hiring some fancy pants. He was hiring someone to work. Nevertheless, Ferran combed his hair with his fingers and smoothed it to the side, then walked up and politely waited for the man to take notice. The drover had a couple of whole walnuts in his hand that he'd bought from the ale-wife. He cracked one with his thumb and forefinger like it was nothing. Just popped it open and tossed the meat into his mouth.

The ale-wife saw Ferran first. "I don't have any work for you today, son."

"That's okay," Ferran said. "I'm here to speak to the stranger."

The man looked down at him and said in a deep voice. "I'm afraid I've already sent all the runners."

"I'm not here for running, sir," Ferran said and pulled himself up straight. "I'm here to offer you my services. As a drover."

The man grinned and popped another walnut shell in half. "You're so short I don't think the cattle will even see you."

"Sir, dogs aren't very tall, and the cattle pay attention to them."

"You offering to bite my cattle?"

Harm and the ale-wife chuckled.

"I work hard. And I run fast."

Old man Harm spoke up. "Especially when he's stolen one of Chuly's peach pies."

That was years ago. It wasn't fair to bring that up now and besmirch Farren's name in front of this man. But Farren wasn't going to let it divert him, so he brushed it off. "That's long in the past when I didn't know better. The good news is I'm even faster now."

"And stealing bigger pies," Harm said and grinned.

"Pay no attention to the venerable man in the chair," Ferran said. "I believe his drink has gone to his head."

"Oh, he's just starting," the ale-wife said. "He'll need two more mugs before he begins with his stories."

The drover motioned at Ferran's fading black eye and asked Harm. "Is this one a troublemaker?"

"What would you say?" Harm asked the ale-wife.

"Not a troublemaker," she said. "But he's not one to back down either."

Ferran said, "I do not fear a long trip. I'll be a good as another dog, I will. And a hard-working one at that."

The drover looked him over, then ran his hand over his short, gray-streaked beard. "Son, if this were a short haul of a day or two, I'd consider it. But we're crossing some rough territory, and I need men to match it."

Ferran's smile wavered, hope fleeing him.

The lord's agent would be back in three weeks. Ferran needed this job.

"Sir," Ferran said.

Old man Harm spoke up. "Don't bother the stranger. He's given you an answer. Now show some respect."

The one thing Ferran didn't want to do was irritate the big man, for then he never would get the job. "Of course," Ferran said, then gave the drover a slight nod and backed away.

The drover watched Ferran go, and then the ale-wife asked the drover what he'd heard about Osson and their raiding parties, and the drover began to talk about the war everyone knew was coming. Queen Conwenna, may the ancestors bless her, was not some lesser ruler that lacked the blessings of the earth. She wasn't a petty queen. She was a mage queen. A possessor of the high power. And she had refused to back the rotted king of Osson as high king. So the rumor was he was coming to bring her and the lords of Akken to heel.

Ferran listened for a bit. It would be terrible if the mage king of Osson attacked. Gallas the Bloody they called him. And he'd bring a host of men. But who knew when that would be or if it would even occur? And what could Ferran do about it anyway? Those were matters for the queen and her lords to sort out.

So Ferran left the conversation. He had to get hired and needed to be thinking about that. He turned and walked over to the end of the ale-wife's house and looked out toward the drover's field. There was a wagon out there and a goodly number of cattle. He imagined the drover would have plenty of food in that wagon. Enough to feed a crew of men. His mouth watered at the thought.

He knew he could be of use. And the man didn't need to pay him as much as others. Surely there had to be a way to convince this stranger that Ferran was worth his salt. The problem was that none came to mind. He didn't want to beg or pester. That would only irk the man. But maybe the smith or miller could speak for him. In fact, if any of the men of the village that were friendly toward Ferran were hired, maybe they could put in a kind word.

He decided that's how he would do this. He would wait and see who took the job and get them to speak for him. And then he would offer to work for three-fourths the going rate.

———————

Ferran waited and watched as the men of the village, plus some women and children, gathered to hear the drover. Farmer Hellum came, saw Ferran and doffed his rich man's hat, but Ferran didn't give him the pleasure of a response.

A dark-skinned man who looked to be the drover's companion took a position at the back of the crowd. He was smartly trimmed, with black boots, gray pants, and a richly brocaded green shirt. He wore a hat with a splash of colorful feathers on one side. He'd rolled up the sleeves of his shirt, exposing well-muscled arms.

Ferran wanted to get a closer look, but then Caswal and Lome showed up. They saw Ferran and began walking toward him, but Ferran moved to a different part of the crowd and took up position next to Loth the plowman. Loth was a big man who was at odds with Caswal's father, and that was enough to keep Caswal and Lome from approaching.

A few of the men purchased a mug of ale and sipped it while they waited. And when there wasn't anyone else on the paths and trails who looked to be headed this way, the drover was given a wooden box. He stepped up onto it, rising head and shoulders above the crowd.

"Good people of Buckle Hill," he said. "Your drover's meadow is splendid."

"And costs a splendid penny to boot," someone said.

A few of the men laughed.

The drover continued. "I am Borros from Three Hammers. I come

37

here on what you might call the queen's mission. Her agent has contracted for these cattle to support her troops against Osson."

"Blackhearts," a man said.

"Whoresons," called another.

Old man Harm said, "I like to think of them as the south ends of north-bound rats."

The drover smiled. "Indeed. They pillage our coasts. And our mage queen is going to teach them a lesson. But she can't if her troops have no meat."

The crowd waited.

"I'm looking for four stout men. It's a little over two weeks to Broniss. I'll pay three coppers per day. I also need a couple of dogs that have been trained."

Three coppers, Ferran thought. That was a fine wage indeed. It was worth half again as much as a man earned working in the fields. And Ferran had a dog. Itch had been trained for all sorts of things. He was smart, and would have been with Ferran right now had his mother and sister not headed out to the woods this morning.

"You don't have your own dogs?" a man asked.

"They were poisoned and are in no condition to drive cattle."

"Where's your crew?" another man asked.

"They're the ones that did the poisoning."

A few of the men murmured. One close to Ferran muttered, "What kind of leader is he that his crew turns on him and poisons his dogs?"

The man standing next to Ferran shook his head, "He doesn't smell right, this drover. Showing up without dogs or a crew. And that dark Sorosian with him to boot. No, he does not smell right at all. You won't catch me going to the end of the lane with this fellow, much less all the way to Broniss."

"It's too late in the season anyway," another said. "The fields are just about to turn white."

Loth spoke up, "Osson has been raiding the coast road. This herd will raise a dust and draw their attention. You'll be nothing but a fat prize."

"Lord Pencoy will provide an escort along the coast road."

"That squint-eyed thief?" someone exclaimed.

The drover turned to see who would say such bold words, but Harm spoke up. "Let us say that Lord Pencoy and our lord are not on friendly terms on account of a certain stallion."

"That has nothing to do with me," the drover said.

"Do you know Lord Pencoy?" Old Harm asked.

"I know of him."

"Well, all here can attest that he'll probably extort you half a side of beef for every mile his men ride."

"Half?" a man said. "I'd say that was generous."

"My agreement is fair, I can assure you," the drover said. "And he's loyal to the queen."

The men shook their heads unconvinced.

Loth spoke up again. "Even if the coast road was safe, the barley is almost ripe. Depending on the weather, it may be on in two weeks' time. We'd be leaving it for the birds. How about pay for a part of the way?"

"And leave my cattle stranded halfway between here and Broniss? I need men who will sign up for the whole trip. And I'm willing to pay."

Loth turned to the man next to him, "Doesn't matter what he can pay. It isn't going to work."

Old man Harm said, "Do you have any bonafides? After all, you are foreign to us."

Ferran realized he hadn't even thought of that. Nobody knew what manner of man this drover was. He might be one of those that didn't pay what he'd promised. He might be of a questionable character. The scar on his face and others on his arms suggested he might be a brawler. In fact, he could have stolen these cattle, and any men he hired would only be helping him with his theft.

The drover reached into his vest and pulled out a small folded parchment and handed it to old Harm.

Harm took it and looked at the seal. "It's the queen's seal," he proclaimed loudly, then opened it and read a bit. "Says here the queen has contracted with one Borros of the Longdowns in the Three Hammers district." Harm looked the drover over. "You're not a lord. Are you a merchant?"

"I am not a merchant, but I do hold lands."

A man raised his voice. "How do we know he's the Borros spoken of on that parchment? He could have stolen these cattle."

Harm said, "It's odd you don't have a crew."

"Are you friendly with those in Mossby?" the drover asked.

Mossby was a village south of Buckle Hill.

"There are good people in Mossby," Harm said.

"They will vouch for me. Four brigands stole the sword that hung in the ale-wife's house. I took it from them, and gave both the sword and the men over to the officials."

Ferran had seen that sword. A fine blade. And if this drover had returned it, that spoke well of him. As did the fact that he'd beaten four men.

"Mossby's a half day's journey," a man said.

Old Harm said, "I always told him hanging that sword up where all could see would only bring trouble. Maybe now he's learned his lesson. But even if they do come and vouch for you, we have a new lord here. And he's a stickler for his rents. Can you imagine what he'd say if his agent tells him we ran off during the harvest?"

"Surely some of you can be spared. I'll up it to four coppers per day."

That was double the normal laborer's wage. Ferran looked at the men. They were doubtful. Many were shaking their heads. If the drover had come two weeks earlier, it might have been a different story, but old Harm was right. When the barley came on, you had to work from before the sun rose until after it set. And you needed children and dogs shooing the birds away. A few years ago, a massive flock of sparrows had come and eaten a good portion of the crop. If that flock showed up again this year, it could be ruinous for those here.

Ferran himself would be required to work, but he could put in his required days after the harvest started. The work usually spread over two to three weeks. He could thresh if he had to. And his mother could work her days plus some of his. And if it came to it, maybe she could convince her friend over by Oakhollow to send her boys to stand in for Ferran. Their lands there always ripened about a week after those here.

Farmer Hellum cleared his throat. "I have a different proposition for our friend from Three Hammers."

All eyes turned toward him.

Hellum looked at the drover and said, "I'll offer you twenty coppers per head."

The drover looked unimpressed.

Farmer Hellum continued, "It's clear you're not going to get anyone here to brave Osson raiders, a lost crop, or the lord's ire. It's equally clear that the two of you can't manage such a big herd. So I'll pay you twenty coppers per head."

The drover said, "That's less than a fifth of what cattle sell for in Broniss."

"But you're not in Broniss," Farmer Hellum said.

The drover narrowed his eyes. "Are you insulting me?"

"It's not an insult. It's help. The best I can muster. There might be a few others here who could pay at that price. With our help, you could whittle that herd down to something the two of you can manage. Something is better than nothing."

"Does this thief work for Lord Pencoy?" the drover asked.

A few of the men laughed, but Ferran could see some of them thinking. A full-grown steer or heifer was worth anywhere from ninety to a hundred and twenty coppers. If someone bought six or seven for twenty a head and sold them for seventy coppers profit each, they could make a laborer's annual wage. It would be a boon.

"It's robbery," the drover said.

Farmer Hellum shrugged.

The drover looked at the others. "I'm looking for four men."

"We bear you no ill will," old Harm said. "It's just the wrong time. We're not soldiers to fight Osson on the coast road. We have a crop to bring in. And before turning off into Lord Pencoy's lands, the road bends near the blight. There've been rumors of something there."

"The blight is many miles away from the road to Pencoy's, even at its closest point," the drover said. "However, considering the time of year and your harvest, I'll raise the pay."

But the people in the crowd had stopped listening and were talking to each other. A number turned and began to walk away. The women began to move their children along.

· · ·

"Four and a half coppers per day," the drover said. "You'll not get a chance like this for some time."

But the people were moving off. Farmer Hellum stood in the street looking at the drover, a smug smile on his face. He waited until the crowd had thinned, then doffed his fat hat and said, "I'll come in the morning." Then he walked off, making a show with his fancy walking stick.

Ferran watched the other villagers go. He waited until all but the ale-wife, old man Harm, and the two strangers were left.

"It looks like you were wrong about these folks," the dark Sorosian said. "You owe me a raisin pie."

The drover took off his cap with the scarlet badge and ran his hand over his bald head. "It's not a laughing matter," he said and replaced the cap.

The ale-wife turned to old man Harm. "Supper's ready. Come on in to eat."

Old man Harm got up and moved inside the house. The ale-wife called out to the strangers. "We have pork pies and peas."

"Thank you," said the drover. "But we've brought our own kitchen."

"Pity," she said, and turned away from the window to her work, leaving Ferran alone in the street with the two men.

Ferran bowed his head in respect and said, "Sir, I will go the whole way. And you won't need to pay me four and a half."

The dark Sorosian looked at Ferran. He had an immaculately trimmed mustache. And his green brocaded shirt was even more impressive up close. As was the splash of colorful feathers. One was a brighter blue than Ferran had seen on any bird.

The drover waved Ferran off and said to his companion, "These men will think on it. You'll see. After supper, we'll have the crew we need."

Ferran said, "I have a dog who is excellent with sheep."

The Sorosian motioned at Ferran with his chin. "He says he has a dog."

The drover sighed and looked down. "You're persistent, boy. I'll give you that. Much like a dung fly."

"Or someone who knows how to work hard and is eager to do it," Ferran countered.

The drover grunted. "Even if I did want to hire you, which I don't, I need a crew. Not one bony boy."

"The three of us," Ferran said, motioning at himself and the two men, "plus my dog Itch. We'll get it done."

The Sorosian gave Ferran a considering look.

The drover shook his head. "Boy, have you ever driven cattle?"

"I've herded sheep, goats, pigs."

"Okay, master pigman, do you think Osson raiders or gangs of brigands would find you intimidating?"

"Not particularly."

"Precisely. So you're of no help to me. What I need is a crew. Bring me one, and I'll give you a finder's fee. Now be on your way."

Ferran wanted to argue his case, but he could see now was not the time, and so he nodded his head.

The Sorosian held out a finger for Ferran to wait. "There's a tin mine in the area. Which way does it lie?"

"Miners," the drover said brightly. "Of course. We can get miners."

Ferran said, "You'll get the same reaction there that you received here. Lord Trawn isn't as bad as our new lord, but he will have all the miners working his fields nevertheless."

"How far away is this mine?" the drover asked.

"Five or six miles," Ferran said, "depending on the road you take."

"There," the drover said to the Sorosian. "Not too far. Word of the pay will spread. Mark me. Men will come. And we'll be waiting for them."

"Let's hope," the dark Sorosian said.

"It's guaranteed," the drover said, then clapped his hand on his well-dressed mate's shoulder. "Now, let's eat." And then the two men turned their backs on Ferran and began to walk toward the road leading to the meadow.

"I'll have you a crew by morning," Ferran called after them.

The big drover raised his hand in acknowledgment, but didn't turn to look at him and continued on.

Ferran would have them a crew, although who the other members might be he had no idea.

6

CREW

The next morning before sunrise, a few stars still shining in the sky, Ferran walked up to the drover's campsite with his dog Itch and six other boys. Three of them Ferran had invited to join his crew. Three of them he had not, but they had heard and insisted on coming anyway.

The dark-skinned Sorosian was tending a pot of breakfast that was simmering over a fire and saw them arrive. He wasn't wearing his finely brocaded shirt, but a tunic. However, even this was clean and still had much wear in it. Furthermore, the sleeves also were embroidered with a looping design.

"Ah," the Sorosian said. "The boy with the black eye." He pointed with his stirring spoon at Itch. "That your dog?"

Ferran nodded.

"You have matching black eyes."

"I just wish my dog had been there when I got mine," Ferran said.

The Sorosian turned to the others. "And I suppose this is your crew."

"We're all hard workers," Ferran said.

The Sorosian looked the boys over, then grinned. "Oh, he's going to love this. I'll inform our fearless leader you have arrived." Then he walked over to a figure snoring on the ground by the wagon and nudged him with his foot.

"Go away," the drover said.

The Sorosian nudged him again. "Get up."

"Do you have a death wish?"

"I'd like to see you try."

The drover grunted.

"A crew has arrived," the Sorosian announced.

There was a pause.

"A crew?"

"Applicants for the job."

"Ha," the drover said and stretched. "Did I not tell you men would come?" He sat up in his bedroll. "Where are they?"

"Waiting right over there," the Sorosian said. "Seven of them, plus a dog."

The drover rose with enthusiasm and looked around. "Where?"

"Right there."

The drover rubbed his eyes. "The boys?" he growled.

"Last night you were thinking of doing it with just the two of us."

"They're boys," the drover said, incredulous.

"Better than nothing."

The drover pointed at the younger Berryman boy. "Look there. You want me hiring that?"

Everyone looked. The younger Berryman boy, who Ferran had not wanted to come, was staring at the ground like a moron, lost in thought with his finger deep up inside one nostril. He then removed his finger from his nose, examined his diggings, and brought it to his mouth.

Ferran winced. The Sorosian and half of the other boys groaned.

"Booger eaters," the drover said in disgust. "You want me to hire booger eaters."

"We only need four."

"And at least one of them is a booger eater."

"Better a few weeks with booger eaters than financial ruin."

"They're boys."

"How old were you when you first went out?"

"That was different."

"Oh?"

"Sir," Ferran said. "You wanted a crew. Well, I brought one. And they're all hard workers." Except for that younger Berryman, but Ferran was going to ignore him and hope he went away.

Ferran's actual picks had been his best friend Winwalom, Ranoc, who was the only one in the village who knew how to ride a horse, and the older Berryman boy, who was now tainted by his booger-mining brother.

However, those three had not kept their mouths shut. Ranoc had told Krov, the youngest of the woodsman's sons who wore a black patch over his eye. Krov was huge and already had a beard, even though he wasn't much older than Ferran. He was strong enough to count as a man and would have been perfect for the crew, but he and Ferran did not get along on account of the fact that the woodsman and his sons were supposed to protect the lord's woods and creeks from poachers, and Ferran, through no ill intent, had seemed to have accidentally borrowed a few fish from the lord's creek this summer.

As for the others, the older Berryman boy had thought it a splendid idea to bring his nose-picking brother as well as a boy from Spring Creek, who wasn't a bad fellow, but had a vacant and wide-eyed look to him that reminded one of a cow.

"Just talk to them," the Sorosian said. "What have you got to lose? If they don't pass muster, you can sell your cattle off to these villagers for a cabbage and three scrawny chickens."

"We'll wait," the drover said, clearly not impressed. "Men will come."

They waited until noon. But no men came. At least, not to offer their services as a crew. Farmer Hellum showed up with two other prominent men. Hellum asked the boys what they were doing here, and when they replied, he smirked, then strode on to make his offer to the drover a second time, saying that a number of other men of the area had joined him and that together they should be able to help the drover in his plight and purchase a good portion of the herd.

"You can leave," the drover replied.

"There are no men in the area who will hire out," Hellum said. "It would be folly."

And Ferran figured Hellum had made sure to convince them of that. Which probably hadn't been hard. All he would have needed to do is get them imagining the lovely profits of purchasing cattle for the price of carrots.

"The mage queen will hear of Buckle Hill's willingness to come to her aid."

"Many would be willing to help you drive them to Broniss but are prevented by the requirements of our lord. Shall we disobey him?"

"If I do sell these cattle," the drover said, "it won't be to you. So you can scoot off."

Farmer Hellum raised a hand and said, "I won't take offense. I would feel the same way you do. We'll remove ourselves to the ale-wife's. You know where to find us."

Then he doffed that hat of his, and the three of them walked back the way they'd come.

———

The hours passed. The sun moved across the sky. And still, nobody came.

Ferran and the others visited the two poisoned dogs that lay in the shade of the wagon. They didn't look long for this world. Ferran asked why they'd been poisoned, and was told it was because the men were cowards.

After that, the boys played stones in the dust, watched the cattle, then asked the Sorosian about his homeland, including whether the women there truly filed their teeth. They learned his name was Lagash. So it was Borros of Three Hammers and Lagash the Sorosian that they were hoping to hire with.

Ranoc got impatient and stood to leave, but Ferran convinced him to stay. The younger Berryman wandered off, and Ferran exhaled a huge sigh of relief, but an hour later the boy returned with burrs in his hair.

Farmer Hellum had not gone home, but mingled and chatted with folks down in the village. Every once in a while, he would walk out from whatever he was doing to show himself between the cottages and look toward the drover's camp. One time he was holding a mug, another a hand pie, another his smoking pipe. Someone would say something, and he'd laugh, then turn away again.

The fourth time it happened, Borros said, "That man is beginning to annoy me." The fifth time, Borros asked Lagash, "Do you think he'd mind if I stuffed that pipe down his throat?"

"He's got a good position," Lagash said.

"He's got nothing," Borros said and looked at the boys.

As the afternoon grew late, a number of the villagers began to eat their dinner in front of the cottages. Someone brought out a fiddle and played a jig. People began to dance. Ferran figured they were celebrating the good fortune of having a drover stranded just outside their village. Hellum showed himself again and spread his arms out as if to ask Borros if he was ready yet.

Borros said to Lagash, "Nobody is going to come, are they?"

"Would you if you stood a chance of purchasing cattle for nothing?"

"I do not like that man," Borros said.

"Neither do I. He's something of an eel. On the other hand, these boys have waited all day."

Borros looked over at Ferran and the other boys, his weathered face sour with annoyance.

Lagash continued, "They have not complained or made a nuisance of themselves."

Borros rubbed the back of his balding head in irritation.

"And they have a dog."

"Fine," he rumbled and put on his cap with the scarlet badge. "We'll hire the booger eaters."

"The mountain has changed its mind? Are you sure?"

Borros said, "They'll get us to Lord Pencoy's. I don't have to hire them for the full trip. Pencoy will have men. And when the boys come back with their pay, they can rub the coin in that farmer's smug face. And every one of those Buckle Hill boneheads will rue their lack of charity."

Ferran's hopes soared. The drover would hire them after all.

Borros walked over to where the boys waited. Ferran stood, and the other boys joined him.

"Right," said Borros. "I'm thinking that since you're not quite men, I'll need five of you to help me get these cattle to Pencoy's lands."

"Sir," Ferran said. "We'll help you get them all the way to Broniss."

"Pencoy will have an escort."

"His soldiers won't want to chase cattle. Besides, you'll want them focused on watching the seas for bloodthirsty Osson rot, not the backsides of a bunch of cattle. We can get you the whole way."

"We'll see," Borros said. "Right now the job is to Pencoy's." He pointed at Itch. "He yours?"

"Yes," Ferran said.

"He looks a bit bony. Is he trained?"

"Yes, sir," Ferran said.

"Any of the rest of you have a trained dog you can bring?"

They all shook their heads.

"Any of you ever worked with a spear before?"

None of the boys had.

"Sword?"

"They're not going to have the money for swords," Lagash said.

"Do you have any weapons at all besides your bad looks?" Borros asked.

"Slings," Ferran said.

Krov said, "I'm a good shot with a hunting bow."

"But not a war bow?"

"No."

"How does that work with one eye?"

"He can hit a button out to fifty yards," Winwalom said.

Borros pointed at Winwalom. "That hair. Are you from up north?"

Winwalom's hair was straight, dark, and long. He normally gathered it at the back of his head with a leather or cloth tie so that it hung like a horse's tail. The girls seemed to like it and his long eyelashes, but Ferran could never grow his hair like that. His was too unruly. Besides, he liked his hair short. Easier to maintain. Easier to avoid lice.

Winwalom shrugged. "It's how my father wears his hair."

Borros was still not impressed with them. He looked over at Lagash as if rethinking his decision.

"Show us what you can do with your slings," Lagash said. He pointed at a slender tree growing by the corner of a field fence. "See that tree about thirty yards away. Hit the trunk."

Ferran looked at Winwalom and Ranoc and grinned. Was he kidding? That was an easy shot. The boys removed their slings from where they'd tucked them along their belts, and one by one, they aimed at the tree and slung. They all hit it easily except for the younger Berryman, but even his stone was still close.

"Bird boys," Borros said. "Is that what you are?"

"Sometimes it's birds," Ferran said. "Sometimes it's hares. We can hit rats. Grasshoppers."

"Ever killed a man with a stone?"

Ferran blinked. A man? None of them were soldiers, and he began to wonder what they might face on this job.

"Bruised one?"

Ranoc began to slowly raise his hand. When the others saw it, they followed.

"Not necessarily a man," Ranoc said.

"What are you saying?" Borros asked. "You attack women?"

"Other boys, sir," Ranoc said.

"We've got lots of bruises," Ferran said because sometimes, even though they'd been forbidden to target each other, they slung dirt clods and other things.

Borros turned to Ferran. "Is that how you got your black eye?"

"No," Ferran said. "That came from a fist."

The tiniest of grins cracked Borros's weathered face. "Do your parents know you're here?"

They all nodded yes.

"And do you all dine on nose diggings like that one," he said.

Ranoc said, "He's an idiot."

"You didn't answer my question."

And then Ranoc realized that by not answering straight, he'd implicated himself in the habit, and his eyes went wide in surprise.

"No," Ferran said.

Borros motioned at the wicked-looking scar on Ranoc's neck. "What happened there?"

"He tried to ride a bull," Ferran said.

"Multiple times," Winwalom added.

"There was a stick that caught me as I flew past," Ranoc said.

Borros raised his eyebrows and looked at Lagash.

"A lively lad would be good," Lagash said.

Borros nodded and looked the boys over. "Well, you're skinny and hungry, and that's good. But I only need five." And then something caught his eye, and he looked past the boys.

Ferran turned to see what had caught his attention. Caswal and Lome were walking up the path. One of the bigger boys from the mine was with them as well. Ferran groaned inside. That's all he needed.

"You part of this crew?" Borros called to the newcomers.

Caswal smiled and opened his arms wide to take the three of them in. "We figured you'd want to hire help that was older and bigger. The three of us, and Krov there, we'll get the work done."

Caswal was what a number of the village women called a well-formed and attractive young man. He had a quick smile for those he wanted to suck up to and dark eyes girls seemed to like until they got to know him.

Borros nodded, and Ferran saw his chance for work start to slip through his fingers.

"Sir," Ferran said. "You need someone who can run."

"And they can't?"

"Not as fast as me. And none of them has a dog like this one."

"A dog would be good," Lagash agreed.

Borros motioned at Ferran. "He's skin and bones."

"If I can run, what should that matter?"

"It matters a lot when facing Osson raiders."

"I thought we were just going to Pencoy's. Besides, those three have no experience fighting grown men. They'll be slinging stones just like the rest of us. Except we're better shots than they are. If you want someone to get you to Pencoy's lands, we can do it."

"Yeah!" the younger Berryman shouted enthusiastically.

Borros raised an eyebrow

By the king's farting goat, Ferran wished that boy would wander out amongst the cattle and not find his way back.

Borros rubbed his jaw and said, "Well, it's easy enough to find out. We'll make this fair and square. We'll have ourselves a little competition. I will hire the top five."

There were ten boys. Ferran was confident he could beat cow-face and the two Berrymans. But what about the others? It would all depend on what the contest was.

"What I want," Borros said, "are the strongest, fastest, and most able to inflict harm. We'll have three contests. Your score in each is how you place. So the winner would score a one because he came in first. The next would score a two. And so on. In the end, we'll add up your three numbers. The five with the smallest totals win. Make sense?"

The boys nodded.

"Good. Let us begin."

SLING AND TOSS

"We'll start with a slinging contest," Borros said.

Lome grunted in protest, but Ferran smiled.

Borros said, "There will be three stationary targets and two moving ones." Then he ordered Ranoc, Krov, and the older Berryman to set up the stationary targets. They were stones the size of a dog's head. The first was set atop a fence post about twenty-five yards out. The next was set on another fence post about fifty yards out. The final target was set in the crook of the branch of a tree about seventy yards out. "You'll get two chances to hit each of those. And two to hit the moving targets. Every accurate strike earns a point. So ten points total."

"That last one is a good distance out there," Lome muttered under his breath.

"Don't worry about it," Caswal said. "Nobody will hit it."

"Who's going to go first?" Borros asked.

Pok, the oldest Berryman boy, raised his hand and stepped forward. Borros motioned for him to proceed. He hit the first target twice with ease. Hit the fifty yarder once. He missed the seventy yarder both times but was close.

For the moving target, Borros wrapped a stone and a whole bunch of dried meadow grass in a cloth and knotted it. The result was a cloth ball about the size of a man's head. Borros had tied it so that the knot had two long tails of cloth coming out of it. He stood behind a tree, took the tails, then swung the ball up and around and launched it into the air in a high arc. He did this at twenty and forty yards out.

Pok hit the closer target both times and the farther target once. His total score was six.

Lagash wrote it in the dirt with a stick.

"Next," Borros called.

Caswal went next and hit six. He hit the first two stationary targets easy enough. Missed the seventy. And missed one each of the two moving ones.

The cow-faced boy went next and, to everyone's surprise, hit seven, only missing the seventy-yard target and one of the closer moving targets.

Ranoc stepped up next, rubbed his hands together, then proceeded to hit nine of the targets, only missing the seventy-yarder once.

"That's quite a feat," Lagash said.

Ranoc shrugged and smiled, pleased with himself.

Winwalom went next with eight. Krov got six and said he'd have gotten all of them if he'd been able to use his bow. The younger Berryman got five. The miner boy three. Winwalom got eight. And then Ferran stood up. At this point, it was Ranoc, Winwalom, and Cow-eyes in positions one, two, and three with Krov, Caswal, and Pok all tied for fourth. Ferran knew he had to do well with this because he would prob-ably not do well in whatever the contest was for strength.

He nailed the first two targets easily. He selected one of his best stones and slung it at the seventy-yarder. It arched slightly, and he feared for a moment he'd overshot it, but the stone flew true and nailed the target with a satisfying smack. He selected another excellent stone and set himself.

"He'll miss," Caswal said.

Ferran ignored him, swung his sling and launched. The second stone flew as true as the first, and he smacked the target again.

"Whoa," Lagash said. "I think we've got ourselves a slinger."

Ferran tried not to smile and prepared for the next targets.

Borros threw his grass and cloth ball, and Ferran hit it. Borros threw it again, and Ferran hit it the second time. It was easy compared to hitting birds on the wing. Borros moved back and threw the ball farther again, and Ferran hit it, his excitement rising.

"One more, and it's a perfect score," Lagash said.

This wasn't a hard shot. He was going to take first place. Caswal would be fifth. Lome and the miner boy even lower.

"Cheese fart," Caswal said. "I heard your mother and Hellum were meeting this evening." Then he thrust his pelvis.

Anger boiled up in Ferran. "You goat dribbler," he said, then saw Borros winding up. Ferran scrambled for a stone, but the ball was already in the air before he slipped the stone in his pouch. He hurried his swing and released. The stone whistled across the meadow at the target, but it missed by an inch and stone sailed out into the meadow while the ball fell to the grass.

"Pity," Lagash said and scratched the score in the dirt. "Looks like we have a tie for first and fourth."

Ferran sighed. He should have ignored Caswal. He shouldn't have gotten cocky.

"So close," Winwalom said and clapped Ferran on the shoulder.

Ferran shot a glare at Caswal who was grinning and whispering something into Lome's ear.

Borros came in from the field carrying his ball.

Lagash pointed at Ferran and Ranoc. "Those two were impressive. Made me think of the Balorians the Lord of Kee hired."

Balor was a group of islands in the south middle sea that was known for its slingers. Various lords hired them as mercenary skirmishers.

"When they do it with a horde of soldiers coming at them," Borros said, "then I'll be impressed."

"We have a number of ties," Lagash said.

"Well, I expect this next contest will sort a few out," Borros said. "We're going to test your strength." He walked over and put his foot on a log that was maybe six feet long and about seven inches in diameter on both ends.

"I figure this is around eighty to ninety pounds. You're going to carry this log from here," he said and strode twenty yards away, then raised his voice, "to here." He dug a line with the heel of his boot in the dirt.

"When you get to this line, you will toss the log as far as you can. Whoever tosses the log the farthest wins. You cross this line, and your toss won't count. Also, there's a time limit with this one. Our dark friend there is going to count to one hundred and twenty. When the time's up, you stop. Are we clear?"

The boys nodded.

"Quickly then, let's get this done."

Pok went first again. When Borros said go, the boy walked over to the log, squatted, and struggled to lift it, but he finally got it up and began to walk. However, before he'd taken a dozen steps, he dropped it. He squatted and lifted it again, took another few steps, and dropped it again. Then he grabbed one end and began to drag it.

Borros shouted, "I said carry, not drag."

Pok stopped and picked it up. But the load was too much for him, and he kept dropping it. When Lagash counted one hundred and twenty, he hadn't even reached the line. Then he was told to drag the log back for the next boy.

His brother went next and did worse. Lome hefted the log onto his shoulder, easily covered the distance to the line where Borros stood, then tossed the log a few yards farther. Cow-face did better than the younger Berryman, but not as good as his brother. He dragged the log back and sat back down muttering how heavy it was. Caswal hefted it on his shoulder, went to the line, and tossed it almost as far as Lome.

Krov went next. He picked up the log like it was nothing. As he approached the line, he began to run. When he neared the line, he heaved the log up and out. It flew yards past Lome's mark and rolled even farther.

"The one-eyed woodsman has some strength," Lagash said.

"You should see his father," Ranoc said. "He wrestled a bull to the ground."

"Now that I would like to see."

"It's true," Ranoc said. "He can out-pull a horse."

Lagash rolled his eyes.

Winwalom went next, followed by the miner boy and Ranoc. When they were done, it was Krov in the lead with Lome and Caswal in the next two positions. Next came the miner boy, Ranoc, then Winwalom.

As each boy went, Ferran added their scores from the first contest to their scores according to how they were placing in this one. As Winwalom was dragging the log back, Ferran finished updating his numbers. At this point, Krov had a total of five points, Ranoc six, Caswal seven. Winwalom and Lome tied for the next slot at eight. That right there was five boys.

Ferran had no idea what other contests Borros would give them. He had talked about speed, so Ferran imagined there would be a foot race. He knew he was faster than many of these boys, but what if Borros marked a course that was long?

Ferran, with his diminishing stamina, would flag and any number of the boys would pass him. Furthermore, he didn't want to give Borros any cause to exclude him for weakness. He needed to show he had some strength. He had to keep himself in the top five. He didn't want this Borros from Three Hammers deciding between him and the others on some whim.

He double-checked his calculations and saw that if he beat Pok, he'd make a three-way tie with Winwalom and Lome. If he beat Winwalom, he'd tie Caswal.

Ferran rose. If nothing else, he had to beat Pok's mark.

He had watched the boys and decided that it would be easiest if he put the log over his shoulder. But when Lagash shouted go, and he squatted to lift the log, he found the log far heavier than eighty pounds.

It had to be over a hundred, and he struggled to get one end up. There was no way he could heft it up on his shoulder as the bigger boys had done. So he crouched down and worked his way to the halfway mark and stood.

The log's ends moved up and down, and he almost lost it. He knew immediately that there was no way he was going to keep its crushing weight on his shoulder for very long. So he tried to run, found that impossible, and ended up walking as quickly as he could. But before he went very far, the log twisted. He tried to right it, but it was too heavy, and he dropped it with a thud. He hadn't even reached the booger boy's mark.

He squatted again, heaved, and struggled more than he had the first time to get it up. But get it up he did. He moved to the middle again, tried to center himself better, and stood. His shoulder immediately started to weaken, and so he hurried forward. He tried to walk more smoothly this time, and as his shoulder sagged, he passed the mark of the younger Berryman.

Behind him, Lagash counted to ninety. Ferran continued walking, straining with the weight. Ahead of him was Cow-face's mark. But Ferran's arms lost their strength, and he dropped it.

He squatted and tried to lift the end again and found it too heavy. He knew he was stronger than this, but he'd been starving for too long. He tried again, heard Lagash count one hundred and ten, then pushed with all his might, using every muscle in his leg and back and buttocks, and the log's end rose. He got his other shoulder under it, balanced it, staggered forward.

Lagash counted a hundred and seventeen. A hundred and eighteen.

Pok's mark was still a few strides away, and Ferran was losing the log again. But he wasn't going to fail. He couldn't! He mustered all his strength and surged forward.

The log began to fall, but Ferran held on and pumped his legs. And then he was off balance and stumbling forward, but he continued to grip it with all his might and pump his legs. The log dropped. He crashed over it and tumbled, painfully skinning his shin on the log and getting a face full of dirt.

But when he'd wiped the dirt from his mouth and eyes and looked back, he saw the log was a foot beyond Pok's mark.

Relief flooded Ferran. He'd made a fool of himself, but he was still in the race.

Borros walked over, looked down, and called out his score.

"Not the best form I've seen," Borros said.

"Me either," Ferran said, climbing to his feet. "Next time I'll find a log with better manners."

"Drag it back," Borros said.

Ferran quailed at the thought, but he wasn't going to show any lack of willingness to work. So he lifted an end and hauled backward, dragging it along. He dropped it a number of times, and when he was still some distance out, Borros shouted at him to leave it and join the others.

Ferran's arms were jelly, and he was glad to be rid of it, but it was also an embarrassment. He flushed with shame as he trudged over to join the others. Then Caswal made some comment that made a number of the other boys laugh, and Ferran's shame doubled. Ferran was still breathing hard when he took his place among the other boys.

"The mighty mouse returns," Caswal whispered loudly enough for the other boys to hear.

Ferran gritted his teeth and pretended the comment didn't sting.

"The final contest will be a foot race," Borros said. "If you're going to dog my cattle, you need to be swift and have the stamina to do it again and again." He pointed to a path that led from his campsite out between two fields. "You'll run along this path, out to that knoll there, then run up the knoll and hug the trunk of that first tree you see almost at the top. Then you'll run out to the main road, follow it back through the village, and then up this path to the starting line."

The course was almost a mile long, and Ferran began to worry, for he was definitely going to flag at that distance.

"You want us to hug the tree?" Krov asked.

"Would you rather lick it?"

"No, sir."

"Now here's another thing. When you turn to run back up this path to the starting line, you will twirl three times. Understood?"

They all nodded, a few of them looking at each other in confusion over the strange requests.

Ferran wasn't ready to run. He still felt weak from the log, and his throat was dry. He raised his hand. "Sir, would you mind if I got a little drink before this race?"

"Me too," Ranoc agreed.

A few of the other boys murmured agreement.

"Fine," Borros said. "Be quick. There's a barrel on the side of the wagon."

The boys hurried over. Lome shoved his way to the front.

"Make a line," Borros said.

The boys lined up, and Ferran was happy to take a spot toward the end with Winwalom. Cow-eyes was in front of them, and when he finished, he handed the dipper to Ferran and walked back to join the others.

Ferran sank it into the barrel three times and drank every drop. The water was old and had the taste of the wood of the barrel to it, but it felt good and refreshing.

He handed the dipper to Winwalom, then pitched his voice low. "You, me, Ranoc, and Krov need to place in the top five in this race."

Winwalom took his first drink. When he finished, he dipped again and said, "Pok's pretty fast. So is Caswal. And that miner boy."

"We need to beat them," Ferran said.

"Then we'd better get in front of them right from the start. Because if we don't, they'll block us the whole way."

"You tell Ranoc and Krov," Ferran said.

Winwalom nodded and finished another drink, and as they walked back, he said, "What's with the twirls and tree hugging?"

"No idea," Ferran said. "He is from down south. I hear they're odd folk down there."

"There are a number of odd things about this drover," Winwalom said.

"Aye," Ferran said, but he didn't care. Coin was coin, and it didn't matter where he got it.

They joined the other boys, and Borros said, "Line up."

Ferran pointed and told Itch to stay where he was, then loosened his shoulders and took a position on the line Lagash had drawn in the dirt. Caswal took the position next to him. Lome muscled Winwalom out of the way and took a position on the other side. Ferran tensed. What were they doing?

"On my mark!" Borros said.

Ferran and the others set themselves, and, in the jumble, Caswal pinched Ferran ferociously on the back of his arm.

The pain burned like a hot poker. "Hey!" Ferran growled and wrenched his arm away.

"Go!" Borros said.

The other boys shot out, and as Lome took off, he swung his fist backward with violence between Ferran's legs, hitting him hard in the groin.

Ferran gasped.

The other boys thundered away.

He took a breath, screwed up his face.

Borros looked at him with puzzlement. Itch rose, knowing something was wrong. "Stay," Ferran said, then ran after the boys despite the ache.

8

SELECTION

The pain made it hard to run, but he pushed through it. Oh, how he wished he could sic Itch on those two farting, goat-brained, fly-infested turds. But he knew what would burn them worse. The best way to get back at those two was to win this race and push their faces in it.

The boys were about fifteen yards ahead. Winwalom was trying to break away from a knot of boys, his horse-tail of hair flowing behind him. Ferran expected one of the boys to grasp it, but Lome and the miner threw some elbows instead and blocked him. A few moments later the boys sorted themselves out into a line. In front were the two Berryman boys. Next was Ranoc, then Caswal, followed by Lome, and the miner. Winwalom, Krov, and Cow-eyes brought up the rear with Ferran trailing behind.

He didn't know how all the boys would place, but he knew if he was in the top five, he would be safe. He also knew he couldn't wait until the end of the race to make his move, so he increased his speed and caught up and passed Cow-eyes.

The pain from Lome's blow was lessening, and Ferran flitted over the dirt in his bare feet. Ahead, the second Berryman boy began to flag. The other boys skirted around him. And then Ranoc made a move and shot out in front so that it was Ranoc, followed by Pok, Caswal, Lome, and the miner.

At this point, Ferran's crew was not doing well. And there wasn't space on the sides of this path to pass. Certainly not around Caswal and Lome who would likely knock them into the rock walls on either side.

But the path opened up at the base of the knoll, and that's where he'd have to make his move. The boys paced themselves. Ferran began to breathe hard, but his strength was holding. And then they came to the base of the knoll and Caswal, Lome, and the miner spread out, trying to prevent the others from passing them.

Pok faded, and Caswal's crew sprinted past, but then they slowed. The knoll was steep, and the tree was up toward the top. Even Ranoc had to stop and hike a few paces before running again.

Ferran decided his opportunity would be on the other side, running down the hill, and so when the others flagged, he put on speed to close the gap. Winwalom and Krov must have made the same calculations, for they did the same.

Ranoc reached the tree, hugged it, and began to jog down to the trail that led out to the road.

Caswal didn't hug, but merely pressed his chest against the tree. Lome did the same. The miner didn't even pretend to hug. He simply reached out and touched the tree and took off toward the road.

Ferran, Winwalom, and Krov quickly hugged the trunk, and then Ferran saw the line he should run and let loose, running as fast as he could down the hill, taking huge flying strides. He ran with abandon, knowing this was his chance.

Caswal, Lome, and the miner heard him too late.

He flew past Lome the Miner on his left, focusing all his attention on the ground out in front of him for anything that would trip him up.

"Get him!" Lome called out. Caswal was ahead of them, but he was on their right, and Ferran raced ahead into second place.

He felt like the wind. And then he was at the bottom, his weight trying to bear him to the ground, and he had to shorten his stride. He ran to the trail leading out to the main road and glanced back.

Winwalom was back a little way. Then Caswal, Krov, the miner, and Lome. Ferran's crew was going to make it. He was going to make it!

The trail opened up onto the main road, and Ferran turned. He ran down the road, slipping past the stone walls of the fields on either side. He ran probably another hundred yards and suddenly found it hard to keep his pace. He tried to push himself, but couldn't, and slowed, breathing hard. A dozen strides later, he struggled to keep even that pace and had to slow again. And then his lungs gave out altogether, and he had to walk.

He glanced back. Winwalom was right there. Caswal was a few strides behind. Pok had regained a position and was in front of Krov.

"Go!" Winwalom shouted.

Ferran started to jog.

"Come on!" Winwalom said and passed him.

Ferran glanced back and saw Caswal blowing hard but running steady. Ferran tried to pick up his pace.

He ran past the first cottage and garden. Then the next. There was a wide gap between it and the next one. And by the time they reached it, Caswal was right on his heels.

Ferran tried to relax and lengthen his stride. He tried to keep his gait smooth and avoid the wasted motion of bopping up and down. But he was flagging.

Behind him, Caswal began to pick up his pace. Ferran tried to match the speed but he couldn't. Caswal was just off his shoulder.

They ran a few paces that way, and Ferran's hopes rose. Maybe Caswal was just as blown as he was!

But as they passed the next cottage, Ferran discovered that wasn't the case. For as soon as they were out of the sight of the drover, Caswal sped up.

Ferran moved to cut him off, but Caswal shoved Ferran in the back of the head, making him stumble forward.

Ferran caught himself, saw Caswal's line, and stepped wide to trip him. But Ferran's exhaustion had stolen his speed.

Caswal side-stepped the move. He shoved Ferran hard in the side of his head this time and sent him careening away into a push cart that was parked in front of the cottage.

Ferran crashed into the corner and felt like he'd run himself onto a pole. He came to an immediate halt and fell to the ground in massive pain.

The miner ran past. Then Krov and Lome. And then Pok was kneeling at his side.

"Are you okay?"

"That whoreson!" Ferran said.

"Get up! Come on!" Pok said and helped Ferran to his feet. "Come on!" he said and began to run. "We can't let them win."

And Ferran noticed what looked like a bruise forming on the side of Pok's face. Had one of them hit him?

Ferran's side was killing him, but he jogged after Pok, and then stretched his stride.

"Come on!" Pok said.

And Ferran put all of his strength into it.

A number of the villagers were watching the race and cheered him on, but when he saw the head of the trail leading back to the starting line, he knew he was too far behind.

Caswal finished a twirl and took off up the trail after Winwalom. Krov began to twirl. The miner reached the trailhead, did one twirl, and sped past Krov. Pok and Lome reached it about the same time and began the ridiculous twirls. They completed them and raced for the finish line just as Ferran arrived.

He completed his twirls as fast as he could then ran for the starting line. He crossed it, the eighth man in, and bent over to put his hands on his knees and catch his breath.

When his breathing began to slow, he calculated the scores, and his heart fell. His total score was not in the top five. Or six. He was number seven.

Seven.

Itch woofed and wagged his tail, and Ferran held out his hand, inviting him over for a pet.

He'd failed.

He scratched the dog on his gray mottled neck, hardly aware he was there. He'd failed. There was to be no money. Only bondage.

Caswal was whooping with the miner and Lome.

Borros said, "Line up."

The boys lined up.

"What are the scores?" he asked Lagash.

"Our lanky bull rider with the scar has seven," he said and pointed at Ranoc. He motioned at Winwalom, Krov, and Caswal. "Those three each have ten. The other two big ones have fifteen. Black Eye there with his dog has sixteen. And the other three are eighteen, twenty-one, and twenty-five."

Ferran's hopes were dashed. He was about to protest the blows at the beginning of the race and the shove by the cottage, but discarded the idea. He'd complain. Lome and Caswal would say they didn't do it. And the drover would just get annoyed.

Ferran cursed Caswal. Cursed himself. He should have moved to another part of the starting line as soon as Caswal and Lome had lined up next to him. What had he been thinking?

"Looks like we need a tie-breaker between those two," Lagash said and motioned at Lome and the miner.

"Oh, that's easy," Borros said. He pointed at the miner. "That one didn't run the race."

"I did," the miner boy said indignantly.

"No, you did not. I told you to hug the tree. You did not hug it. I told you to twirl three times. You didn't do that either. Therefore, you did not complete the race. Anyone who works for me will perform the tasks I give them with exactness. I don't run a nursery for children. You failed the test, and so you're out."

The miner boy scowled and looked at the ground.

"Well, then we have our five," Lagash said.

"Sir," Ferran said.

Borros looked at him.

"I think you're overlooking something important."

"Oh?"

"My score was sixteen. But that does not take into account my dog. You'll get more work out of the two of us than you ever will with him," Ferran said and pointed at Lome. "You need a trained dog. I have one."

"We do need a dog," Lagash said.

"And Ferran should have had a better score in the race," Cow-eyes said.

Everyone looked at him.

"Had it not been for some dirty play down in the village, he would have come in fourth or fifth."

"What kind of dirty play?" Borros asked.

Cow-eyes shrugged. "The kind that shoves a runner into a cart and makes him lose four places."

"Sometimes shoving is part of racing," Borros said.

"You said you wanted speed," Cow-eyes said. "Just thought you should know Ferran was faster."

"Fine," Borros said. "Dog Boy is in. The big one is out."

"What?" Lome said in protest.

"That's hardly fair," Caswal said. "He won."

"I'm not trying to be fair," Borros said. "I'm moving cattle. And I will hire who I think suits the task best."

"But you said—"

"Do you want to join your friend and stay here?"

Caswal swallowed his next words. "No," he said.

"Good, because I don't have time for any more nonsense."

Relief flooded Ferran, and then his heart soared. He was in! He was going to actually make some good coin.

Borros looked at him. "Don't disappoint me."

"No sir," said Ferran. "You're going to be happy with your choice. I promise you. I—"

Borros held up his hand for Ferran to stop and addressed the boys. "Now before you accept, you need to know my rules. I have three. And if you're going to drive with me, you'd better be ready to keep them. Rule number one: you will treat each other with respect. There will be no fighting or bickering or provocation.

"Rule number two: you will treat the possessions of others with respect. This means you will ask before you use. You will not steal. Not from me, not from our cook here, not from each other, and most definitely not from anyone along the way.

"Rule number three: you will work willingly. From the moment we leave until Pencoy's escort joins us, you are in my employ. When you're not working, you'll be sleeping, and I will tell you when you can sleep. I don't want any sass or complaint. I don't want any dragging of feet." He motioned at himself and Lagash. "When either of us makes a request, you jump to it. Do you understand?"

The boys nodded.

"I'm not going to nag you to keep any of these rules. I'll treat you like a man and pay you like a man, and I expect you to keep your agreements like a man. I may give you one warning, but only if I think that maybe you were just too dumb to understand. But you will never get more than one. Now for your work, I will feed you two sound meals a day. And I will pay you what you're due the very day we arrive at Pencoy's. Are you agreed?"

"And that's at four and a half coppers per day?" Ranoc asked.

"That was the wage for full-grown men. I'll pay you two."

"We'll be doing the job the men would have," Krov said.

"You're only going to Pencoy's," Borros said.

"Three," Ferran said.

"I'll do two and a half," Borros said. "Not a birdseye more. Are we agreed?"

It was more than any of them would earn at any job they might be given.

The boys agreed.

"Then go inform your parents and get back here with whatever you'll need for the trip. We will be leaving in less than one hour."

Three pennies per day would have been a better deal, and he wished the other boys had held out, but two and a half for ten days would earn him twenty-five. His mother owed the lord 120 pennies, the price of two year's rent on their cottage. They had saved forty since the debacle with the cheese vessels. His wages from droving would add to that for a total of sixty-five pennies. Surely such a sum might induce the lord to reconsider giving them more time.

But Ferran wasn't going to rely on that alone. He didn't want to stop at Pencoy's. He wanted the higher wage that would be paid for risking his life along the coast road. What he needed to do now was prove himself valuable. And then at Pencoy's, he would offer his services again.

Ferran was ecstatic. He'd gotten the job!

Cow-eyes turned to him and said, "Good luck."

"I owe you," Ferran said.

The boy shrugged. "Caswal and Lome are maggots."

And Ferran realized that Caswal and Lome had probably made it a point over the years to search the boy out to pick on him.

Pok said, "They spoil everything."

Ferran pointed at the fresh bruise above his eye. "Did you get that during the race?"

"Caswal's elbow."

And suddenly Ferran felt bad for the feelings he'd harbored toward these two earlier. "I wish I could share some of my earnings, but--"

Pok cut him off. "We don't want any of your earnings. The satisfaction of seeing Lome get what he deserves is enough."

"I wish we could say the same of Caswal," Ferran said.

"You watch him," Cow-eyes said. "He's going to make you pay."

Usually, Ferran could simply escape Caswal, but that wasn't going to be possible on this trip. "I'm not afraid of him."

"You'd better be," said Pok.

"You watch out for Lome," Ferran said.

"At least with us, it will be two against one."

"I've got Winwalom," Ferran said, although that might not be enough if Caswal convinced Krov to join in on one of his plots.

And with that, he bid both boys farewell. He even waved to the younger Berryman, but the boy didn't see him because right at that moment he tripped over a log while chasing something in the air. Ferran shook his head, then took off at a run to share the good news with Mother and gather his kit.

9

PROMISES

Ferran found his mother and sister Lily by the mill pond. Today was the monthly wash day, and they were there with many of the village women and children washing a month's worth of under clothing. There were large wooden tubs full of under linens, some soaking, some being tread by children. There were fires, and cauldrons of heating water, and short, fat laundry bats for beating the clothes, plus a few barrels of urine for bleaching, and piles of ash for making soap. There were a dozen laundry lines strung in tidy rows and hanging with washed clothes looking like a white vineyard.

His mother was rinsing and wringing clothes in a round, wooden tub of steaming water. Her sleeves and trouser pants were rolled up. She saw him, finished wringing the undershirt she working on, and set it aside. The hair framing her face was wet with moisture.

"I got the job," he said.

"Truly?"

"I'm going home to get my kit."

"Wait," she said. "I'm wondering if this is wise."

"What?" he said.

"There's talk about this drover."

"What talk?"

"He has no references."

"That's Hellum talking," Ferran said. "Spreading his lies so he can cheat the man out of his livelihood. He's the last maggot we want to listen to. The drover has the queen's contract, written and sealed."

"His crew left him."

"They poisoned his dogs. They wanted to rob him. And they didn't leave him. He fought them and tied them up for the headman of Mossby to handle."

"He fought them?"

"Yes, him and his mate."

"That is not what I heard."

"The Sorosian told us the whole thing. Has nobody gone to Mossby yet?"

"Hellum convinced them it wasn't worth it."

"And that right there should tell you the worth of all of these rumors."

"You're right," she said. "But even so, the drover's taking you into dangerous territory."

"Mum," he said, and looked her in the eyes. "I'm going to be all right. We're going to pay our debts. This job is two and a half coppers per day."

"I just don't feel right about it."

And Ferran realized this was the real issue. She had not felt right when Father had gone out on that week-long patrol of the western range and never returned. And she condemned herself for not listening to that feeling and preventing him from going.

"Mum," he said. "You know what will happen if we don't come up with the payment. He's hired us to get him to Pencoy's. So it's not the full distance. Although I intend to go all the way. But even if I only go to Pencoy's, that's seven days. It's seventeen and a half coppers. If I'm going to be sold, that would be seventeen and a half less for me to work off."

"Hellum," she said with disgust. "Him and his poison."

"Yes. Dripping it in everyone's ears. This is our chance. And if we convince him to use us for the whole way to Broniss, we'll be able to pay the debt in full."

"It's so far," she said. "Who else is going?"

He told her.

"That's a good lot of boys."

"Except for Caswal."

"True," she said. "Two and a half coppers per day?"

"Yes."

"Were there any witnesses to the agreement?"

"Just the other boys."

"We need more than boys. This drover's a stranger. You get your kit. I'll bring the miller and smith."

Ferran raced home, took their sturdy hemp pack and filled it with a large wooden cup, a wooden spoon, his cloak, a chewing stick, the goatskin water bottle the widow had given him, plus his bow drill for making fires. On the way back he wanted a fire, and he wanted to be able to make it on his own because he wasn't going to travel back with Caswal.

He took some cord, a long tree-thorn needle, plus one of the two knives they owned and the whetstone. If he had to, he could sleep on the ground, but he saw the sackcloth they weren't using right now and figured Mother wouldn't mind. So he took two large pieces almost as long as he was tall, folded them, and slid them into the pack as well. He intended to tie them together and then stuff the bag with grass, leaves, and other material he might find to make a softer bed to sleep on.

He thought that should do it, but knew his mother would worry about injuries and so took the small crock of poultice and a couple of cloth strips she used for bandages. Surely that would set her mind at ease.

Finally, he fetched his shoulder bag and stuffed it with about three-dozen sling stones, all about the size of a hen's egg, some a little smaller. Ferran had made it a habit to gather good stones when he found them. In the evenings, he'd used an old claw chisel and a wooden mallet to carve the stone into the shape of an egg or elongated sphere since rocks flew the farthest and straightest when they were that shape. At one time, his collection had included half a dozen projectiles made from lead that his father had been given as part of his military duty. But Ferran had sold them and the chisel earlier this year to help pay for their cheese vessels.

When the last stone was in, he went through a mental list of what he thought he needed, but couldn't think of anything else, and hurried back to the drover's field.

The others boys were already there. Ranoc's parents had come, as had Winwalom's widower father with his long and graying hair. Nobody from Krov's family was there. Nor Caswal's.

Lome was there with his da who was having words with Borros.

"It's an insult that you're hiring a flea-infested backtalker over the son of a man with a full thirty acres," Lome's da said.

Ferran realized Lome's da was talking about him.

"He brought the better value," Borros said.

That only made Lome's da angrier. "You're a fool."

"We all are fools," Borros said.

"You'll rue this," he said. "Come on, Lome. With such poor judgment at its head, this drive is obviously destined for failure." He turned on his heel, saw Ferran, and gave him a withering glare. And then he and Lome marched back to the village. They passed Hellum coming the other way.

Hellum was with the two other richer farmers he'd come with before. He saw the boys and shook his head in amusement. "Master Drover," he said. "You've had a night to sleep on it. We've collected money to purchase a hundred head."

"I'm not interested," Borros said.

"Come, sir, you think these boys will get you to Broniss?"

"They're lively and fit enough for my purpose."

"Fit enough to contend with raiders? You're going to lose all of your cattle that way. And the lives of these boys. Be sensible. Let's negotiate a price."

"I keep hearing the sound of farting," Borros said to Lagash. "Do you hear it?"

"Now that you mention it, there is a peculiar odor," Lagash replied.

Hellum narrowed his eyes. "You are being a fool."

"People keep telling me that."

"Okay, fine. We'll raise our price to forty per head. That's our final offer."

"They're not for sale. These are contracted to the queen. So you can take your pittance and hang it for all I care."

Hellum narrowed his eyes.

"You're still here?" Borros said.

"These boys can't help you. They are duty bound to their days of service to the lord."

"Not for a fortnight or more," Ranoc's father said. He was tall and lean and wasn't cowed by the likes of Hellum.

Furthermore, what he said was true.

Hellum knew he was beaten, but he smiled anyway. "Have it your way," he said, then raise his voice so all could hear. "We'll all pray your journey is safe." He looked meaningfully at Ranoc's and Winwalom's parents and then addressed the boys. "You're going off with a strange man whose own crew turned on him. You're going into danger. Mark me; if you come back at all, you're going to come back empty-handed."

Ferran and the other boys just stood there and looked at him.

"I'm only thinking of you," he said. "It's not too late to avoid a foolish and probably mortal risk." And then he and the other two men departed like three snakes in the grass.

"That stinking fish," Borros said.

Just then Ferran's mother and sister started up the trail with the carpenter and miller.

Borros rolled his eyes. "What now?"

Ferran raised his hand. "Sir, they are here to witness the agreement."

"Well, at least one of them is easy on the eyes."

"That would be my mother," Ferran said.

"No, the stout one on the left," Borros said. "See how he kind of rolls from side to side."

Ferran looked, but could not see how that was attractive.

Borros cracked a smile.

The miller called out to Krov, "Your father agreed to this?"

"He did."

"And you?" he asked Caswal.

"Yes."

The miller nodded and said, "We are here to witness the agreement."

Borros nodded. "So I heard."

"Well, then let's hear it," the miller said.

Borros explained his rules, the meals he'd provide, and the pay. Then he added, "And they need to deliver the cattle to Pencoy's with no more than a one percent loss."

"How many is that?"

"Two head."

"Two? That's not much margin. What if some of them are old and simply die? Surely, it's not their job to cure your aged and sick cattle. The one percent should apply only to those that wander or are stolen through their neglect."

Borros sighed. "Fine, it will apply only to those that wander or are stolen."

"And what if it's more than one percent?" the miller asked. "What if it's two? Surely, they still deserve some pay for helping with the other ninety-eight percent of the cattle."

Borros looked at Ferran. "Was he your idea?"

"He was so easy on the eyes," Ferran said. "I couldn't help it."

Borros's eyes rounded a bit, and Lagash laughed.

The miller beamed.

Borros said, "If it's two percent, I cut their pay in half. If it's three, they don't get any pay at all."

"Six head," the miller confirmed.

"Six."

Six wasn't a lot. Two was less, and Ferran realized they would all need to be alert and working hard because he didn't want to lose one bit of the promised payment.

The miller looked at Ferran's mother and the smith. "Anything else?"

They shook their heads, and the miller raised his voice and addressed those gathered. "Does everyone here understand and agree of your own free choice?"

"What about some surety against the payment?" Ranoc's father asked.

Borros raised an eyebrow.

Lagash said, "That's a reasonable request."

"Are you on their side or mine?"

"I'm on whatever side gets us moving. Give them one of your dandy silks."

"That will work," Borros said and went to the wagon, opened a barrel, and fished out a silk scarf the light blue of a robin's egg and brought it over and showed his sign embroidered in the corner.

The miller nodded, but the smith said, "We shall keep this and your ring as proof of the agreement, to be recovered upon your return and validation of your payment."

"My ring?"

"I'll keep it safe," the smith promised.

Borros sighed, but removed a large ring from his finger and handed it over to the smith. "Satisfied?"

"Yes."

"At last," Borros said and motioned at the boys. "The job starts now. Get your packs in the wagon. We're moving out."

Ferran's mother took him by the shoulders and looked him in the eye. He knew she was thinking of Da.

"I'm going to be alright, Mum. We're going to pay our debts."

"Demonstrate exact obedience. Don't give him any reason to claim you didn't fill your part of the agreement."

"I won't."

Lily took off the braid she wore around her wrist from which hung a small acorn, a tiny blue stone, and the skull of a small bird. "Take this," she said.

"I'll lose all three of those charms for sure," he said. "You keep it safe. And take this." He removed a braid from his wrist that was far plainer but had his father's initials woven into it and gave it to her. "You keep that safe for my return."

She took it and hugged him.

"Where's your hat?" his mother asked.

"I'll be fine."

"Take mine," she said and removed it from her head.

"I'm not taking your hat."

"Take it," she said.

"I don't need it."

She raised her eyebrows in warning.

"Mother," he said, and she relented and embraced him.

"Be safe," she said.

"I will."

Lily squeezed Itch, and then Ferran took his pack to Lagash who stowed it in the wagon then joined the boys waiting for Borros to give them their tasks. But Ferran's mother was talking to Borros.

She was probably talking about hats and baby stuff. Ferran's cheeks burned with embarrassment. But when she finished, Borros gave her a couple of coins.

"What was that?" Ferran asked her.

"I'm going to take care of his dogs. He'll pick them up on the way back."

Ferran's embarrassment turned to surprise and then pride in his mother. She'd seen the opportunity to earn more while he'd been blind. She was good with animals. If any could nurse the dogs back to health, it was her.

"I'm going to go borrow a wheelbarrow to transport them," she said and hurried off with Lily.

Borros held up a small ram's horn that was painted with various symbols. It also had a leather strap to hang it from your neck. "If you hear this," he said and blew three high notes, "that means I want you to stop." He blew a long note that went from a lower to a higher pitch. "That means to start again. Understood?"

The boys nodded.

He pointed at Ferran. "You'll bring up the rear. That's the best place for a dog. Get behind them. We'll see how good the two of you are. The rest of you form up on the sides." He grabbed four poles with dirty yellow pieces of cloth tied to the ends and handed them out to the other boys. He pointed at Caswal. "You're in charge. I want two on a side. Make sure everyone does his job."

Ferran groaned inside at Caswal's appointment, but the adults seemed always to pick him, and Ferran wasn't going to start his job by arguing. He went to the gate, entered the meadow and made his way through the cattle to the back corner. Ferran had learned that calm animals were more biddable than scared or angry ones, so he didn't send Itch barking and snapping. He simply clapped and shouted a few times. Itch too knew his place, and he barked a couple of times.

It was more than enough for the cattle, and they began to move. Very soon the last cow left the field, and Ferran and Itch walked in a wide zigzag from one end of the back of the herd to the other pushing the cattle along. Borros took the lead, scouting ahead. Lagash came behind on his wagon. He wore his wide-brimmed hat with the feathers on the side.

Caswal and Krov took one side of the herd, Ranoc and Winwalom the other. They followed the trail from the drover's field onto the main road and along a stretch that traveled straight for about a quarter mile, then curved. The cattle seemed to know to follow the road and began to disappear around the bend.

When Ferran reached the bend, he stood in the warm dust of the road in his bare feet and looked back. His mother and Lily were still standing on the road at the edge of the village. They waved. He waved back. And then he faced forward and followed the cattle until Buckle Hill village was out of sight.

10

THE ROAD

They drove the cattle for three miles, skirted the village of Nob, and continued. Lagash said they didn't want to hurry the animals. He said they had many miles to go and a comfortable but steady pace was the best. And so Ferran and Itch simply walked back and forth in the curve of a half moon and allowed the cattle to set the pace.

A couple of times a few of the cattle lagged, and the herd began to string out, and it was at these times that Ferran would urge them forward with some claps. Itch had done this enough with goats and sheep and knew that was the time to bark as well.

They traveled another few miles and passed the road to the village of Narsk which is where the Haver family lived. The Havers had seven daughters, and each was as pretty as the last. Beyond Narsk was Wood-hill, which is where a tailor lived who also bred dogs that had been sold as far as Dob's Port on the coast. It was from him that Ferran wanted to buy a puppy mastiff to add some muscle to Itch's speed. He could visit the tailor to see how much a mastiff might cost.

And then he realized that a puppy in arms might be a good ploy to get the notice of one of the younger Haver girls. That thought grew, and he decided he was going to get a puppy when he got back.

They continued. The road was dry, and the cattle kicked up a cloud of dust that he and Itch had to work in. He quickly pulled his old scarf up to cover his nose and mouth. But that didn't keep the dust from his eyes, and they soon began to feel gritty and sting.

They came to a creek, and the boys had to hold the cattle back and let them at the water in groups of twenty or thirty so as not to cause trouble. When all the cattle were on their way again, he went upstream to avoid the water the cattle had muddied and washed the dust off his face and topped off his water bag.

They continued, herding the cattle up and down hills and around corners. The other boys held their positions on the sides, now and again waving their cattle flags or clapping to keep the animals from straying into the woods.

Borros walked almost a quarter mile ahead of the herd, scouting, and Ferran rarely saw him. But he did see a badger hiss its way through herd from one side of the road to the other. He saw a hawk dive at something out in a meadow. A little later they passed the victory tree where Ulam, a blackhearted Gorman raider, had been hung when Ferran's mother was a youth.

They passed through another village, and Ferran felt an odd pride as the people looked on. This was the farthest spot he'd ever traveled in this direction, and he felt excited about going beyond it and seeing what lay ahead. As they passed through, an old, skinny farmer with a thin beard that fell to his chest asked where they were from.

Ferran replied, "The herd is from Three Hammers, but the other boys and I are from Buckle Hill."

"We used to get delicious cheese out of there. But I heard the cheese wife fell on hard times. Was robbed and killed."

Ferran realized he was talking about Mother. "Robbed," he said, "but not killed."

"It's a pity," the man said and shook his head. "And I would say you're heading for trouble as well. You know the coast road isn't safe."

"We have an escort arranged at Pencoy's," Ferran replied.

"There's something else out there, stealing livestock in the night."

"Something?"

The farmer shrugged. "All I know is that people have been losing livestock."

"Thieves?" Ferran asked.

"This herd's a pretty thing," the farmer said. "You boys had best watch yourselves."

That was ominous, and Ferran wanted to know more, but the cattle were getting away from him, and a few were starting to crowd next to a garden fence, eyeing something on the other side. So Ferran thanked the man and raced forward to keep the animals from doing any damage. The last thing he needed was for a couple to crash into someone's garden and have the drover get after him.

Ferran and Itch got the cattle moving again, and as they left the village behind, he began to think about that warning. The next village was Pencoy's, and that was days away. They were going out into land where there weren't a lot of people. Which meant he'd have to stay alert. He had his sling and stones. They all did. They'd just have to stay alert.

And he did as they trudged through the late afternoon and into the early evening. Or at least he tried. He'd run out of water a few miles back, and his throat was dry. And it didn't help that so much road dust covered him that when he slapped the front of his tunic, dust poofed up in a cloud. And then the sun began to sink in the west. Itch's mottled gray coat was covered in it as well.

He lagged back to where Lagash rode in his wagon. And Ferran noticed it was as well-maintained as Lagash was. "Shouldn't we be stopping?" he called.

"Sometimes, if the moon is bright enough, we drive them through the night."

"The night?" Ferran asked in dismay.

"Where I'm from it gets hot in the day. Too hot. Much better to drive them at night. And sometimes you need to keep your position secret from prying eyes. But look, it appears we've come to our destination."

Way up at the front of the herd, Borros stood in the middle of the road, turning the cattle into a break in the trees. When Ferran got closer, he saw Caswal and Winwalom directing the cattle into a small, fenced field. One section had fallen into disrepair, and Krov and Ranoc stood there to keep the cattle from breaking out.

11

WATER JOB

Borros joined Ferran as the tail end of the herd began to move into the field, and when the last cow was in, he swung the wooden gate shut and secured it. The cattle quickly went to munching the grass in the field. Lagash drove his wagon over to a campsite and stopped.

Borros said, "I'll take Krov and Ranoc to help me repair the fence. I want the rest of you to fill those troughs with water, fetch Lagash whatever he needs to cook supper, and gather firewood. There's a stream on the other side of the field. And we need a trench for a latrine well away from the camp." He pointed at Caswal. "Get them organized and get it done. Buckets are in the wagon."

Ferran sighed. He didn't know if he could bear that maggot being the boss the whole trip.

Caswal motioned at Winwalom and Ferran. "You two fill the troughs. I'll help Lagash."

Of course, Caswal would take the easy job. It irked Ferran to no end that Caswal was giving him orders, but he didn't want to give the drover any reason to say Ferran hadn't kept his part of the agreement, and so said nothing, just walked over to the wagon. There were four wooden buckets. He and Winwalom grabbed two each and headed out for the far end of the field.

Borros took an axe, some wedges, and a saw out of the bed of the wagon and headed toward the break in the fence.

Lagash set Caswal to unhitching Carrots the mule and wiping him down with grass.

Ferran surveyed the huge herd of cattle. "How many buckets is it going to take to water this mob?"

"Two each," Winwalom said. "So about five hundred."

Ferran groaned. "We're going to be carrying water the whole night through."

"Why don't we just lead them to the stream in small groups?" Winwalom asked.

That sounded like a good idea, but when they arrived at the edge of the narrow stream, they saw there was no bank on this side, just a five-foot drop-off. There was no way to get the cattle down and back up again.

"The king's stinking feet," Ferran said. "Who chose this as the site for a drover's field?"

"Look," Winwalom said and pointed. "Fish."

Ferran looked. Someone had built a rock dam across the stream here so there was a pool maybe fifteen feet across. The brown backs of fish were visible.

"Look at that one," he said and pointed at one that had to be almost three feet long.

"Dinner," Winwalom said. "Catch him." And then he gave Ferran a huge shove.

Ferran yelped as he flew over the ledge and splashed into the cold, deep water. He touched bottom, came up, and cleared the water from his face. After that hot, dusty road they'd walked, the water felt glorious.

Winwalom was grinning. "Make way. Make way!" he called and stepped back a few paces to get a good start, and then he ran and took a flying leap. He soared out over the pool and made a big splash next to Ferran. Itch barked and jumped in after them.

When Winwalom came up, Ferran dunked him, but Winwalom simply went down and grabbed Ferran's leg and yanked him under. Ferran reached down, felt Winwalom's long hair slip through his fingers, and came back to look for him, but he wasn't anywhere to be seen. A few moments later he popped up at the far end of the pool.

Ferran moved in the opposite direction to the part of the rock dam where the water cascaded down the other side and slaked his thirst. Winwalom wrung out his horsetail, then hucked a glob of mud and weed at Ferran. Ferran ducked it and thought about getting his own mud missile, but then he remembered his mother's words about working hard. What if the drover found them messing around?

"We'd better get hauling," he said. "We don't want to get in trouble our first day."

"You're right," Winwalom said and lobbed another weed glob.

Ferran thought about the warning the old farmer had given him. "Did you talk to anyone in that last village we passed through?"

"No."

"An old farmer there told me there are thieves in the area. Somebody is stealing livestock."

Winwalom narrowed his eyes.

"That's what he said."

Winnwalom shook his head. "Lovely. And who better to steal from than a herd guarded by a bunch of boys."

"Thieves," Ferran said in disgust.

"Let's just hope they're not the throat-slitting kind."

Ferran felt his throat, then looked nervously at the woods around them. Certainly, Itch would alert them if someone was coming. That is if he smelled or heard them, but what if he didn't? They were going to have to stay alert.

He looked around for a way back up the ledge and saw a little trail of tall steps leading up from the edge of the dam to the field above. He clambered across the rocky dam up the trail, the dirt sticking to his wet, bare feet. Winwalom and Itch came behind.

They found four wooden troughs at this end of the fence placed directly up from the dam. Ferran expected the troughs to be warped beyond use, but they only had a few gaps that the boys easily plugged with grass. And when they had plugged all the holes, the two boys began to haul water. One of them would dip the buckets and place them at the top of the ledge while the other hustled to the troughs and emptied them out.

The cattle saw the water and immediately began to mosey over to drink. Very soon there was a crowd of them around the troughs. Ferran and Winwalom dipped and hauled and traded places several times and then found that they could haul faster if both of them just carried their own buckets.

Ferran kept glancing at the woods. He wished he could order Itch to stand guard or power some contraption that would help them finish sooner. But he'd never taught Itch anything like that. So they worked, while Itch played in the water and explored the area. It took them about an hour to carry five hundred buckets, and then they had to get another hundred more because the cattle weren't finished. By the time they finished, the sun was just about to set, and Ferran's arms, shoulders, and hands had passed from being on fire to barely being able to move.

He tipped the last bucket in. "I think it would have been easier to dig a ramp down and another back up."

"I bet that's what every crew says, and the next time through they decide to stop somewhere else."

Ferran said, "I swear my arms are six inches longer than when we started."

"I guess that means you'll look normal now," Winwalom said.

"Oh, funny."

"Little frog arms," he said and wiggled his fingers up close to his chest.

Ferran scooped a bit of water from the trough with a bucket. Winwalom ducked, but Ferran was too quick and splashed Winwalom squarely in the face. "Oops," he said.

"I'll show you oops," Winwalom said and lunged for a bucket, but Ferran grabbed the other three buckets and danced away. "It must be sad to be so slow," he said with a grin.

Winwalom tried to grab a bucket, but Ferran darted away. However, both boys were so tired, they left it at that and trudged back to the campsite. They passed the split rail repair job that Borros, Krov, and Ranoc had made on the fence and found the others already eating a supper of porridge. Lagash motioned them over to the cook fire. It was in a hole in the ground about a foot across and a little more than a foot deep. Two metal rods lay across the hole. On top of the rods sat an iron cooking pot with some delicious-looking porridge in it.

"A fire in a hole?" Winwalom asked.

Lagash said, "Indeed. It's easier to cook over. I don't need a tripod or anything like that. These two iron rods lying across the opening are more than enough. I just set the pot on them. It's easy to start and keep going in a wind. Burns hotter with less wood. Makes less smoke. And it's hard to spot from a distance because the flames are below ground. It's especially good when you have a lackey to dig it."

There was another hole a little over a foot away. "What's this hole for?" Ferran asked.

"Air," Lagash said. "Put a fire in a hole, and it's going to run out of air. So you dig a tunnel between the two holes. The air goes into the empty hole and over to the base of the fire. It's part of what allows it to burn so hot. When you need to give the fire some life, you just fan that hole."

"That's ingenious," Winwalom said.

"And easy to conceal when you're in enemy territory and don't want to leave tracks," Borros said. "You just shovel the dirt back in and tamp the turf down. You have to be almost on top of it to see it. And even then, some still miss it."

"You were a soldier?" Ferran asked.

"I've been a lot of things," Borros said and took another spoonful of porridge.

Lagash handed each boy a wooden bowl and spoon. Then he ladled in two heaping portions of the warm porridge out of the iron pot. It was made with barley and peas and flavored with herbs and what looked like some bits of meat. It smelled delicious.

Ferran's mouth began to water, and he spooned a bite. "Whoa," he said in surprised delight. It was savory and smooth with melted tallow. The meat was jerked pork. He took another bite, and a wave of delicious desire washed over him, and then he couldn't help himself and stuffed two more bites in his mouth. "This is amazing," he said around a mouthful of food and took yet another bite.

"Slow down," said Lagash.

"Right," Ferran said; then Itch whined. "What about Itch?"

Lagash looked at Borros.

"If he wants to feed his dog, it will have to come out of his wages," he said.

"You're not going to feed him?" Ferran asked.

"I hired five boys," Borros said. "I promised each pay and food. I have no agreements with a dog. If the boy had been thinking, he would have tried to bargain with me and ask that I cover his dog's meals."

That wasn't fair. Itch had worked as much as any of them. In fact, he'd worked more, and the drover knew it. Ferran looked down at his bowl of porridge and then at Itch. He could share his portion, but it wasn't enough for both of them. Not with the work they were doing. Which meant he needed to help the drover see the light.

12

ITCH

F erran cleared his throat, then said, "My mistake. That was indeed the bargain. But I have a question."

Borros raised an eyebrow.

Ferran didn't want to anger him. The last thing he needed was to be kicked off this job. But he thought he saw a way to fix the issue and began to speak.

"Master cook," Ferran said. "Since you had the best view of my labors today, would you say that my dog and I performed the work of one boy. Or did we perhaps do more?"

A smile tugged at the corner of Lagash's mouth. "I would say you did the work of one boy. But your dog there did the work of another, maybe two."

"But the dog has no agreement with the drover, correct?"

"That is correct."

"If I were to lend you a horse, would you ever think of making an agreement with the horse itself?"

"A horse is a thing that's owned. I would make an agreement with the horse's owner."

"And would you pay him for the use?"

"I would," said Lagash.

"I see," said Ferran. "I agree. It appears that today, in gratitude for being hired, I employed my dog in the services of the drover. I wonder if he would like the services of the dog tomorrow."

Borros said, "You are the one who said you and your dog were a package deal. But you never said anything about feeding it. That's part of what made you more attractive than that large whining knothead and his bigger knothead of a father."

"That's what you assumed. But I never offered my dog's services for free. I merely said that you needed a dog."

"O, ho!" Lagash chucked. "He's got you there."

"He's got nothing."

"What do you say, boys?" Lagash asked.

"It sounds like an oversight," said Winwalom, grinning.

Lagash looked at the others.

Krov and Ranoc nodded in agreement.

Caswal said, "It sounds to me like he promised one thing and is now wanting to go back on his word. On his own, he wasn't worth anything close to Lome. And so he threw in the dog, hoping to make himself more attractive. I say the dog was part of the bargain."

"Ha," said Borros.

Ferran turned his back on Caswal, the maggot, and addressed Lagash, "Do you remember what the witnesses confirmed with the agreement? Was there any mention in the agreement of a dog?"

"Now that I think of it, no mention was made of a dog. Only boys."

"I tell you," Borros said. "You're a traitor, through and through."

Lagash just smiled.

Ferran said to Borros, "Sir, I would love to put my dog into your service for the rest of our journey. I don't ask for the rate you promised us boys, even though he does the work of a man. My price is simply a portion of food twice a day."

Borros's dark eyes glittered, and Ferran felt like Borros was testing him.

"That sounds reasonable," said Lagash.

"We'll have no more comments from the cook," Borros said calmly.

Ferran said, "And you need a dog if what I heard today was true."

"Oh?" Borros asked.

"An old farmer in that last village said that livestock was being stolen at night and that this herd made a pretty picture."

"You're talking about that skinny fellow with five hairs for a beard?"

"Yes."

Borros nodded. "He talked to me as well."

Krov looked alarmed and asked Ferran what he'd said. Ferran repeated the conversation, then said, "A dog would help keep watch."

Borros sat back and crossed his big arms. "Okay, I'll give him half a portion."

"A full one in the morning, and a half a night," said Ferran. "Surely you want his full energy."

"You're costing me."

"He'll add far more value than what you pay. He's a good watchdog. So he'll be of use at night."

"Fine. A full portion in the morning and a half a night."

"You will be happy you hired his services," Ferran said.

Caswal shook his head in annoyance. "I would not have made such an agreement."

"I didn't ask your opinion," said Borros, "did I?"

Caswal said nothing to that.

Lagash took a bowl and spooned a half portion of porridge in it. "For Itch, who is now officially a dog of the crew."

Ferran turned with both his bowls and looked around for a spot to sit and found a nice piece of grass. He sat, blew on Itch's porridge until he figured it was cool enough, then set it on the ground. Itch buried his muzzle in it and slurped with gusto.

Ferran went back to his porridge and took another bite. There was a strange herb in it, but he decided he liked it. He took another bite and decided he liked it a lot, and very quickly found himself scraping the bottom of the bowl. He looked over at Winwalom, hoping he didn't like the taste, but Winwalom was cleaning out his bowl as well.

Ferran was still hungry. He said to Lagash, "Do you have any fishing nets or hooks?"

"You see something in the stream?"

"Maybe."

"You catch some fish, and I'll happily cook them."

"Deal," Ferran said.

Lagash rummaged around in his wagon and came up with some bone hooks and linen line. "You know how to use these?"

"Oh, he knows how to fish," Krov said sourly.

Ferran said earnestly, "We wouldn't be trespassing on a lord's land, would we? I would never want to trespass or poach."

Krov groaned at the lie.

Borros said, "I don't see any lord claiming this specific creek. Do you see one?"

"Can't say that I do," Lagash said.

"I always like to obey the law," Ferran said.

"A very smart thing to do," Lagash said and held out his hooks and lines.

Ferran selected one of each.

"If a lord does come along," Lagash said, "you didn't get these from me."

Ferran grinned. "If one comes, I'll say they're Krov's."

"Not if you value your life," Krov said.

Ferran took Itch and Winwalom with him. On the way, they lifted several stones in search of worms. When they had a handful, they proceeded back to the dam. Ferran ordered Itch to stay back from the edge, and then they tied the line to a stick, baited the hook, and quietly lowered it from a hidden position among the shrubbery to the deep, shaded part of the pool.

They didn't have to wait long. The big fish here were hungry, and they soon had four large trout, which they took back to the camp. They gutted them and gave Itch the offal, which he bolted. Then Lagash cooked them with tallow and herbs. It smelled delicious. When they were nice and crispy on the outside, an equal portion of the fish and fish heads were shared out to all, including Itch.

By the time they finished eating, Ferran felt full for the first time in weeks. A relaxed happiness suffused him, from his legs and fingertips to his face. It was the feeling of starving body parts all sighing in relief and satisfaction. And then he thought about his mother and Lily and felt a little pang of guilt because they wouldn't be eating much at anything right now. He wished could have taken them some of Lagash's excellent porridge and fish. And he realized again just how important this job was.

Lagash looked at Caswal. "Time to clean up."

"Me?" Caswal asked.

"Did you not assign yourself to help me?"

"I thought—"

"Up. Let's go."

Ferran glanced at Winwalom. They shared a small smile of satisfaction at Caswal's discomfort, and Ferran decided he liked this dark Sorosian.

Lagash loaded Caswal with the pots and knives and bowls and spoons. "Off to the stream with you. I expect them to be scoured. If they're not, you'll go right back and do them again."

Caswal lumbered off, none too happy about having to work.

The rest relaxed, digesting their fish and porridge, while Lagash began to put things back into the wagon in a very particular way. He was an orderly man, that was for sure.

"Should we set a watch?" Ranoc asked.

"We will," Borros said. "My guess is that any thief wanting to try his luck here will do so in the dark of night. Not now."

Ferran relaxed a bit more at that news. The fire popped. Lagash reached up his sleeve to scratch his arm and revealed a tattoo.

Ranoc peered at it. "Is that a raven tattooed on your arm?"

"I've always thought it looked more like a duck," Borros said.

Lagash shook his head at what appeared to be a long-standing tease.

"Raven?" Winwalom mused. "I've heard of that." He thought for a moment, the brightened. "The Raven Guard."

Lagash smiled.

"What's that?" Ranoc asked.

Winwalom said, "It's the elite company of soldiers that protect the Sorosian emperor."

All of the boys looked at Lagash.

What was an elite Sorosian soldier doing cooking for a drover here?

13

SECRETS

Ranoc's eyes went wide. "You're part of this Raven Guard?"

"Having a raven on your arm doesn't mean you're part of the Raven Guard," Lagash said. "If you haven't noticed, I'm a cook."

"A Sorosian cook," Winwalom observed.

"So you cooked for the Raven Guard?" Ranoc asked.

Borros laughed. "And washed between their toes. And shined their boots."

"Really?" Ranoc asked.

"Oh yes," Lagash said. "I shined lots of boots."

"I would imagine that's a high station for a servant," Ranoc said, impressed.

Ferran shook his head. Ranoc was sometimes so oblivious.

Borros chuckled. "Why, he was practically a lord. The lord of boots, toe cleaners, and other foot gear."

"Don't believe them," Winwalom said. "He's Sorosian. With a raven on his arm. Over there that means something. And I don't think they give mere cooks such a badge of honor."

"Mere cooks?" Lagash asked threateningly.

"Oh, now you've done it," Borros said with delight.

"I didn't mean any offense," said Winwalom.

"A mere cook?" Lagash demanded.

"A fabulous cook," Winwalom said. "A porridge man without peer."

Lagash grunted.

"So you *were* a cook for the Raven Guard," Ranoc concluded.

Borros laughed.

Lagash said, "Don't you have some job for them?"

"Indeed I do, Master Cook," he said. "Indeed I do. It's going to be dark soon, and I want a patrol made of the area around us. I want to know what's there. As we've seen, a herd attracts attention. And I want to know what's looking at us. Dog Boy and Long Hair can do a half circle on the other side of the road. Make the radius about a half mile. If you see a good tree or knoll, climb to the top to get a view. Eye Patch and Ranoc take this side of the road. Be silent and alert. I expect a detailed report of the terrain and what's there when you come back."

Ferran was still tired. What's more, his limbs were all stiff. And he did not want to go out where some throat-slitting thief might be, but he climbed to his feet with Winwalom, and then the two of them moved out with Itch trailing behind.

They walked up the road what they gauged was a half mile, then turned off into the trees to make their circuit. Itch darted ahead, but Ferran hissed for him to come back and told him to stay at their side.

"You think they're worried about thieves?" Ferran asked.

"I think they just wanted us out of their hair."

"Right," Ferran said, but still wondered.

They walked another pace, Itch padding at their side.

Ferran said, "How did you know about the Raven Guard?"

"My da tells me stories about the campaigns he was in across the seas."

"Do you really think Lagash was part of it?"

"He never said he wasn't, did he? He kept misdirecting us."

"Borros thought it was hilarious, us thinking he was a cook for them."

"Which makes me think we hit the truth."

"But wouldn't he still be part of it? Can you retire from being the sworn bodyguard of a Sorosian emperor?"

"I don't know. And I don't know if the Raven Guard just protects the emperor's person, or if they do other things. All I know is that my da said they were a fearsome unit."

A sunlit clearing showed through the tree trunks up ahead, and they changed direction to skirt around it to keep themselves in the shadows.

"Could he be here as a spy?" Ferran asked.

"It's possible."

"A sworn man from Soros would only be here on official business, right? Maybe he's going to see and report about what's going on in Broniss. Or maybe he has other business. It wouldn't be the first time Soros sent an assassin."

"Soros has no argument with our queen."

"That we know of. Maybe Osson convinced them otherwise."

"Maybe, but he could also be here to simply take a message. Or nothing. Maybe he truly is a cook."

"You ever know a cook to carry a short sword like the one he has?" Ferran asked.

"He has a short sword?"

"Under the seat of the wagon," Ferran said, keeping his voice low, and stepped over a fallen log. "Right within easy reach."

"Drovers need protection."

"Spears maybe. Slings. What kind of drover can afford a sword?"

"What kind of spy takes the guise of a drover traipsing across the countryside? If I were a spy, I'd go right to Broniss and blend in there."

Ferran shrugged and scanned the woods about him. "Whatever they are, they're an odd pair."

"As long as they pay, they can be as odd as they like."

"Agreed," Ferran said and thought about carrying their pay back to Buckle Hill. "You know of course that we'll need to return home a different way. Everyone knows we're going to Pencoy's. Someone just might wait for us on the way back, hoping to lighten our purses. And we need to separate from Caswal. I'm not traveling with him."

Winwalom didn't answer.

"Win?" he said.

"Right."

But Winwalom was hiding something. "What is it?"

"Well, you might want to go with Caswal and the others."

"You can't be serious. You want to go with him?"

"No. It's..."

"What?"

Winwalom struggled for a moment to find the right words, then said, "You can't say anything."

Suddenly a squirrel began chittering a warning. A branch cracked, and both boys stopped to look and listen. Itch alerted as well, his dark ears perking. They scanned the woods, but after waiting for some time found nothing there. The squirrel chittered again, and Itch looked like he wanted to bark, but Ferran shushed him, then gave him a pet and a word of praise for staying silent.

They walked a minute or so in silence, Ferran waiting for Winwalom to finish what he'd been about to say, but when he didn't, Ferran prompted him. "So what can't I say?"

Winwalom hesitated, then said, "I'm not coming back. I'm going on to Broniss."

"He hired you for the full trip?" Ferran was in shock.

"No," Winwalom said. "I hope he hires me, but either way, I'm going on to Broniss. I'll be staying with a friend of my father's."

"Doing what?"

"A sort of apprenticeship."

Itch smelled something and trotted out a few paces and stopped to sniff, but he didn't make any noise, and Ferran allowed it.

"You're a bit old to start an apprenticeship. Did the former apprentice run off or something?"

"Not exactly."

Ferran furrowed his brow. "What does this friend of your father's do?"

"He's a, well..." Winwalom thought. "A felter or something."

"You're going to apprentice to someone, and you don't even know what he does?"

"He felts."

"You're lying."

"I'm not."

"Win," Ferran said.

"What?"

"Out with it."

"It's nothing," he said. "Just a friend of my father's. And I'm going to work for him for a time."

"And leave me with Caswal and Lome?"

"My da thought it was best."

Ferran thought about living in the vale without Winwalom, and his heart sank. It was so unexpected. So odd. He knew Winwalom was hiding something.

"Is this some marriage thing?" Ferran asked.

"No."

"Is he a relative?"

"No. And I probably shouldn't have said anything. You can't tell anyone."

"I won't," Ferran said. And he wouldn't, although he couldn't see any reason to keep such a thing a secret. "Tell me what this is really about."

"I can't," Winwalom said. "Not now. Please."

Ferran sighed, but he didn't press, and they continued their patrol with Itch staying close.

As for threats, they heard and saw more squirrels, saw the hoof prints of some deer by a boggy spot, crossed a few thin animal trails, and passed through a clearing that was thick with dragonflies. They both climbed a tree and saw the woods for miles around. Winwalom said he saw the smoke of a village far to the west by the mountains, but Winwalom had uncanny eyesight, and Ferran couldn't detect any smoke. They continued, keeping quiet, and returned at dusk.

They reported on what they saw and drew in their half the map that Ranoc and Krov had already drawn in the dirt. Borros nodded and asked questions, and when they finished, he said, "There are seven of us. We will have seven watches during the night, one hour each. That way we won't wear anyone out. I will be first. Lagash will be last."

Ferran thought about the farmer's warning and realized this was going to be a true watch.

14

FIRST WATCH

Borros continued, "Your job is to patrol the outside of the enclosure. We have a lot of cattle. If you see something, your job is to alert us." He motioned at Caswal, "Organize the rest of the watch hours."

Caswal again. Ferran groaned inside.

Caswal assigned himself second watch, followed by Krov, then Ferran, Winwalom, and finally Ranoc. Ferran didn't want to be the one having to watch in the middle of the night, but it wasn't worth arguing over, and so he and Winwalom grabbed their packs out of the wagon, then found a nice flat spot a number of paces from the fire hole.

Ferran said, "The drover obviously has this figured out. Going first or last basically means you get a full night of uninterrupted rest."

"If they were my cattle, I'd do the same," Winwalom said.

Ferran opened his pack and was surprised. Sitting on top of his gear was a single strip of dried beef. He hadn't put that there. And then he remembered his little sister fiddling with his pack. Mother must have bought it with part of whatever she'd earned washing, and Lily had sneaked it in. He shook his head. They needed the food far more than he did. He blew out a breath.

"What's wrong?" Winwalom asked.

"Nothing," Ferran said and sniffed it. It smelled of the herb blend of his mother's friend who lived out by the great willow trees. It was going to be tasty, and he decided that he and Itch would share it during their watch that night.

He searched the pack for any other surprises, but only found the items he'd packed, so he grabbed the two large pieces of sackcloth he'd packed along with his tree thorn needle and the cord. He placed one piece of sackcloth over the other, then used a super wide whip stitch to sew the two pieces of cloth together. He only sewed three sides, making a bag.

He put his needle and cord away, then gathered up a large quantity of dried leaves and grass and stuffed the bag full. The other boys were doing the same. When he finished, he had a good six inches of padding that would keep him warm.

The other boys had each brought some canvas and were finishing makeshift tents. They made the tents by driving two sticks about three-feet long each into the ground so they formed an X with extra long bottom legs. Next, they laid one end of a branch that was a few feet taller than the boy in the crook of the X. The other end lay on the ground, making a long triangular frame. Then they fastened their canvas over it and slipped their browse bags inside.

Such a tent would be nice to keep the dew and bugs off, but Ferran's family didn't have any spare canvas, so he would be sleeping only with his cloak.

Borros and Lagash had opted for other methods. Borros had moved some things aside in the bed of the wagon and set up his blankets there. Lagash set up the strangest thing Ferran had seen. It looked like a fish net strung between two trees.

"That's your bed?" Ferran asked Lagash.

"It's called a hammock. It keeps me up from the bugs and snakes and such."

"It looks painful," said Winwalom.

Lagash just smiled, laid a wool blanket in the netting and straightened it just so. Then he settled himself in the netting and pulled the blanket around him.

"Looks kind of nice to me," Ferran said.

"Enjoy the spiders and snakes," Lagash said.

There was a slight breeze, so Ferran laid his browse bag in the lee of Winwalom's tent and lay down there. The bag was thick and soft and felt heavenly with his tired limbs. He laid his cloak over himself and got situated, the dry grass crunching underneath him. Itch came over and laid down on the bag with him

"Dog Boy," Borros said. "We don't want your companion stirring up the cattle in the night. Tie him up."

"I'll be happy to put a leash on Winwalom," he said.

"You know what I mean."

"Sure," Ferran said. And he got out of bed, grabbed some cord from his pack, then tied one end to a small bush not far away and the other to Itch's old leather collar. If Itch were determined, it wouldn't hold him, but Itch knew the routine and would behave.

Ferran settled back down. Itch came over and lay next to him again. By this time the light had faded, and a thousand stars were twinkling in the dark sky. Ferran always enjoyed watching them, hoping to see one of those that streaked across the heavens, but the next thing he knew, Krov was nudging him awake with his big foot to take his watch.

Ferran got up, still dead tired, and stretched. He grabbed his walking stick for defense, because even if there weren't robbers in the shadows, there might be other critters. He untied Itch and stood. A little crust of moon illuminated the dark shapes of the cattle in the corral and the surrounding trees. About him, the crickets chirped. He noted the position of the lodestar and the cup constellation so he could tell the time, then turned to the field.

He decided that if he wanted to steal some of these cattle, he'd go to the far side of the corral, remove a few rails from the fence, and just walk them out. He wouldn't go for the big ones. He'd go for calves and yearlings.

He looked at the far corner. It was dark there, hidden by moon shadows. But he knew if he was going to conduct a proper watch, that's where he had to go.

And so he made his way bare-footed to the black water of the stream and splashed his face to wake himself fully. He listened to the water cascade down the little dam and scanned the woods on the far bank, then climbed back up and continued his patrol of the enclosure.

His heart raced as he approached the dark corner. He was glad he had Itch with him, and Ferran watched Itch, but Itch didn't seem the least bit alarmed. And so Ferran walked into the shadows, his heart thumping, and inspected the fence. He found all of the rails present and heaved a sigh.

And then something snapped in the dark woods. The hairs on the back of Ferran's neck stood on end, and he brought his stick up in a defensive position.

Itch alerted to the sound as well.

"What do you see, boy?" Ferran asked.

Itch sniffed the air, looked eager.

"Go," Ferran said, and Itch ran out into the trees. His mottled gray coat soon disappeared in the darkness, but Ferran could hear him. He rushed through the brush and trees, stopped for a moment, but then came back again, wagging his tail.

So maybe it had been just a falling branch. Or some small animal that had gone to ground. Ferran gave him a pet, and they moved on.

He made a few more rounds, each time his heart thumping as he inspected the dark corner. He watched the movement of the cup and moon, and when he'd judged an hour was up, he went back and nudged Winwalom awake, relieved that no whoreson thief had decided to steal cattle on his watch.

Winwalom rose, pulled his hair back, and tied it on his head. Ferran yawned, then sat down on his stuffed bag, and let himself fall backward. But instead of the soft bag he'd left, he struck something hard and pointed that speared his back. He cried out and rolled off.

"What are you doing?" Winwalom whispered.

Someone had stuffed a huge sharp stone into his browse bag. He felt around and found two additional stones. And as he ran his hands over his bag, he poked himself on a tree thorn sticking up out of the cloth right where his head would have been. He tossed the offending items away from his bed.

"You thought a thorn would be funny?" he asked Winwalom. "It could have put out my eye. Skewered my ear."

"Thorn?"

"Don't play stupid."

"I have no idea what you're talking about. I was in dreamland until you nudged me."

Ferran looked at the other tents. Nobody was moving, but his mind immediately went to Caswal. He wanted to dump the rocks on Caswal, but he remembered Borros's rules. He'd agreed not to fight. And it was a fact he'd learned by hard experience that the one who starts the fight rarely gets caught. It was always the one who defends himself.

Ferran sighed. "Never mind." He felt around one more time to make sure he hadn't missed any more nasty surprises, then lay back.

"Can I take Itch?" Winwalom asked.

Ferran kind of wanted Itch by his side, but he thought about facing that dark corner without him and said, "Sure. Then he pulled his cloak up and closed his eyes.

He was awaked again by Winwalom shaking him. "Get up," he said urgently. "Get up."

15

BATS

Ferran still had the images of his dream looping about his mind. He'd been galloping a tiny horse. It was so tiny he could only sit on it if he drew his feet up onto the saddle. He'd been riding it, trying to escape a pack of cattle thieves.

"What?" he asked groggily.

Itch licked his face, and Ferran pushed him away.

"I think I saw something," Winwalom said urgently. "Get up."

A jolt of alarm ran up Ferran's back. "Thieves?"

"No. Something up in the sky, circling over the camp and field. Something large."

Ferran looked up, but there were too many branches here to see anything clearly.

"Come on," Winwalom said.

Ferran got out of bed and followed him out from under the trees and onto the moonlit road. He scanned the night sky. "I don't see anything."

"It was there. Huge."

Ferran looked again but didn't see anything except the stars. "Did Itch see it?"

"He watched it."

"It was probably an owl."

"It wasn't an owl."

"A bat?"

"It was large. It had a long neck. Kind of like a stork."

"Storks don't fly at night."

"It was not a bird."

Ferran wondered what kind of creature would be large and fly at night and couldn't think of any. "Large like an eagle?"

"It was bigger. Much bigger. It wasn't swooping or flitting like a bat," Winwalom said. "Just circling, way up there, like a hawk looking for prey."

Ferran scanned the skies again in all directions. "There's nothing there." And then he began to suspect this was another prank. "You put those rocks in my bed, didn't you?"

"No," Winwalom said earnestly. "I think your black eye is affecting your sight."

Ferran looked at the sky again. "You said it was up high?"

"Yes."

Ferran looked again, then shrugged, still suspecting Winwalom was having a little joke. "Whatever it was, it's long gone. I'm going back to bed."

"If I'm missing tomorrow morning, it will be on you."

Winwalom had probably been some big owl. Maybe a big bat. Ferran himself had seen a bat once with a wingspan almost two feet across. And while seeing such a thing would be interesting, it wasn't when you were dead tired.

Ferran waved off the warning. "If you're missing tomorrow," he said, "it's because you were dumb enough to let it take you."

"Ferran," Winwalom protested.

"Good night," Ferran said and left Winwalom to his watch.

Ferran was awaked the third time by the sound of Lagash thumping an iron pot with a spoon and calling for them to rise and report. Ferran groaned. He'd definitely not gotten enough sleep, but he pulled his cloak down from his face and saw, to his surprise, the stars still twinkling above.

"It's still night," he said.

Winwalom groaned. "He's worse than the harvest master."

"Oh, you're still with us?" Ferran asked. "That big bat you saw didn't come and carry you away?"

"It wasn't a bat."

"Rise and report to work," Lagash called.

Ferran rose, stretched, and, with Winwalom and Itch, walked over to Lagash's fire in a hole. As he did, he caught a whiff of more porridge, and he perked up at the thought of the delicious food.

"Take a bowl," Lagash said and pointed to a stack.

Ferran picked up two wooden bowls plus a wooden spoon for himself. He salivated as Lagash spooned his and Itch's portions into the bowls, then he carried them over to a log where he could sit and eat. He blew on Itch's bowl to cool it and got a good sniff. The porridge had oats, carrots, onion, and something else.

"Is it garlic I'm smelling?" he asked.

"Yes," Lagash said.

"Smells wonderful," Ferran said

He continued to blow, his mouth watering, until he figured it was cool enough, and then he set the bowl on the ground. Itch immediately began to slurp it up. Ferran took a bite of his portion and sighed in delight. Two solid meals in a row that didn't feature weeds or sickly sparrows. It was glorious.

Winwalom said excitedly, "It's got salt in it."

Ferran just sighed again. He spooned in a few more mouthfuls, then asked, "So did anyone else see a giant bat?"

"Giant bat?" Lagash asked and ladled some porridge into a bowl for Ranoc.

"Circling way up high," Ferran said.

"It wasn't a bat," Winwalom said.

"Oh, that's right," Ferran said. "It looked like a stork."

"Storks don't fly at night," Lagash said.

"That's what I told him," Ferran said.

Winwalom groaned. "It wasn't a stork. It had the rough outline of one."

"He saw it through the trees," Ferran said and blew on another spoonful. "I think it was a big bat. We have those around here, you know. I saw one with wings this wide." And he showed Lagash how wide it had been.

Lagash said, "There's an area in Soros called Karamore. There are bats there with wings four feet across. Huge."

"Goh," Ranoch exclaimed. "Do they attack humans?"

"Fish mostly. Although they've been known to carry off small animals and snakes. They're aggressive. They'll dive right at your face. If they're angry enough, they'll try to rake you with their claws. And you don't want those wounds. They fester and corrupt quickly."

"I had a bat lodge in my hair once," Ranoc said. "It was trying to escape my cat. It careened around me and disappeared. But it was hanging right on the back of my head. And then my cat jumped at my shoulder. And I ducked, thinking the cat had gone feral. But he was jumping for the bat, which flitted around to hang right on my face."

"And then what?" Lagash asked.

"I yelled and knocked it away. It flew up and into the night."

"What happened to your cat?"

"It went over to sit and lick itself."

Lagash smiled. "The bats of Karamore would have had you for breakfast."

Ranoc shuddered.

They shared a couple of other tales about wild animals attacking folks, and then Borros asked Winwalom to describe his giant bat again.

Winwalom did. Borros nodded, but instead of disregarding it, he told Winwalom that if he saw it again to wake him. And then he gave the work assignments, and they struck camp and began to move the cattle with the stars still shining above.

As they left, Lagash fashioned a quick doll out of grass and hung it from the fence around the field.

"What is that?" Ferran asked.

"An offering of respect to whatever spirits inhabit this place."

"Spirits?" Ferran asked.

"You never know whose land you're crossing," Lagash said. "It's best to approach with gratitude."

"Don't spirits want blood or some such?"

"I don't know what the ones around here want. But recognition can't hurt."

Ferran had heard of various powers, but none around here. At the same time, who wanted to offend one when a little grass doll would do? So he quickly fashioned his own grass doll which didn't look nearly as tidy, and hung it next Lagash's. And then he and Itch followed the cattle into the early morning darkness.

Ferran figured they traveled at least four miles before the sun rose, and as the heat of the day rose and burned the dew off the road, he realized how smart it was to get an early start. There would be less dust, and it would be less tiring on both the drivers and the cattle to move in the cool of the morning. However, it didn't cut down on the number of cow pies he had to walk through, and he decided there was no benefit to being at the back of the herd.

During the day's drive, they met three bearded men on horseback riding the other way. The men talked with Borros for a bit, then rode by.

When they passed, Lagash said, "I wouldn't trust those three farther than I can throw them."

"You know them?"

"See enough of their type, and you can just tell."

"You think they'd come after the cattle?"

Lagash shrugged. "If they do, we have you and your stones, don't we?"

"Yes," Ferran said, not feeling confident that would be nearly enough. He gave the men another glance as they trotted away.

There wasn't much else that happened on the drive that day. The cattle moved along. Itch and Ferran zig-zagged behind them, going all the way out past the end of the herd and then back again. By noon Borros was turning them off into another drover's field, and Ferran figured they'd gone at least thirteen miles.

They set up camp. Luckily, a little stream ran at the edge of this field, so all he had to do for his water job was to check and make sure the fencing on the enclosure was solid. Borros sent them off to survey the area again in a radius of a half mile and told them to be quick and silent. As before, Ferran, Winwalom, and Itch took one side of the road, Krov, Ranoc, and Caswal took the other. The most notable thing Ferran and Winwalom found was an area thick with hares. They killed five with their slings and brought them back for cooking.

With the survey of the area finished, Borros gathered the boys and said, "We're going into some sparsely populated country. Part of your job is keeping these cattle safe. You're good with your slings. But there are many situations where a sling will be useless. You need to learn to fight up close."

"Fight?" Ranoc asked.

"Maybe."

"All I've got is a knife," Ranock said.

"You ever been in a knife fight with a wolf?"

"No."

"Want to be in one?" Borros asked.

"No."

"Let's say its men. Some band of outlaws. Many will be taller than you are. Stronger. Heavier. Have a longer reach. You want to face them with a knife?"

"Maybe lashed to the end of a pole," Ranoc said.

"There you go. What you need is something that will let you strike with a little bit of distance. Something that will give you the ability to cause damage before you're smelling your opponent's breath, be that wolf or man. I hired you to guard these cattle. It's time you learned to do that properly. And that starts with the spear."

16

SPEARS

"**B**ut we don't have any spears," Krov said.

"I know that. I asked you that when I hired you, remember? Your first task will be to make your own spears. You're going to go out and find yourself a sapling with a seven-foot length that's as straight as possible. Something that, when the bark is stripped, will be somewhere between an inch and a quarter and an inch and a half in diameter. You're looking for oak, maple, walnut, ash. Do not come back here carrying some lousy piece of poplar or pine. You need good hardwood. Eventually, I want you to have a practice weapon plus another for the real job. But we'll start with one. Questions?"

"Were you a soldier once?" Krov asked.

"He was much more than that," Lagash said.

Ferran believed him and suspected that's where he'd gotten the scar on his face and the other small ones on his arms. The boys waited for more information, but Borros said, "Off with you. And be quick."

Ferran surveyed the woods around them and spotted a likely group of trees. It would have been much easier to find a straight stick back at the village where the surrounding woods had many trees that had either been coppiced to the ground or pollarded to the trunk. Pruning them that way allowed a mass of straight branches to grow, but he supposed that would have cost Borros extra to purchase such wood and maybe given the parents second thoughts, especially his mum.

Caswal said to Borros, "Have you got an axe I can borrow?"

Borros reached into the wagon bed, pulled out a hand axe, and held it out to him.

"Do you have another?" asked Krov.

This time Borros pulled out a full-sized axe. "That's it. Now get to work."

Ferran went with Winwalom and Itch, but of course, Caswal and Krov and Ranoc had already spied the same likely set of trees that he had and reached them first, so Ferran walked beyond them. Maybe fifty yards later they came across a fine beech.

Ferran knew that from the tip of his thumb to the first joint was an inch. So he used his thumb to measure and found a sapling that was the perfect diameter. "Ooh, this one's mine," he said.

"Fine, I'll take the oak," Winwalom said and trundled up a hill another dozen yards to another sapling.

Ferran searched the ground for a thick stick, found a branch and broke it into something he could wield as a mallet, then knelt at the base of the beech sapling. He unsheathed his knife, set the blade against the base of the branch at an angle, then began to strike the back of the blade with the stick, cutting into the wood. When he'd cut almost halfway through that side, he removed the knife, and did the same to the other side, then pushed the sapling over. It broke where he'd cut with a crack.

He measured off seven feet, finding the sapling much taller than he thought, then used his knife and make-shift mallet to cut the top of the sapling away. He knocked off all the small branches, then stood and picked up his staff. It was strong and straight with a solid diameter and felt like six or seven pounds.

Up on the hill, Winwalom finished cutting his length of oak. Ferran walked up to join him and look for a second sapling, but then Borros's horn sounded through the trees. One long note.

"Hurry up, boys," Borros shouted.

They hustled down the hill with their freshly-cut poles.

Caswal and Ranoc were already there, each with a length of maple. A few seconds later, Krov came jogging out of the trees carrying the axe and two excellent lengths of ash in his big hands.

Borros stood in front of them, his balding head shining in the sun. Lagash stood next to him wearing his brightly feathered hat and holding a real spear.

When they were all together, Borros said, "You'll fashion a nice wicked spike on the end of your poles later. Right now, while it's light, you need to learn how to use these things. Line up and give yourself enough room to easily swing your pole without hitting the man next to you."

The boys lined up and spaced out. Itch lay down and observed from a nice shady spot under a tree.

"Right. So where does fighting with the spear start? What's the foundation?"

"Bravery," said Caswal.

"Courage is a must," said Borros. "But courage will only get you killed faster if you don't have any skills. So what's the foundation of your skill?"

"Strength," Krov said.

"Strength is helpful, but if the battle always went to the strong, then all we'd need to do is set our soldiers to heaving logs and stones and sprinting about. Your strength cannot be employed without the proper foundation. So what is it?"

The boys just looked at him.

"Speed?" Ferran offered.

Borros shook his head at their lack of knowledge, then picked up a stick that was maybe only three feet long and stood just outside of Ranoc's reach. "Okay, Bull Rider. I'm your foe, and I'm bent on bashing your brains out. Are you ready?"

Ranoc lowered one end of his staff and pointed it at Borros.

"Come get me," Borros said, his balding head shining in the sun.

Ranoc took a step forward. Borros immediately moved to Ranoc's right. Ranoc tried to turn with him, but the way he had to move forced him to twist at the waist and reach forward.

"Look at him," Borros said. "Overextended, moving my way, and I'm inside his guard."

Borros grabbed the pole and yanked.

Ranoc stumbled forward.

Borros took a step and rapped Ranoc's head lightly with the stick. "And our bull riding friend here is now has scrambled eggs for brains. Why? Because you've got to do more than stand upright and be strong. You need to be able to move, gracefully, easily, keeping yourself in a position of power, because your opponent, be that man or animal, will be moving. And if you can't move, you will never be able to strike or defend with any effect. It all starts with the proper stance. Your feet, boys. The foundation of all battle is your feet."

Borros motioned at Lagash. "Show them."

Lagash held the drover's spear with a real metal blade. He sank into a stance with his feet a little more than shoulder-width apart. "Look where my feet are. Look at my knees, slightly bent, ready for action. If I want to move forward, I do not walk. I shuffle." He shuffled forward twice, then back. "If someone is coming at me from the diagonal, I pivot over with the lead leg." He pivoted to the left then back, then to the right and back.

Borros spoke up. "Where's our peacock holding the shaft?"

"At the center and back," Ferran said.

"Correct. There are other times when you'll hold it with your hands at the one-third and two-thirds marks. But this is the basic stance. Look at his hands. How is he holding it?"

"His front hand is cupping the shaft," Krov said. "The back hand is on top."

"Good," Borros said. "Okay, let's see it. Take your stance."

The boys dropped into their stances, their poles forward.

"What did he say about the hands, Long Hair?" Lagash asked.

Winwalom looked at the grip of the two boys on either side of him, then changed the grip of the forward hand to hold the pole from underneath.

"Good," said Borros. "Shuffle forward. Think about what you saw our cook do."

The boys shuffled forward.

"Back."

They moved back.

"Forward."

They shuffled forward again.

"Back."

They moved back again.

"Pivot left."

All of them pivoted left except Krov who went right, then saw his mistake and pivoted to match the other boys.

"Left is the direction of your eye patch," Borros said.

"Right," Krov said.

"Left."

"I meant left was right."

Borros cocked an eyebrow at him.

"Left," Krov said and pointed at his patch.

"You are now going to drill," said Borros. "You're going to do what's called the Rooster's Foot." He held up three fingers. "A rooster has three front toes, pointing in three different directions. So you will shuffle forward and back, then pivot to the next, and then the next. You will shuffle forward once, then back once. Then forward twice, and back twice. Then forward three times, and back three times so you are in the place you started. That's one toe. You will then pivot and do the same for the left diagonal toe. Then the right. When you've done three toes, you've completed a foot. I want fifty feet. Go."

The boys began, shuffling forward and back in their bare feet. Ranoc was on Ferran's right and was going just a little faster, so Ferran sped up his shuffling to match Ranoc's. Ranoc increased his speed, so Ferran increased his speed until they were almost hopping.

"Heel to toe when you're going forward," Lagash said. "Heel to toe. Keep your form!"

Ferran slowed down and made sure to lead with his heel when moving forward. He noticed it gave him more control in the shuffle. He finished the next toe and pivoted.

Lagash pointed at Caswal. "Don't stand up. Keep your stance lower so you can react quickly. Less weight on that front leg when you're coming back."

They shuffled forward, and back. Forward, back. Pivoted.

"Better," said Lagash.

Ferran kept himself in that balanced mini squat as he went forward and back, noticing the difference. He finished another foot and began again.

The boys kept moving. Forward, back. Forward, back. The dust rose as they scuffled their bare feet. Ferran finished another foot and noticed Caswal was trying to stay ahead of him. Ferran sped up.

By the twelfth foot, he was breathing hard, but he'd passed Caswal. By the time he got to twenty-five, he was out in front of all of them. His thighs were aching, but he was out in front.

Krov stopped for a breather, and all the other boys soon followed suit.

"Did I say to stop?" asked Borros. "Go!"

The boys dropped back down in their stances and started up again. Forward, back, forward, back, forward, back, pivot. At forty-five feet, Ferran's thighs were burning. He was breathing hard, but he was winning this race. Ranoc began to speed up, but Ferran poured on the speed and began to shuffle as fast as he could, the dust rising.

At forty-eight feet, Ferran began to grin. He was going to beat them, but then Caswal suddenly stopped and stood. "Hoo," he said. "That's fifty."

It wasn't fifty. It wasn't even close. Ferran shook his head in disgust and finished out his rooster's feet. Ranoc, Winwalom, and Krov finished behind him.

"Good," said Borros. "Now switch your lead hands. Give me fifty on the other side."

Ferran and the other boys groaned.

"Did I hear a protest?"

Nobody answered.

"Do you think your foes are going to give you a breather?"

"I thought we were avoiding raiders," Ranoc said.

"Did you agree to provide security?"

"Yes."

"Security is all about hoping for the best and planning for the worst. If you don't want to add more scars than what you've got on your neck, you'll get to it. Good soldiers can do 500 feet without batting an eye. Now go."

The boys started again. The others started out slow, but Ferran did not. He continued at his former pace, and by the time he was to twenty feet, the others were five or six behind him.

"Looks like Dog Boy is going to beat all of you," Lagash said.

Ferran tried to act like he didn't notice the compliment, but he couldn't help puffing his chest a bit.

"Let's make this more interesting," Lagash said. "The first one done gets an extra serving at dinner. And it has to be with good form."

Ranoc and Winwalom immediately began to pick up their pace. Krov and Caswal followed. Soon they were all racing, shuffling through the form madly and kicking up a haze of dust. But none of them gained any ground on Ferran. He continued, feeling some of his old stamina returning.

Borros and Lagash watched for a while, then Borros put Lagash in charge and went off to check the cattle. Lagash moved over to the wagon to drink a ladle of water out of the barrel.

When Ferran hit forty-five, it was clear they weren't going to catch him, and they all began to slow down. Ferran slowed as well, breathing hard, his thighs on fire.

Ferran finished number forty-nine, and suddenly Caswal stood. "Done," he said loudly.

Lagash looked over from the wagon.

"No even close," Ferran said. "You're on thirty-seven."

"I'm done, slow boy."

Ferran finished up his current foot and started number fifty. "You're thirty-seven. I've been counting after your last cheat."

Caswal pitched his voice low. "Watch yourself, Dog Boy."

Lagash walked over. "Have we got a winner?"

"No," Ferran said and continued with the drill.

"I'm done," Caswal said.

Ferran finished number fifty and stood. "Now you have a winner."

Lagash looked at the boys. "Ranoc, who's telling the truth?"

Ranoc kept shuffling. "I've been focused on my count."

"Patch?"

Krov kept moving as well. "I'm not sure. I've only got one eye."

"Long Hair?"

Winwalom shuffled forward and back. "We were all behind Ferran. I never saw Caswal speed up enough to catch him, but I wasn't counting."

Lagash considered their answers, then turned to Caswal. "I saw Dog Boy's speed as well. You signed an agreement. You said you'd do what we said when we said it. No loafing. Maybe I should take your meal tonight and give it to the others who are pulling their load."

"I counted every one of my feet," Caswal said.

Lagash turned to Ferran. "How many did he have?"

Ferran didn't want to be the annoying tattle-tale. At the same time, Caswal was robbing him of a prize. "Sir, I will let you decide."

Lagash nodded, then said, "Caswal, you can do another fifty feet or forfeit your dinner. What will it be?"

"Fifty?" Caswal protested.

"Do you want to do a hundred?" Lagash asked.

"I'll do the fifty," Caswal said sourly.

"Krov," Lagash said. "Count them off."

The other boys finished their original fifty, and then stood there watching Caswal finish his extra fifty with Krov counting.

Borros returned. "What's going on?"

"Just helping Caswal with his counting," Lagash said and flicked a speck of grass off his shoulder.

Borros gave Caswal an appraising look, then nodded.

Caswal finally finished and bent over, resting his hands on his knees.

Borros said, "Go get a drink of water, then come right back."

The boys began to walk toward the stream.

"What are you doing?" Borros demand.

The boys stopped, confused.

Borros pointed at their poles lying on the ground. "Your weapons go with you now at all times. You'll herd with them. Eat with them. Fart and dump in the bushes with them at your side. Hope for the best, plan for the worst. Is that not what I said? Don't be caught with your pants down."

The boys turned around and picked up their poles, then headed for the stream. Caswal lagged behind Ferran, and when they were out of earshot of the two men, he said, "You're going to regret that, Dog Boy."

"It's not my fault you don't know how to count past your fingers and toes."

"Well, I can count this," Caswal said and snaked the bottom of his pole between Ferran's legs.

Ferran tried to step clear of it, but his back foot caught the pole. He tripped and slammed into the ground so hard his hands smarted from the pain.

Caswal chuckled.

Krov and Ranoc smiled.

"Don't trip over that weed," Caswal said.

Ferran's anger boiled, and he pushed himself up, but as he got to his knees, Caswal walked past and violently jabbed Ferran in the side with the butt of his pole.

Ferran cried out and clutched his side.

Caswal smirked.

Ferran lunged to his feet, staff in hand.

Winwalom moved between Ferran and Caswal. "Calm," he said and put his hand up to block Ferran.

Caswal took a defensive stance. "Let the little moron come."

17

THREAT

"Remember the agreement with the drover," Winwalom said.
Ferran gritted his teeth. Drill the end of his pole in Caswal's smirking face or take home money to buy his freedom? For a second it was a hard choice. But he wasn't going to waste his life on this bum dribble.

"Hey!" Borros yelled. "What's going on over there?"

"Nothing," Winwalom called.

"Then get moving. You have one minute to get your drink."

Ferran swallowed his anger and turned to the stream.

"Coward," Caswal said under his breath.

Ferran simply gritted his teeth and walked away.

The boys spread out, got their drinks, then trudged back. On the way, Caswal whispered something to Ranoc and chuckled.

Laugh now, Ferran thought. We'll see who laughs last. And he returned to his position in the practice area.

When all the boys were lined up, Borros said, "Here's the next lesson. If you draw a circle around yourself, you'll see eight points of attack. You have been working on the three in front with your Rooster's Feet. But there are three behind you, and then one straight out on either side.

You need to learn how to pivot to those positions so that you can do it quickly and without thinking."

He took his spear and showed them pivoting to the sides. Then he said, "When pivoting to the positions behind us, why don't we want to keep the staff level and just swing it around?"

Ferran raised his hand and said, "Because there might be one of your mates in the way. Or a tree or a bush."

"Correct," said Borros. "So when you pivot to the three positions behind you, bring the end of your spear up and over your head and down. On the way, you switch your hands and simply face the other way. You don't move your feet. Just up, over, and face the other way."

He raised the end of the staff up and over and switched hands. "See, now I'm facing the opposite direction, and the leg that was behind is now the lead leg." He did it again and faced the way he had when he started. "I'm simply turning to face the other way, rotating the staff up and over, switching hands. This is how you pivot to all three points in the rear."

He drew a large circle in the dirt and marked the eight points. "Each of these points of attack has a number. We start straight ahead and go around. Number two is front diagonal right. Three straight out to the side. So where is number five?"

"Straight behind," said Ranoc.

"Correct."

"Number seven."

"Straight left," said Winwalom.

"Yes. You're going to do something called the ring dance. It goes like this." He then began to pivot to the points and call them out as he did. "Eight, two, seven, three, six, four, five." He stopped and stood. "Except here's the kicker. Every time you pivot, that new position becomes position one. One is always straight in front of you. Understand?"

Ferran wasn't sure he did.

"I want 100 rings. Call out each number as you pivot and each ring as you finish it. Go."

Ferran pivoted to eight and called it out, then had to remember that this new direction had now become the one position and pivoted to two.

He went slowly, having to work out the next position in his head. The other boys were going at the same pace.

"Long Hair," Borros said. "You don't take a step when you pivot behind you. That's wasted movement. It's slower. And slow means you get stuck like a pig. You simply turn your body. Front, then back, front, back."

Winwalom tried pivoting to the rear again.

"That's better. No wasted movement, boys."

The boys continued, pivoting and calling out the numbers. Lagash moved off to start making their supper. And then Ferran began to get the hang of it and began to move with more vigor. He began to fly around the ring.

When he passed fifty, Borros said, "Looking very fine indeed, Dog Boy. Caswal, what's your count?"

"Forty-six."

"See if you can keep up."

"Yes, sir."

Ferran knew Borros's comment was only going to make Caswal hate him more, but he didn't care. He was going to demonstrate his quality and shove that in Caswal's face.

Ferran finished first. His head was swimming with numbers, but one thing was for sure—he knew the position of each point.

Borros complimented him with a "well done," and Ferran smiled inside and turned to watch the others. To his delight, Caswal kept screwing up his count. As he did, he became more frustrated and made even more mistakes. Borros had to correct him a couple of times, and he ended up coming in dead last.

Ferran looked at Winwalom and tried to hide his grin.

"Okay," said Borros. "We're going to do the ring dance again. A hundred rings. But this time you're going to do one shuffle forward and back with each pivot. You only need to sound out when you complete each ring. Begin."

The boys began. Ferran worked hard to be exact, to shuffle forward heel to toe, to keep his balance when shuffling back. He moved quickly, calmly. He was focused. However, Ranoc and Winwalom sped up, trying to keep pace. And then Caswal finally got his counts and began to catch up. Soon all the boys were moving as fast as possible, racing through the rings, calling out their numbers.

Ferran pushed himself. They finished in a string of shouts. This time Winwalom came in first, Ferran in second.

"Take that, Dog Boy," Winwalom said with a grin.

"Good work," Borros said. "Caswal and Krov, you two got sloppy at the end. Let me see another five rings. Make them perfect."

Borros watched them, and when they finished, he said, "Practice forms habit. And habit is the only thing that will be there when the fight is upon you. When your life is on the line, everything else is stripped away. So if you practice sloppy, you're only practicing your own doom. Do you understand me? Practice sloppy, and you'll fight sloppy, and you'll soon find yourself skewered on a better man's blade. Accuracy first, then speed."

"Yes sir," the boys said.

"Caswal?" he demanded.

"Yes sir," he said.

"We're going to end with two things to build your strength," he said. He called them the grinders and grips. For the grinders, the boys were to find a branch they could barely touch when jumping. When they had all found one, he had them jump to touch it, land, immediately go into a squat, do a push-up, and then jump up again. He counted them out until all the boys were struggling. For the grips, he had them pick up fat stones in a one-handed grip and carry them back and forth between two points. When they began dropping the stones as soon as they picked them up, Borros said, "We're done. Now go get a drink and then report for dinner."

Ferran rejoiced, picked up his pole, and headed with the others for the stream, Itch trailing behind.

"That was murder," Ranoc said.

"My hands," Caswal lamented.

"Yours?" Krov said. "Did you see the size of stones he made me carry?"

"I saw Ferran's," Caswal said. "Little baby pebbles."

"They were as big as yours," Ferran said.

"Hardly."

Ferran rolled his eyes. It wasn't worth the fight.

"He's putting us through the paces," Winwalom said. "But I don't know how one day's practice is going to help."

"With thieves?" Ranoc asked.

"It's better than nothing," Ferran said. "I now know how to shuffle and turn and pivot; I can tell you that."

"But is that going to be enough?" Winwalom asked.

Caswal spoke up. "Dog Boy can prance in front of the drover, but it's not going to mean anything when it comes time to fight."

"Whatever," Ferran said and moved to take the path to the stream, but Caswal turned and blocked his way.

"What do you think you're doing?" Caswal asked.

This was beyond tedious. "Get out of the way," Ferran said.

"You can get your water downstream, Dog Stink."

Ferran bristled. "I'll get my water wherever I please."

"No, I think not."

Ferran clenched his fists.

"Ferran," Winwalom warned.

Caswal said, "Both you and your dog stink, and nobody here wants to smell you on the water."

"He doesn't stink any more than the rest of us," said Winwalom.

"You can join him."

"It's okay, Win," Ferran said. "He's got to have some alone time to sniffle and cry about his inability to perform like the rest of us." Ferran turned and angled upstream. Caswal tried to flank him, but Ferran quickened his step, and Caswal let him go.

A few seconds later, Caswal sniffed loudly. "Ah, that's better."

Ferran shook his head. He hoped they did fight and that Caswal got stuck by a blade. Ferran found a good spot upstream and walked down the bank to the stream's edge, and then realized the opportunity this gave him. He looked downstream, saw Caswal scooping up the water.

Ferran turned to Winwalom. "You think he'd enjoy a little pee in his drink?"

"He'll kill you."

"It would be worth it," Ferran said.

"No, because then you'd be dead."

Ferran stood there a moment, then decided against it. He splashed his face and dunked his head and drank cupfuls with both hands. Itch ran through the water and up the bank to the other side to explore.

Winwalom splashed his face to clean the sweat and dust off and sat back on his heels. "You shouldn't let him get to you."

"He's a stinking swine."

"You've got a job to do. Just ignore him."

"That's easy for you to say."

"Keep the goal in mind. A week of putting up with a smear of dog turd, and you're that much closer to keeping your freedom."

"He's a maggot," Ferran said.

"No doubt about it."

"A mouse dropping."

"Worse."

Ferran sighed.

"Just be level-headed," Winwalom said. "Like me." And then he rose. "I'm going to the jacks. I'll meet you back at camp."

Be level-headed like him, Ferran thought and rolled his eyes. Except the truth was Winwalom was level-headed. Ferran drank a bit more, then rose and whistled for Itch. He waited, but didn't see the dog and whistled again.

"You think you're something."

Ferran turned.

Caswal stood at the top of the bank, staff in hand.

"I'm just working hard, Caswal," Ferran said. "You might want to try it sometime." Ferran whistled for Itch again.

"You're trying to put me in a bad light. Get my pay docked."

Ferran waved him off. "Whatever, Caswal." And he scanned the far bank. Where was Itch?

Something struck Ferran in the back of the head. He felt a stab of pain and saw bright lights. The force of the blow sent him stumbling into the stream with his bare feet. He stepped on a sharp rock, then stumbled and fell to his knees in the water, striking more sharp stones.

Anger burned through him, and he rose with clenched fists.

Caswal was standing at the top of the bank, staff in hand, smiling.

"Having a bit of a problem, Dog Boy?"

Caswal had that look of his, and Ferran knew he was planning on violence. Ferran's staff was on the bank, and he couldn't get it without risking another blow from Caswal, so Ferran reached down and picked up a river stone.

Someone needed to teach Caswal a lesson. Itch appeared at the top of the far bank, ears alert, his patch face dappled with shadow. And Ferran began to think now would be a good time for such instruction. Siccing Itch on the worthless rot would teach a wonderful lesson. And while Itch was biting him, Ferran could add his blows.

"Back away, Caswal."

"It should have been Lome the drover hired."

"Lome would have been worse than you. He'd probably still be out there trying to figure out where position number eight was."

Caswal's expression turned menacing, and he changed his grip on his shaft. "You think you're so funny."

Itch splashed through the water and came to Ferran's side. "I'd think twice, Caswal."

Caswal looked at Itch and then the stone in Ferran's hand.

"One wrong move, and you're going to feel his teeth."

"If my pay's docked, it's coming out of your portion."

"If your pay's docked, it will be your own stupid fault."

"You'd better be careful, Dog Boy," Caswal sneered. "You never know what might happen on a trip like this. You might not make it back with even half a birdseye."

"Is that a threat?"

"It's whatever you want it to be," Caswal said. And then he turned and walked away, leaving Ferran standing in the current.

So that was Caswal's plan then? To beat him and take his money?

He could try. But, dumb rock that he was, he'd revealed his plan, and Ferran would be watching for him. And then another thought struck Ferran and turned him cold.

Maybe Caswal wouldn't try. Maybe he'd let others do the work for him. Suddenly Ferran thought about the thieves that had attacked him earlier this year. They had known about the coin he carried. They'd be waiting for him.

And how could they have known unless somebody told them? The more he'd thought about it, the more certain he was that's exactly what had happened. Why else would they have been there?

Had Caswal done it? It certainly wasn't beyond him. And if he'd done it once, he'd do it again. And it wouldn't be hard to spread the word around Pencoy's. Just a few loud comments in a tavern here and at an ale-wife's there. A few comments about a lone boy on the road with a fat purse full of money.

The news would travel. It wouldn't be long before it reached someone who'd grin and figure his ancestors had just blessed him with an easy target for some coin.

All this meant Ferran could not linger at Pencoy's. As soon as he was paid, he had to get away from Caswal. But there were only so many roads back from Pencoy's. It's not like he was going to be able to just disappear.

He picked up his shaft from the side of the stream and climbed up the bank. And then an idea struck him.

Ferran needed more money than what he'd receive for driving the cattle to Pencoy's. He needed the pay for the full job. He needed to work the whole distance to Broniss.

And if he went to Broniss, he could avoid having to travel with coin completely. The new lord was from Broniss. And if he wasn't there, someone the new lord trusted might be. Some banker or merchant. Which meant Ferran didn't need to risk traveling with all that coin. He could receive his pay from Borros and then immediately hand it over to the new lord or one of his agents in Broniss.

He smiled, despite the throbbing pain at the back of his head. There was no way Caswal could stop that. Of course, it all depended on Borros hiring him for the second leg of the journey. And how was he going to get Borros to do that?

He walked back to the camp, pondering how to convince him.

18

THE LILLY OF WELLSDROP

The meal was the same as it had been the evening before with one exception. They had the same barley, peas, and herbs, but Lagash had also included the hares they'd caught. The porridge was a delight despite the hard stare Caswal gave him, and Ferran and Itch both licked their bowls clean.

There was another lidded black, iron pot with legs sitting next to the fire. Lagash heaped some coals onto the top.

"What's in there?" Ferran asked.

"Crickets," said Lagash.

"Crickets?" asked Ranoc.

"They're delicious."

The boys looked at each other dubiously.

Lagash kept his face straight, and Ferran couldn't tell if he was pulling their legs or not.

Borros said, "Well, there won't be any cricket pie until you finish your spears. You need to get a good hard point on them. So when you finish your porridge, I want you to remove the bark on the last foot of your shaft. Then you're going to cut it to a point, but don't start that until I show you how."

Ferran took out his knife and began to shave off the bark. The others soon joined him. When they had exposed the wood, Borros took a little stick from the fire that had char on the end, then grabbed Krov's staff. "We're going to create a seven-inch spike. So start seven inches back from the end like this. Then draw a triangle to the tip. You'll cut the wood away. Then we'll turn it, draw another triangle, and cut that away."

The boys all grabbed a stick from the fire and drew their lines, then Ferran and Winwalom worked together to cut theirs, one boy holding the shaft firmly against the wagon while the other set his knife on the wood and used a stick as a mallet. The other boys saw how quickly they were making their cuts and soon followed their lead.

"When you finish your first cuts," Borros instructed, "it will look like a tall pyramid. Then you'll whittle the edges of the pyramid off until you have your spike."

The boys finished their cuts and began whittling. And Ferran began imagining having to use his spear. Could he stick a man with this? He supposed he could if it was stick the man, or die.

When they finished, Borros held up a stone and said, "I want you to find a rough stone like this one. You're going to rub the cut wood until it's fairly smooth."

They found their stones and began. As they worked, Borros made sure each was doing it right. As they were finishing up, he said, "This is looking good. You'll thank me for this. Every man needs to know how to make a spear. And with the maggot king of Osson making threats, your lord may very well muster you to use it."

Winwalom asked, "Do you think raiders will spot you on the sea road?"

Lagash said, "There's no doubt they'll spot us. The question is whether they will risk a landing."

"And Pencoy is going to escort you?"

"That's what he promised."

"Would having an extra man with a spear help?"

Borros said, "Your contract is to Pencoy's lands."

"What if you had two spears?" Ferran asked.

"Or three?" Krov put in.

"Four," Ranoc said.

"Five," Caswal said.

"It's a dangerous road, boys."

"How big would an Osson raiding party be?" asked Ferran.

"Depends," said Borros. He removed his cap with its scarlet badge and scratched the top of his head. "They can be as small as a dozen men or up to three or four ships, which would be a few hundred." He put his cap back on.

"That's a small army," said Ferran. "Pencoy doesn't have that many men."

"There are patrols from Broniss," Borros said.

"How many?" asked Winwalom. "It's a long stretch of coastline."

"There won't be any waiting there for us," Borros said. "But Osson doesn't know that, does it?"

Fighting Osson sounded great in the stories, but there wouldn't be any fighting against two hundred of them. There would be fleeing. And probably dying. But Ferran needed the money. He looked at Winwalom who just raised his eyebrows at the prospect.

"I'd still go," Ferran said. "One more spear is better than one less."

"You practice with a spear for two hours and figure you're the match of a seasoned soldier, is that it?" Borros asked.

"No, but we are practiced with our slings. And that's something."

Borros grunted.

"Why do you all want to go to Broniss so badly?" Lagash asked. "For the money?"

Ranoc said, "I wanted to see the Queen's Rangers. I've been told that all may compete to take their oath."

"You want to be a Queen's Ranger?" Borros asked with a grin.

"Why not?"

"Have you got family in Broniss with any type of position?"

"No."

"A horse?"

"No."

"You're going to just walk in and impress them, eh?"

Ranoc shrugged. "Maybe they won't look at me. But it's worth a try. And it's as good a reason to go as Krov's."

"Hey," Krov said in warning.

The boys all grinned.

"What's so funny?" Lagash asked.

"Nothing," Krov said. "I wanted to see a bit of the country is all. And earn some coin."

"There's a girl," Ranoc explained.

"Oh?" Borros asked.

Krov gave Ranoc a withering glare.

"Tell us about her," Borros said.

"He doesn't even know her," said Ranoc.

"That's not true," said Krov. "She looked at me. We exchanged a meaningful glance."

Borros cocked an eyebrow. A grin tugged at the corner of his mouth. "A glance. Well, we must hear all about her then."

Krov ran his finger along the eye patch cord that ran above his good eye and said, "She came through the village last year. She and her family."

"In a white dress," Winwalom added.

"She was a lily," Krov said, enraptured with the memory. "A pale dress against dark hair and brown skin."

"A brown lily?" Lagash asked. "Or was the dress the lily?"

"She—" Then Krov thought about it. "Well, the dress I suppose."

"So you're going to Broniss to see a dress?" Borros asked.

"No. Look, I was carrying a three-point stag over my shoulder. It was field dressed. I was taking it back for the lord's agent. I came to the edge of the wood, and there she was. Like a vision, shining in the sun. Something out of the tales. Then she turned and looked at me. And..."

"Yes?"

"She waved."

"Oh, a wave," Borros said. "Now that's something."

"Exactly," Krov said. "And more. She remarked on the stag, noting its quality. And then she smiled at me."

"A wave *and* a smile," said Lagash as if impressed.

"She had all of her teeth, at least those that I could see."

"Teeth are good," said Lagash.

"And then," Krov said, reliving the wonder of the moment, "she asked me my name. Of course, I gave it to her."

Borros was grinning. "And then?"

"Well, as I said she and her family were on the road. I came upon them at the end of a rest. So they departed. But as they went, she looked back at me with mischief in her eyes."

"That was the meaningful glance?" Borros asked.

"Oh, no. It's what came next." He heaved a sigh. "She winked. Very deliberately. And then I stood there and watched her until they disappeared around the bend."

Borros sat back. "Well, I'd say that's as good as a betrothal."

Krov's eyes widened. "Do you think so?"

"Of course." He looked at Lagash. "What do you say?"

"Definitely."

"Her eyes haunt me. I have to find her."

"Did you get her name?" asked Borros.

"Not exactly," Krov said.

"She didn't give you her name?"

"Not then. But later I went back to the village and found out they'd stopped at the ale-wife's window. Her father's name is Kut from Wellsdrop, just outside of Broniss."

"But you don't have her name."

"No, but I have her face. And her hair shining in the sun, and that pale dress."

"I see," Borros said. "Well, that's a very good reason to risk the danger of Osson raiders and possible death."

Lagash said. "Have you written her any poetry?"

"Poetry?" Krov asked.

"Good grief, you expect to show up without poetry?"

Krov got a worried expression. "I don't know the first thing about poetry."

"Alas," said Borros. "Alas."

Krov looked up at Lagash, worry in his eyes. "How does one do poetry?"

Borros said, "It's mostly metaphors. Her hair was like fire, her eyes like flame. She burned me to a crisp, but didn't give me a name. Stuff like that."

Krov looked dubious.

Lagash shook his head. "His verse will woo no woman. It takes the right metaphor."

"Like lily?" Krov asked hopefully.

"Maybe," Lagash said.

"Will you help me?"

"I might," Lagash said.

"Oh, this is the lord's delight," said Borros. "I can't wait. His last verse wooed him a cow."

"The lady Efor was not a cow."

Borros shrugged.

"You wooed a lady?" Ranoc asked.

Lagash said, "I've wooed many, including ladies." And then he looked pointedly at Borros as if daring him to challenge the truth of that statement. Borros just grinned.

"Who was one of these ladies?" Ferran asked.

"Later," Lagash said and turned to Winwalom. "What about you, Long Hair? Are you a lover too, or do you want to present yourself to the Rangers?"

"No. Nothing like that. It's just me and my da. My mother died some years ago. Our oxen are getting old, and we thought this was a good way for me to earn some extra coin to replace them."

Ferran furrowed his brow. "What about the—"

Winwalom gave him a warning look.

Ferran changed his course and finished with, "The horse you wanted?"

Winwalom smiled. "We're going to get the oxen first."

Ferran looked at Winwalom. An apprenticeship was a thing to be proud of. Why was he hiding his?

"Broniss has a fine horse market," said Borros. "I intend to buy me an Elboran stallion."

Ranoc whistled. "Those are a pretty penny."

"Indeed," said Borros. "On the way back, you will see me riding in style."

"What about you, Caswal?" Lagash asked.

He shrugged. "I figured why not."

"Nothing more?"

He shrugged again.

"I thought you wanted to view the sea," Krov said. "Look at the ships." Caswal had talked for years about getting out and going to other places, but it has always been south to Sordis, the island kingdom.

Caswal shrugged.

"New lands," said Borros. "New sights. Young men are always running off to the sea."

"Maybe," said Caswal.

If Ferran had Caswal's da, he would have run off the sea long ago. Caswal's father was liberal with his hands and feet and whatever else he might have to beat his boys.

"Well, if you go down to the docks, be careful of the crews from Norrson. Their press gangs are notorious. They'll either knock you senseless or get you drinking until you've drowned your wits, and then you find yourself waking up on one of their ships. Ale contracts they call them. I knew a man who was forced onto one of their ships and didn't see home for almost three years."

"That's not right," said Ranoc.

"Lots of things aren't right," said Lagash. "But they happen. The wise man seeks to make himself aware of the risks in the things he does so he can avoid as many of them as possible."

"Like taking the sea road with two hundred fifty plus head of cattle when raiders are about?" asked Winwalom.

"I think he's questioning my judgment," said Borros.

"Are you questioning his judgment?" Lagash asked.

"No," Winwalom said. "No, I've always wanted to face a horde of Osson raiders. And maybe I'll get my chance. With this stick."

Borros laughed out loud.

Ferran laughed as well, but the truth was that if they had to face raiders, it would not go well. It would end up with them facing axes and swords and having their body parts being hacked off.

Lagash motioned at Ferran. "What about you, Dog Master?"

Ferran shrugged. "It's simple. We need the coin."

"They're massively in debt to the new lord," said Caswal. "His father abandoned them. Ran off. Now either he or his sister will be sold. And Ferran made it all worse."

Caswal made it sound like his father had slunk off like some coward. "He didn't run off," said Ferran. "He was part of a patrol in the Western mountains."

"And he ran off."

"He didn't run."

Caswal shrugged. "Okay, he walked. Whatever."

Ferran's anger rose, but he tamped it down.

An awkward silence ensued, which Lagash broke. "So you're shouldering the responsibility, eh?"

"Yes," Ferran said. "My father was a good man. He had a good trade. But he disappeared. The men with him on the patrol said so. They heard him yell, and then nothing."

Lagash nodded. "And you're the oldest?"

"Yes."

"Well, let's hope everything goes well along the way, and that Borros makes your purse fat and heavy, and you return with enough and to spare."

"Knowing Ferran," Caswal said, examining his fingernails, "he'll lose it on the way back. In fact, I'll bet on it."

Another clumsy threat. Ferran ignored him and turned to Borros. "A slinger with an excellent aim would come in handy where you're going. You saw my aim. I can strike targets well past a hundred yards."

"The agreement is to Pencoy's," Borros said. "That's all I'm worried about right now. And that's all you should be worried about, which means you should focus on finishing your spear so you can help get me there. The same goes for the rest of you."

Ferran nodded. It was clear Borros wasn't open for more discussion about it now. Ferran would have to try again.

Borros said, "The last step, after you've got a good spike at the end of your spear, is to dry and burnish it. You want the spike to be hard and smooth. Our wooing cook will give you some lard. You'll smear on a thin coating, then rotate your spikes over the fire until the wood changes color. And then you'll get charcoal and a smoother stone and rub them to a finish."

The boys worked at it until evening, rotating the spike ends of their shafts over the fire. The wood turned color. Ferran burnished his until it was smooth as glass.

Borros held his hand out to inspect it. Ferran passed the spear to him.

"This looks good," he said. "Very good." And then he passed it back. "Now I want you to strip the last three inches of bark from the bottom. I don't want a point. Just a round end. Then get a strip of leather from Lagash, get it wet, and then wrap it around a few times and tie it to keep that end from splitting."

They all finished, and wrapped the wet strips, which would shrink. It was at this time that Lagash moved his pot of cricket pie off the fire. Inside were nine small hand pies that Lagash had baked. He served one to each of the boys and Itch and two to himself and Borros.

The boys looked at each other questioning who was going to eat the crickets first, but Ferran didn't care what was in them. Food was food. And he took a bite of the hot pie. He was rewarded with a sweet crunch.

"Honey," he said and then pulled out what looked like a small body. "What's this?"

"A cricket," said Borros.

It wasn't a cricket. There was no head or sockets of legs or any coloring. "It's some kind of nut," Ferran said delightedly.

"It's a cricket," Borros said.

Ferran blew on his pie, took another bite, and made a small groan of satisfaction. The other boys, seeing his enjoyment, took bites of theirs with similar results. In just a few minutes, the pies were gone, and the boys were licking their fingers. And Ferran decided he didn't care if they were crickets—they were delicious.

By this time, the sun had dropped low in the west, and suddenly dozens of swallows appeared and began to flit and swoop over the cattle.

"What are they doing?" asked Ranoc.

"Eating," Winwalom said.

"We love swallows and bats," Borros said. "Anything to keep the rotted flies down."

They watched the aerobatic diners flutter and fly, and when the light was gone, Lagash said, "It's time to start the night watch. Time to watch for things more dangerous than swallows and bats."

19

BURRS

They hauled their browse bags from the wagon. Ferran found himself a nice spot while the other boys set up their tents. The watch order was the same as it had been the night before, and so Ferran, Winwalom, and Itch lay on their bags stuffed with leaves and grass, looking up at the sky as the last of the light faded. Lagash's fire in a hole crackled in the background.

Ferran said, "You're not going for oxen."

"Shush," Winwalom said.

"What are you hiding?" Ferran whispered.

"Nothing."

"That's such a lie."

"It's not."

"I'll find it out. I always do."

Winwalom was silent.

"What could be so bad you can't say it?"

"What do you think about the road ahead?" Winwalom asked.

That was Winwalom's way of saying he wasn't going to talk about it, and when Winwalom didn't want to talk, he didn't talk. So Ferran dropped the mystery even though it was killing him. "I'm thinking we're out on a lonely road, and that if I were some scum outlaw and spied all these cattle being guarded by nothing but a bunch of boys, it would be prime pickings."

"I was thinking about the coast road and Osson," Winwalom said and put his hands behind his head. "My da says if the Osson raiders don't kill you, they take you as slaves to sell in the markets in the east."

"Well, you don't have to worry about slavery," Ferran said. "You're so ugly, they'll kill you straight off."

"No, that's what they'll do to you. When they see me, I'll look so nice in comparison, they'll spare me in gratitude."

They fell silent for a moment. Itch licked Ferran's hand, and Ferran gave him a scratch behind the ears.

Winwalom said, "Do you think Lord Pencoy's men are any good?"

Ferran shrugged. "You heard Old Harm. He'll probably chintz the drover and send a bunch of toothless old men as his escort." And as he said it, Ferran realized hiring on for the second leg of the journey would put him at greater risk. "Your troubles and mine—why can't we be like those that seem to move through life with nothing but smooth sailing?"

"Have you ever thought about not going back?"

"To Buckle Hill? If I'm not there when the lord's agent returns to prove I've paid, my sister will be sold off to pay the debt. I can't allow that to happen. I have to go."

"Your mother taught her the cheese craft. She could end up as a dairy maid somewhere."

"Or, because she's pretty, she might also be sold to some piece of filth to abuse as he sees fit. No. She's not going anywhere. If anyone is to be sold, it will be me."

"I hope you don't get sold."

"Not that you'll be around to enjoy my brilliant wit if I do stay."

"I never wanted to go to Broniss," Winwalom said. "But sometimes you have to do things you don't want to do."

Aye, Ferran thought. Wasn't that the truth.

The two of them didn't say anything else but simply lay in silence, watching the stars appear as the last of the sky faded to black.

Ferran felt a strong nudge in his side from someone's foot and woke to find Krov standing next to him, the night stars shining above.

"Your turn," he said, his spear in hand.

Ferran sat up. "See anything?"

"Smelled a skunk. Smelled the cattle. That's all."

Ferran nodded. "Okay, I've got it." He turned to Itch. "Come on." And then he rose out of bed, the images of a dream still playing in his mind. In it, he and the others had been fighting a monstrous creature from the sea that was trying to drag the cattle off the coast road. The monster had tentacles as long as trees.

He grabbed his spear and stood. In the field, the cattle were darker smudges against the even darker backdrop of the woods. The night breathed with the soft chirrup of crickets and other insects. But such a night could easily conceal other things. This camp was a long way from any village. And he realized that if anything did happen out here, there would be no calling for help, for there would be nobody to hear.

He looked at the cattle and identified the spot where he would go were he a thief, and then he and Itch slowly walked around the perimeter of the field toward it, stopping every ten or fifteen yards to listen.

He patrolled the dark spot where any proper-minded thief would lie in wait. After those tense moments, he finished the first round, and then another and another. He stopped to take a leak and then continued. He gauged the turning of the stars, and when he was at the far end of the field, something dark moved in the sky. He turned to get a better view of it and thought he saw a shadow, high up. He startled, his eyes going wide. And then the shadow disappeared, obscured by the tops of the trees.

He moved to get a view that was clear of tree branches and scanned the sky. He thought he saw it again.

"Do you see it, boy?" he asked Itch. He snapped his fingers and pointed at the sky to direct Itch's attention.

Itch looked, but then lost interest. Ferran tried to find it again, but after ten minutes of looking and seeing nothing, he chided himself. This was simply his mind building up his fears and playing tricks on him. It was Winwalom and his dumb bat all over again. He shook his head at his foolishness and made the rest of his rounds. And when he figured an hour had passed, he went back and woke Winwalom.

"Did you see anything?"

"A bat," Ferran said. And then he felt his bag for rocks and thorns. When he found none, he lay down, pulled his cloak over himself and fell asleep.

———

He woke again to Lagash banging his big cooking spoon against the side of the wagon and ordering them to rise. Ferran yawned, looked at the stars, and then tried to sit up, but something pinched his hair. The hair on the whole side of his head he'd been lying on was attached to the browse bag.

"What the...?" He tried to run his fingers through his hair to free it, and found it matted and snagged, rising in odd prickly shapes.

It was full of burrs! Burrs that were sticking it to the sackcloth.

Where had he gotten burrs? Had he stupidly laid his browse bag next to some weed? But there weren't any weeds around. This spot was grass. When could he have picked up so many burrs?

And then he noticed Itch biting the fur at his side. Had he picked them up and transferred them to Ferran?

Ferran pulled himself loose from the sackcloth with a small cry of dismay, his hair pinching and pulling. He ran his hand over the bag and found burrs all over around where his head had been. How?—and then he knew exactly what had happened.

This wasn't Itch. Someone had dumped the burrs on him and Itch during the night.

Caswal.

Ferran pressed his lips together in irritation. That maggot.

Winwalom woke, stretched, rubbed the sleep sand from the corner of his eyes, then looked at Ferran.

"What's going on with your hair?"

"Burrs," Ferran said sourly.

Winwalom chuckled.

"Yeah, real funny," Ferran said. He was going to be picking them out all day. He stood, felt Itch, and shook his head. Itch was covered in them. And you couldn't just leave them because they could irritate the skin. Some of them worked their way right in.

"Come on," he said to Itch. The firelight would help him see the size of the problem. They walked over to Lagash and the porridge.

Lagash turned. "Get a bowl." Then he peered at Ferran's hair. "I don't think I've seen morning hair stick up quite like that before."

"It's full of burrs," Ferran said.

Lagash reached out, felt it, and laughed. "What did you do, make your pillow from hounds-tongue?"

"No."

"You're going to be picking that out all day."

Ferran pulled out one burr, then tugged on another, but found it was knotted and impossible to pull out. He cursed.

The other boys began to arrive.

Ranoc took a look at him. "Hoo," he said and pointed.

"Did you do this?" Ferran demanded.

"Not me," Ranoc said and laughed.

Caswal walked up behind the others and smiled, but his reaction was too subdued.

"Rocks, thorns, and now this?" Ferran demanded.

"Don't blame me for your stupidity. You probably brought it back on your pants after your watch."

"Then they would be on my pants, not on my head."

Caswal laughed.

Ferran sighed in irritation. "Is this some drover's prank?" he asked Lagash.

Lagash said, "Dog Boy, I don't have time for pranks."

Ferran shook his head.

"Shave it off," Borros said. "That's my advice."

"The dog?"

"Both of you. Neither of you is going to any fancy wedding celebration."

"No, we're not," Ferran said.

Caswal smirked. "What a cheese brain."

"Take your bowls," Lagash said. "We need to get fed and on the road."

Ferran folded his arms and decided he was done taking Caswal's pranks. If Caswal wanted to play this game, Ferran was more than happy to play with him.

The boys lined up. Ferran took the last spot because he'd found Lagash always seemed to have a little extra in the last portion. He picked another burr out and winced at the tug. And then an idea came to him. It was a splendid idea. A brilliant next move. Something Caswal would surely appreciate.

20

TARGET

They struck camp, and then Borros ordered Ferran and Itch to push the cattle out of the field and onto the road. Ferran whistled and waved his staff with the yellow scarf tied to it. Itch wanted to bark and snap at the cattle, but the cattle were moving fine without that, and Ferran figured there was no reason to rile them up, so he kept him back. The cattle were soon trailing down the road with the other boys keeping the sides of the herd from straying too far.

At one point during the drive, they stopped at a stream to let the cattle drink. Ferran had picked and cut all the burrs from his hair by this point. During the break, he cleaned Itch up.

Krov and Ranoc found a wasp nest high in a tree and began to unloop their slings, but Borros lit into them, telling them the last thing they needed was angry wasps stinging the cattle. When the cattle finished drinking, they moved on. They traveled around fifteen miles that day, then came to another pasture, drove the cattle in, and checked the split-rail fencing to make sure it was secure.

They practiced again with their spears, but this time after they were done with their legwork, Borros took a piece of charcoal from the fire and walked over to the fat trunk of an old oak.

"Normally, we'd use straw men, sometimes real men, but a tree will work. This is a face," he said and drew an oval on the trunk. "Neck," he said, then outlined a neck. "Body," he said and outlined the torso and legs. He then sketched a side view of a man on either side of the trunk and the rear view of a man at the back. As he sketched the outline of each view, he made a dot in the center of the head, neck, chest, thigh, and foot.

"All of you will work on this tree," he said. "The trunk will be like the hub of a wagon wheel and your spears the spokes. Find a position."

Krov said, "There are five of us, but only four drawings on the tree."

"That's fine. There are eight points of attack and defense, remember? Four attacks that are straight into the target and four at a diagonal. Just find one. You'll move from position to position around the tree."

The boys each took a spot to start.

"Look at the man. You're looking at his front, back, or side. I've marked five targets on each view."

"He's talking about the dots for the head, neck, chest, thigh, and foot that you see on each drawing," Lagash said.

Ferran noted the positions.

Borros said, "After knowing where to strike, the next thing you need to learn is the correct distance."

He walked a few paces away, then set himself and slowly lunged at the target. He ended up having to stretch to reach the target. "You don't want this. Look at me. Totally off balance. Open to an attack."

He stepped a pace closer and slowly thrust the spear, touching the tree with the tip of the spike. It looked like he was the perfect distance.

"You don't want this either," he said. "I'm tapping the tree with the tip. Do that in a real battle, and you'll fail to kill even your grandmother's flea. You need to push into the target. You should be far enough away that when you finish your lunge, the tip of your blade would be a foot or two into the trunk of the tree. Why? Because, unlike a tree, a man might move, and that gives you enough space to adjust. When you strike, you want all of your body weight and force transferred to this tip and pushing through. So, no taps."

"Measure your distance," Lagash said.

Ferran stepped his off and found his first guess was still too far away. So he wiped away some old acorns with his bare foot at a spot that was closer, and found the tip of the spear hit the tree before he was fully extended.

"Dog Boy's got it," Borros said. "Patch is good. Long Hair. Good. You all look good. Okay, here's the next part. A spear is a stabbing weapon. It's also a staff, and a good clout can send a man to his knees. And when you get a weapon with a proper head, it will be a hooking weapon as well. Nothing like a good hook on the reverse stroke to pull a man off balance or hook his shield or pierce his neck. But for you, with these weapons, it's about stabbing. A spear has a tip. And you need to hone your ability at putting that tip where you want it to go. So this is how you're going to practice."

He took the solid stance, then lunged in slow motion and touched the tip of the spear to the dot on the man's face.

Caswal scoffed.

"Something funny?" Borros demanded.

"Well, how is that any better than a tap?"

"Because it's accurate. Because it can become a killing blow when speed and force are applied. But a tap will forever be a tap. What you don't understand, because you're a snot-eating boy and have never been in a battle, is that accuracy comes first. And after you are accurate, which I will be the judge of, only then will you increase your speed. And so today you will lunge and strike the very center of your dots. And you'll do it with the speed of a turtle.

"If you're at one of the four positions that face the man in the tree directly, you will attack those targets. If you're on a diagonal, choose the man in the tree to your left or right."

Ferran was on a diagonal at the back view of the man. So he decided he would strike the targets at the back rather than the side.

"There are five dots, five targets, on each view," Borros said. "You will strike each dot ten times from your current line of attack. When you finish those fifty strikes, you move to the next line of attack."

Winwalom said, "Fifty times eight—that's four hundred strikes total."

"He can count," Borros said. "Caswal, did you hear that?"

"Yes," Caswal said.

"Slow and accurate," Borros said. "See your target, strike it. And if you go too fast, I will make you start again."

Ferran lowered his spear, lunged slowly, and stuck the tip in the dot on the face.

"Aim for the very center of the dot," Borros said. "Aim at a large target, and you will only train yourself to hit somewhere in a large area. Aim at a tiny target, and you will train yourself to strike with pinpoint accuracy."

Ferran set himself again and slowly lunged and struck the center of the dot on the man's face.

"Slower, Long Hair," Borros called out. "Slower."

The boys slowly lunged forward and back, the tips of their spears poking their targets.

"Focus," Lagash said. "Don't look away. Don't let your eyes slide. See your target. Strike your target. Think about pushing through."

The boys continued, and Ferran soon found that the slow movement was making his legs burn. He switched arms and continued, lunging with the other leg.

"Dog Boy's getting tired," Caswal said.

"No, just trying not to faint from your odors."

"Focus," Lagash said.

The boys continued.

After a few more strikes, Borros said, "Patch, you're in charge. Don't go any faster than you're going now. Make sure everyone does their full count."

"Yes sir," Krov said.

Lagash and Borros left them to put a new shoe on Carrots the mule.

The boys finished another line of attack and moved to the next position.

Caswal said, "You need a rest, Dog Boy?"

"Does anyone else hear that?" Ferran asked. "It sounds like a farting cow. Oh, wait. It's Caswal. I'm sorry, what did you say?"

Ranoc laughed.

"We'll see how funny it is when the real fight comes," Caswal snapped, "and Dog Boy's all tired out and can't hold his pole."

Ferran had a sudden urge to change the direction of his lunge and stab Caswal, but he refrained and slowly lunged forward and struck the mark for the neck on the tree. "I can outrun and outwork you any day of the week Caswal."

"Both of you be quiet," Krov said. "You're messing up my count."

Caswal grunted, but Ferran smiled with satisfaction because he knew what was going to happen tonight.

A few strikes later, Caswal said, "This is stupid."

"Says the snot-nosed boy who hasn't been in a battle," said Krov.

"Like you know anything. Borros was probably assigned to be the ditch digger in his army. A mighty digger of latrines."

Ranoc slowly extended a lunge. "Whatever he was, I wouldn't want him after me."

"Do I hear talking?" Borros called from over by the wagon.

"No sir," Krov said and glowered at the other two.

The boys focused on their practice and continued in silence, the spears poking the trunk of the tree in a ragged rhythm. And soon Ferran found that what was happening around him faded away, and his whole focus became the tiny dots of charcoal and his burning shoulders and legs.

Ranoc finished first, then Caswal stopped.

"Getting tired, Caswal?" Ferran asked.

"No, I'm just done."

"I think I'll do an extra fifty," Ferran said.

"Whatever," Caswal said and turned away.

But Ferran wanted to do the fifty. He might need this later. Also, he wanted Borros to see he was eager to follow orders and learn. And so, even though he was hot and sweaty and his legs and shoulders were burning, he moved to the next line of attack and practiced fifty more strikes. And then he regretted it, for Borros put them through the grinders and grips again.

When they were done, Borros ordered those that didn't have a second spear to go cut another sapling and bring it back to work on it so that each boy had two. By the time Ferran and Winwalom came back with their second shafts, Borros had gone to scout the road they'd just traveled.

"It's like he's expecting someone," Winwalom said.

"We're not in the safest territory," Ferran said.

"When in doubt, always watch your back," Lagash said. "Now get your bowls."

Ferran realized that is precisely what he needed to do with Caswal.

21

PAYBACK

The watch followed the same sequence as it had before. Except this time when Krov came and nudged him awake, Ferran got up willingly. He and Itch made their rounds, and then, when his watch was about half over, he commanded Itch to sit next to the fence.

Itch whined, but Ferran shushed him. Then he quietly went to the wagon. Borros was there snoring loudly, which made it easier for Ferran to remove one of the spades that was affixed to the side of the wagon.

He went into the field. There were a lot of clouds in the night sky, dimming the moon, but the clouds broke momentarily to let a thin crescent of moon shine through. Ferran spotted what he was looking for, scooped up a great quantity, then walked as quietly as he could over to Caswal's narrow little tent. Caswal was inside on his back, breathing loudly with his mouth open.

Ferran wanted to dump the load of wet manure right into his gob, but instead, he deposited it where he figured Caswal would crawl when he exited the tent. He deposited two more large loads to either side to widen the area.

He then cleaned the spade on some tall grass outside the field, returned to the wagon and the snoring Borros, and put the spade back.

He made another two patrols around the cattle, then went and nudged Winwalom awake.

"You see anything?" Winwalom whispered.

"Nothing but cows," Ferran said and felt his bed and cloak for burrs and sticks.

Winwalom yawned. "Okay," he said, then called Itch.

Ferran suddenly realized that the best time for Caswal to play his stupid pranks was when Itch wasn't here. "Can you leave him here tonight?"

"I kind of like having him along," Winwalom said. "He's got teeth."

"Well, your spear's got one nice big tooth on it. Just tonight."

Winwalom sighed, "Okay, fine." And then he tied his hair up on his head and left.

Ferran put his arm around Itch. "Now's our revenge," he whispered into the dog's ear. "Bark if you hear something." And then he fell asleep.

———

He woke the next morning to Lagash banging his pot. Ferran felt his head, found no burrs or anything else around his bag, and sighed in relief. Itch was up already and came over to give him a lick. Ferran checked for burrs and found none. Everything was perfectly normal.

Lagash banged his pot a few more times, and Ferran looked over at Caswal's tent, anticipation bubbling in him, but Caswal was taking his time. So Ferran walked over to the fire, his stomach growling for breakfast, Itch padding beside him.

Ferran waited and waited, and then Caswal cried out in dismay and cursed.

Ferran forced himself to keep a straight face.

"Who put this here!" Caswal demanded and cursed again.

"What's he going on about?" Lagash asked.

Ferran shrugged. "I have no idea."

Caswal rose, and then he spotted Ferran and pointed. "You!" he cried and stormed over, but as he approached, Itch must have read Caswal's mood, and began to growl.

"You're dead," Caswal said.

Ferran tried not to grin. "What seems to be the matter, Caswal?"

Caswal stopped a couple of paces away from Itch. "You think it's funny?"

"What are you talking about?" Ferran asked.

Lagash sniffed. "What is that?"

"Someone dumped three or four cow splats next to my tent. My hand was lying in one all night."

Ferran couldn't contain himself and blurted out a laugh. "What an idiot. Who puts their bed next to a cow pie?"

"I didn't," Caswal spat. "You dumped it there."

"Not me," said Ferran.

Lagash lifted an eyebrow.

Ferran held his arms out. "Do I look like I've been moving manure? I'm clean as a whistle."

Krov and Ranoc were yawning and making their way over to see what the commotion was about. As they drew near, Krov wrinkled his nose. "Hoo, that stinks," he said.

Lagash said, "Did either of you see anyone over by Caswal's bed last night?"

They shook their heads.

Ranoc motioned at Caswal's clothes. "What did you do, roll around in the grass by the cattle?"

Lagash said, "It appears Caswal made his bed in an unfortunate location."

"It wasn't there when I went to bed."

"Your knees are black with it," Ranoc said.

Caswal glanced down, then looked up and glared murder at Ferran.

Borros came into the camp and sniffed. "Some cow must have eaten something rotten. Do you smell it?"

Ferran couldn't keep himself from laughing.

"Line up," Lagash said.

The boys moved to form a line for food, but Lagash waved Caswal off. "Not you. You wash first. You're already attracting flies."

Caswal turned to leave.

"Cheese brain," Ferran said under his breath.

"What did you say?" Caswal demanded.

"Please rain. I'm hoping for a little water to keep the road dust down. It gets bad at the back."

Caswal scowled, then marched to the stream.

"He's going to kill you," Krov said, the bowl looking small in his huge hands.

"Unlikely," said Ferran. "Besides, it could have been you that put it there."

"What would my motive be?"

"Do you need a motive with Caswal?" Ferran asked.

Krov considered the question for a second, then nodded. "That's true."

Ferran got his and Itch's bowls and sat down on a nice log on the outside of the camp to enjoy the early morning sky. Breakfast that morning was the same porridge they'd had since the beginning, but for some reason Ferran found this morning's serving particularly delicious.

He'd almost finished when Winwalom strode out of the trees and marched directly toward him. "You need to come with me."

"Sit down," Ferran said. "Enjoy breakfast."

"I need another pair of eyes." There was an urgency in his tone.

"What's going on?"

"It wasn't a stork."

Ferran narrowed his eyes.

"It was something else. Hurry!"

22

FUR AND BONE

Ferran didn't know if he wanted to go out into the dark of the early morning to investigate a monster. But he slurped the rest out of his bowl, picked up his spear, and followed Winwalom out to the road. Itch glanced at them, but saw the remainder of Ferran's breakfast and began to lap it up.

"What's going on?" Ferran asked.

"Maybe nothing," Winwalom said and began to walk down the road.

The dark shadows looked threatening. "It's not still out here, is it?"

"I saw it land."

"Last night? When?"

"I'd come back from my watch and couldn't sleep. It circled high above the cattle a few times, then went off and perched on an outcropping of a hill."

"Is this some dumb joke?"

"I saw something," he said.

"You're sure it wasn't a figment of your mind? Some bug flying around your head?"

"I saw it plain as day. And it wasn't above my head. It was up in the sky."

"Clouds gathered at the end of my watch," Ferran said. "I could hardly see the stars."

"I could see well enough."

Winwalom suddenly turned off the road. "This way," he said and disappeared into the dark trees.

Ferran swallowed and followed, his bare feet crunching twigs and other forest debris.

Winwalom pushed through some branches that whipped back and hit Ferran in the face.

"Nobody sees well enough without some kind of moon or starlight," he said. "And especially not with clouds."

Winwalom didn't respond, simply kept climbing. Ferran kept his eye on Winwalom's hair. Another bush whipped back, but Ferran heard this one and raised his arm to stop it.

"Do you even know where you're going? It's too dark."

"Quit your whining," Winwalom said. "I can see just fine."

Ferran blinked. Was he losing his sight?

Winwalom picked up his pace, and Ferran had to scramble to keep up. But then he tripped in the darkness over a branch and fell.

"Will you slow down," he called.

Winwalom stopped and waited.

Ferran brushed himself off, and they continued up the hill.

"I don't know how you can see a path through this," he said.

"You must be going blind."

"I'm not going blind."

"I think we're almost there," Winwalom said. And another dozen yards or so later, they burst out of the trees and onto a rocky part of the hill where Ferran could see. To the east, the sky was beginning to lighten. To his left were a ledge and a drop of maybe forty or fifty feet. Beyond it lay the drover's field. The cattle were just visible from this distance.

"It had to have left some sign," Winwalom said.

"We're not going to see it in this dark. How big was it?"

"A ten-foot wingspan. Maybe fifteen."

"Fifteen feet?" That was enormous.

"Something that big must have left something behind," Winwalom said.

"Maybe it left a big poop. Maybe that's what was around Caswal's bed."

"Laugh all you want. You didn't see it."

"Why didn't you say something at the time?"

"Because," he said, then pointed at some shrubs. "Ha! Look."

Ferran looked, but it was still too dark. "I don't see anything."

"Here and here," Winwalom said and pointed down at the bushes by his feet.

Ferran opened his eyes wide to let in all the light he possibly could, then crouched down, and he could just barely make out some broken branches. A lot of them.

"And the dirt is scuffed over here," Winwalom added.

Ferran could barely make it out, even when looking right at it. Winwalom had always had good eyesight, but this was ridiculous. Were Ferran's eyes going bad?

"I think it's stalking us."

"Anything could have made these marks. Could have been a bear. Could have been some elk bedding down for the night."

"On the edge of a cliff? No elk is going to bed down here. And they look for grass beds, not a bunch of poky sticks."

He was right. "Okay," Ferran said. "So something was up here. But there's no sign that clearly tells what it was. If it were day, we could look for fur and other prints."

"What's that?" Winwalom said and pointed off the side of the ledge.

Ferran looked in that direction. About ten feet below the edge of the cliff was an outcropping of rock. On it lay something gray. It was large and oblong and looked like it had fallen there.

"A poop," Ferran said surprised.

But when they scrambled down and got a look at it, they found that it was not a poop of any kind.

It was maybe two feet long and a foot and a half thick, the shape of a pig bladder. But it wasn't smooth like a bladder. It was made up of hair and bones compacted and matted together.

The sky was lighter now, and some things in the mass were visible. "Those are teeth," Winwalom said.

"It's a jaw," Ferran said.

"A deer jaw?"

"With canines? No, that's something else." Ferran reached out and wriggled the end of the bone with two fingers.

"There's more than one set of teeth," Winwalom said. "More than one set of bones."

And then it struck Ferran. "This is like those pellets regurgitated by owls."

"Except four hundred times bigger."

"Did you see a giant owl?"

"It was not an owl," Winwalom said.

"Whatever it was, it likes to gulp its food."

"And it was eyeing the cattle."

Ferran suddenly had a bad feeling and looked up, but the sky was clear.

"Why didn't you wake Borros when you saw it?"

"Yeah, well..."

"How long was its body?"

"I don't know. Six feet. Eight feet."

They looked down at the hard, compact mess of fur and bones.

"We need to take this back," Ferran said.

Winwalom nodded, and they wrapped in it his cloak, then climbed back up to the top of the ledge. Ferran turned to make his way down the slope, but Winwalom grabbed him by the arm. "Don't tell them about how dark it was."

"What do you mean?"

"Tell them you saw it. And wanted to investigate."

That was silly. "Me?"

"Please," Winwalom said earnestly.

Ferran looked at his friend. Winwalom was acting odd. First the apprenticeship in Broniss that wasn't an apprenticeship. Now, this. "What is going on?"

"You saw it," Winwalom said. "You saw it land, and you spotted this mess of fur and bones."

"It isn't my eyes, is it. You're worried someone will know you can see in the dark." There were only three sorts of people who could do that. Those who had been anointed with sight, demon spawn, and those of the Old Blood. And some figured those last two were one and the same.

Old Blood. Ferran's heart missed a beat.

The blood of the Old Ones was black and tainted. It had been purged from the population in the War of Four Kings more than a century ago. But tales were still told of them coming in the night to touch folks with some spell that would make them their servant. Anyone showing any sign was to be taken to the inquisitors.

"You're making me uneasy," Ferran said.

Winwalom sighed. "It's not what you think."

"What is it then?"

Borros sounded his horn, one long note.

"Later," he said. "He's calling us back. Just don't make a big deal of the dark."

Ferran looked at his friend.

"I've always been able to count on you."

"And you always will," Ferran said.

Winwalom nodded. "Let's get going then."

They scurried down the hill and back to the camp. Everyone was packed up, waiting.

Borros gave them a look. "Nice of you two little lords to show up."

"I thought I saw something during my watch," Ferran said. "But of course it was dark, and I just chalked it up to my eyes. But then I got to thinking this morning that we should investigate. We found this."

He set the cloak on the ground by Borros and unwrapped it.

By now there was enough early morning light to see. The coloring of the matted fur was indeed that of a badger. And something else. Borros crouched down, then pulled his knife out and used it to flake a section away.

Lagash said, "Where did you find this?"

Ferran pointed. "Just below the lip of that ledge over there."

Borros looked up at Lagash, but Lagash just shook his head and shrugged. Borros flaked off another hairy bit with pieces of vertebrae in it. "This looks like it's from a sheep."

The words of the skinny farmer came back to Ferran. "That farmer's warning," he said. "I thought he was talking about thieves. Maybe this is what's been taking the livestock."

Borros nodded. "Tell me exactly what you saw."

Ferran made up a story of seeing something dark against the stars out of the corner of his eye. He said that it looked like it had flown over the cattle and lighted in the top of the tree. He didn't think he should say what it looked like, because who could have seen it in the darkness, only that it was big and silent, and that he'd thought he'd heard the distant sound of leaves rustling.

"You should have awakened me," Borros said.

"I thought it was just night fears getting the better of me."

"Better safe than sorry," Borros said. "How many times do I have to say that?"

"Sorry," Ferran said.

"If any of you see this thing," Borros said, "you wake the whole camp. I'd rather have a few false alarms than get caught with my back turned to a threat. Understood?"

The boys nodded.

"What could it be?" Krov asked.

"Did you find feathers?" Lagash asked.

"We didn't see any," Ferran said, "but more light might reveal other spoor."

"There are giant birds in the lands beyond Soros," Lagash said. "But they run on the land. They don't fly."

"What about the blight?" Caswal asked. "Maybe it came from there."

The blight was an area not too many miles to the north and west in the mountains. Ten years ago, a mage and his troop had been running blackmeal to a garrison posted on the border or Gorland. The blackmeal would grant power to the men in the garrison who were anointed to wield it. But the blackmeal had become volatile and burst out in a chaotic riot of wild magic. The mage and his subordinates had contained the calamity but lost their lives in the process. The blight had contaminated the land for miles around. It sometimes took years for such things to heal. And it was forbidden to go into a blight until the mages proclaimed it clean.

"I doubt it," said Borros.

"Why?"

"Did the queen send her mages and grimsmen into the blight?" Borros asked.

"Yes."

"Just once?"

"No."

"No," Borros agreed. "They go in every year because sometimes it takes the twists a few years to manifest themselves. Something this big would be too big to miss."

"It could have been hidden up in some crag or cave," Winwalom said.

"That's true, so it's possible the hunters might have overlooked some cleft, but they have dogs to sniff. They know what sign to look for."

"What if they sent some lazy slug-a-bed to do the job?" Ferran asked.

Borros nodded. "It's possible. I knew one grimsman that was drunk most of the time. If they sent someone in who did a piss poor job, then it's possible anything is in there. Even so, a creature like what you've described would have a large territory. It's a big animal. It's going to have to travel to find enough food. If it had been living there all these years, surely someone else would have seen it, and news like that would fly. You would have heard it back in Buckle Hill. The queen would have heard about it in Broniss."

"It's just odd," Caswal said, "that it shows up now, when we're getting closer to the area."

"It's the herd," Lagash said. "The smell of prey. It draws predators."

"So if it's not some twist from the blight, what is it?" Krov asked.

Borros shrugged. "There are tales of all sorts of things that used to fly the skies. It could also be some filth cooked up by Osson wizards."

Lagash nodded. "That's a possibility."

Ferran glanced at the other boys who all looked alarmed.

"Fifteen feet," Ranoc said, then walked five long paces away and turned. "From you to me is about fifteen feet. It was this big?"

"I don't know. It could have been more," Ferran said.

The other boys looked shocked.

"Take heart," Borros said. "It had plenty of chances to eat one of you three nights in a row and didn't."

"Maybe it wasn't hungry," said Ranoc.

"Maybe," said Borros. "So it's a good thing you've got your spears. And it shows you why you need to keep them with you at all times."

Somehow the thought of fighting such a creature with a pointy stick didn't give Ferran much comfort.

"The good news is that this pellet is going to bring some pretty pennies," Borros said. "You wait and see. People will come running to see it. They'll be hanging off the roofs and eaves to hear the story and feast their eyes. Get it in the wagon. Make sure it's wrapped good and tight. We want it in good condition when we arrive."

Ferran hadn't thought of that, but it was true. Lots of people would pay to see this. "Technically," Ferran said. "It was Winwalom and me that found it." He continued in a generous tone. "And we'd be happy to share the earnings with you, Master Drover, if we were hired on for the full trip to Broniss."

Lagash grinned. "Now there's a little bit of brass for you."

"I don't mean to be rude," Ferran said. "It's just the truth."

Borros grunted and folded his massive arms. "But is what you find while you are in my employ mine or yours?"

Ferran took on a thoughtful look. "I don't remember that being in the agreement."

Lagash laughed.

Borros motioned at Ferran. "Get it in the wagon."

"Think about my offer," Ferran said.

"You think about the penalties for theft," Borros said.

Ferran and Winwalom found some weeds with monstrous leaves. They wrapped the pellet in them, then wrapped that in a square of burlap Lagash gave them. Then they packed the whole thing in a barrel with dried grass all around to keep it safe.

They began to move the cattle out, the boys sober and watching the skies.

23

ANOINTING

The drive was dusty, long, and just past noon, they traveled through a rocky place where few trees grew. The Black Mountains were visible in the distance. The old road to Broniss ran through them. It was the fastest way to Broniss, but it was also where the blight lay. So all travel for the last ten years had been funneled to the east through Pencoy's lands to the coast road.

Those mountains were an ominous sight, and Ferran wondered if a slug-a-bed mage hunter had indeed been assigned to that blight and missed something that was lurking back there. It gave him a little shiver just thinking about it.

The cattle were moving well, so he dropped back with Itch to the wagon to talk to Lagash. "What are your thoughts about this creature, Master Cook?"

Lagash looked down from where he was sitting on the driver's seat. "Well, let's look at what we know. It seems to like the dark. It gulps prey the size of badgers and ewes and probably you. We didn't see any horns in there, so maybe it takes down larger prey and rips the flesh. After all, dogs will eat mice, but they're happy to bait a bull as well. I'll need to get a look at it to make any more guesses."

Ferran said, "What do you think of Borros's conclusion about the blight?"

"It might have come from there, but I agree with him on this. Things affected by wild magic tend to be ravenous. They don't pass up opportunities for fresh meat."

"You sound like you have experience."

"I was in the eastern lands on a campaign, long before I fought Borros."

"You fought Borros?"

"I made him my slave."

"He was your slave?" Ferran asked, shocked. Now that was a story Ferran wanted to hear.

"He was. But this was before that. Back in Soros. Some wizard lost control out in the desert. Weeks later tales of a pack of lions start trickling out. They'd come at night to waste and feast on whole villages. People, camels, horses, goats—whatever moved."

"Lions," Ferran said, thinking of the stories he'd heard about them.

"Yes. They were wicked and large. They'd been changed by the magic and had a lot of dark coloring, not the tan of normal lions. Their eyes were wholly black. They had canines this big," he said and stretched his thumb and pinky finger out. "There was a band of us sent in to hunt them down."

"You fought grimmers?" Creatures twisted by feral magic.

"We slew them out in the desert. But they were unnaturally ferocious and quick, and we lost seven good men while we were at it. And these were men with anointings."

Ferran shook his head and then realized what Lagash had just revealed. "So you weren't just a cook."

Lagash smiled. "The cooks of Soros are demons in the flesh."

Ferran grinned wryly. Yeah, right. And then he thought about fighting something like twisted lions. "I've never hunted anything large," Ferran said.

"Well, let's hope we get to Pencoy's lands sooner rather than later. I doubt this thing will attack a whole troop of men."

No, but it would attack single badgers, sheep, and, as Lagash had said, boys. Which meant he'd be a fool to travel back from Pencoy's alone.

"What are you thinking?" Lagash asked.

"Oh, just that I most definitely need to be hired for the full trip."

They arrived at another pasture that afternoon and turned the cattle in. After they checked the stone and log fencing and watered the animals, Borros had them practice with their spears. They did so this time with more urgency and focus.

And after their rounds of rooster's feet, rings, and tree strikes, Borros added exercises to strike targets coming from above such as a man standing higher than you on a hill or standing upon a wall or some winged thing diving at you, wanting to dig its beak into your throat.

Borros finished the session by teaching them how to execute break-falls to the front, sides, and back, saying that you couldn't always expect to keep your feet. You might stumble or get knocked, and you needed to know how to fall and roll without your spear going flying. And so they practiced break-falls until they were covered with dust and sweat and bits of grass and all breathing hard. Then he made them do the grinders and grips. When they finally finished, he ordered them to go to bathe in the stream and get both themselves and their clothing clean.

The boys received soap from Lagash, then trudged over to a bend in the stream where the water was calm, clear, and deep. They took off their clothes and stepped in, scattering water skeeters. Ferran made sure to keep himself well away from Caswal.

The water was cold and felt wonderful against Ferran's flesh. And he dunked himself and enjoyed how it washed the heat and dirt away. He used the soap Lagash had given him to wash his body. He soaped his trousers and was looking for a stone to agitate them against when Caswal exclaimed, "By the king's eyes, look at that."

Ferran thought it was another dig at him, but when he looked up, Caswal was pointing at Borros. He was bathing downstream. He was a hairy, well-muscled man with a scar slashed at a diagonal on one side of his back.

Caswal said, "Look at his chest."

The boys waited, and then Borros turned. There was a pattern there. Like a tattoo. But it was ringed. It was forbidden for any to wear such a marking but those who were anointed by the mages.

Ferran stood in shock. He blinked and peered closer and couldn't imagine it was anything else. Borros was one of the anointed.

Earthgrace was raw power given by the gods. There were rare places where it seeped out of the seams of rocks. Wars and battles were fought over such places and great defenses erected to protect them. The mage lord that possessed such a site gathered the earthgrace and, with his or her fellow mages, turned it into meals of power—blackmeal, redmeal, and others. But the godmeals could not be used except by those that had been anointed to do so. That anointing left runes of power in the flesh of the anointed, which gave the bearer the ability to channel one of the many graces, be that strength, vision, or a number of others. It was all an arcane lore.

"So much for him being a ditch digger," said Krov.

"It could be an anointing for anything," Caswal said.

"Yeah," Krov said. "Maybe they anointed him with the power of super-deadly farts."

Ferran chuckled, but still felt awe.

"It could be for vision," Caswal said.

"They put those anointings on the eyes and brow," said Winwalom and gathered together his sopping wet horsetail of hair.

"Endurance then. He could have been a runner."

"Does he look like a runner?" asked Krov.

Borros was not a runner. The men and women who were anointed for that were whippet-thin. Borros looked like an old oak. Except this oak was made of weathered muscle, sinew, and scars.

"I've never met anyone that was anointed," Ranoc said in awe.

"Except for that sniffer that came through," said Winwalom.

A tracker with thin greasy hair had come through the village a few years ago on the trail of some fugitive. He had been missing many of his teeth.

"I never met him," said Ranoc.

Krov scratched the beard under his chin. "It looks like a warrior's anointing."

"Oh, so now you're the expert on mage craft?" Caswal asked.

"Why don't we just ask him?" Ferran said.

"Did I just hear something dribble out of a goat?" Caswal asked.

"Ferran's right," Ranoc said. "I'll go ask."

They got back to the camp with their clothes and hair still a bit damp and sat down.

Lagash was sitting on a short stool and leaning back up against the wagon wheel, plucking a pheasant.

"Perfect timing, boys," he said. "This fine fellow just walked through the camp and had the misfortune of catching my eye. He needs plucking. Dog Boy, you look like you've got good fingers." He held the pheasant out to him.

Ferran took it and sighed. "Is the plucker going to get any of this?"

"Only if the plucker hurries," Lagash said.

Ferran sat down and put the bird in his lap. He plucked a few of the colorful tail feathers for himself. After the first day on the road, he found himself wishing he'd followed his mother's advice and brought a hat. He'd decided to get one at Pencoy's. And he figured these feathers would go nicely in it.

He continued to pluck. Borros came up from the stream, his beard wet.

The other boys eyed Ranoc expectantly.

Borros came to the camp and hung his washed clothes over a branch, then noticed the boys staring at him. "What are you doing?"

Ferran said, "Ranoc has a question for you."

"Oh, he does, does he?" Borros said.

"Indeed," Ranoc said. "We saw a pattern on your chest."

"And?" Borros said roughly.

"We were wondering if it was an anointing of some kind."

Borros looked at them with an expression that clearly said he expected this conversation to be tedious. "And what would you, a lanky lad from Buckle Hill, know of anointings?"

"Not much."

"Did you ever think that maybe I bathed away from you for a reason?"

"Of course," said Ranoc, "but are you?"

"Am I what?"

"Are you one of the anointed?"

"Anointed with bad taste in women," Lagash. "Or was it ditch digging? I forget."

It appeared the two men had overheard Caswal's slights. Ferran and Winwalom gave each other a look. This was going to be good.

"Why, it was ditch digging," Borros confirmed.

"Really?" Caswal said.

Borros nodded. "Oh, yes, you're full of wisdom and insight."

"I've never heard of anointings for ditch digging," said Ranoc.

"Somebody's got to dig the ditches," said Lagash. "And muck out the stalls. And remove the lint from the belly buttons of fat lords."

"I don't believe it," Ranoc said.

"You were a soldier once," Ferran said. "Lagash said he beat you in battle. Made you his slave."

Borros cut a glare at Lagash who just grinned back at him.

"That was only after I made him my slave first."

"It doesn't matter where you are when you start," Lagash said. "What matters is how the game ends."

Borros dismissed the comment with a wave of his hand.

"You were more than a guard. Lagash said so. What were you?" asked Ranoc.

Borros sighed.

"He was a hammer," said Lagash. "A scourge."

Borros said nothing.

The boys waited.

Borros finally relented and said, "I led a small band of men."

Krov said, "How did you get that scar on your back?"

"A woman."

Caswal laughed.

"She was an Osson assassin. She tried to stab me. I turned, and she missed and slashed me across the back instead. There wasn't a surgeon around to sew it properly, so I had to force the son of a cabbage monger to do it. He did a poor job, but it was better than a gaping wound."

"What happened to her?" Krov asked.

"She got away."

"Her blade wasn't poisoned?" Ranoc asked.

"It wasn't her blade that she sliced me with."

The boys waited for more, but Borros just looked at them.

"Surely there's more to it than that," Winwalom said.

"There's a lot more," said Borros. "But it's getting late."

"But what was your anointing for?" asked Ranoc.

"Ditch digging," said Borros.

"Ha!" said Caswal.

The other boys shook their heads.

"We need another pheasant to go with our porridge," Borros said. "Away with all of you. Bring back something good."

The watch that night was suspenseful—everyone waiting for Winwalom's creature—but the beast never showed. Breakfast was more porridge with a slice of hard, sharp cheese. And then they were pushing cattle again.

The next stop was fifteen miles down the road. When they arrived, they secured the cattle, set up camp, then practiced with their spears and slings. Borros then had them all find another good sapling and make a practice spear so the real spears could keep their sharp points.

That night, Ranoc began shouting during his watch.

Ferran sat up.

"It's here!" Ranoc cried. "It's here."

Ferran jumped out of his bed and grabbed his spear. The others around the camp did the same.

"I saw it! I saw it!"

Winwalom scanned the dark night sky.

"Where is it?" Ferran asked.

"I don't see anything," Winwalom replied.

"To Ranoc!" Borros called. "To Ranoc!"

They all hurried through the darkness, hopping the rail fence, and joining Ranoc on the far side of the field. Above them, a small crust of moon shone in the night.

"Where is it?" asked Borros.

"I think it's over there," Ranoc said and pointed, but it was too dark to see anything but dark smudged against the blackness of the night.

"I don't see anything there," Lagash said.

"There!" Ranoc said.

All eyes followed his finger.

"It moved. You can see its shoulder."

Ferran peered into the darkness and thought he saw it, then looked at Winwalom.

Winwalom shook his head.

"I think I see it," Borros said.

Ferran leaned in close to Winwalom. "It's not here, is it?"

"No," Winwalom whispered.

"We're going to stay together," said Borros. "Quick. Into the middle of the field."

They hopped back over the fence, threaded through the cattle, and took up their positions. All the commotion wound Itch up, and he barked until Borros told Ferran to keep him quiet.

Borros ordered them into a circle and told each of them to watch the sky in front of them. In the beginning, the others called out frequently, saying they thought they saw it, but Winwalom did not. He scanned the night sky, silent and alert.

A breeze picked up. The exclamations and shouts grew less frequent. And Ferran thought about Winwalom's secret.

His friend could see in the darkness. Something one of the anointed might do. But Winwalom wasn't anointed. Winwalom was just a youth from Buckle Hill who thought pickled beets was fare fit for a lord. A youth who was leaving the village to apprentice to a man in Broniss to acquire no skill to speak of.

It was possible Winwalom's father did have a friend in Broniss. It was also possible that Winwalom's apprenticeship was something embarrassing, like having to work for some stinking tanner. But it was also possible that something else was going on. Ferran thought about Winwalom's mother. She had come from across the sea. His father had fought as a soldier in distant lands. Had something happened there? Had one of the Old Blood darklings infected or cursed one of them?

The group stayed out in the field until the sky began to lighten, and it was clear there was nothing around them but open land and trees.

And that was when they saw that a portion of the fence on the far side of the field was newly broken. They went to investigate and found a bloody trail leading away from the enclosure and into the woods. A wide trail where something large had been dragged away through the grass.

24

FRESH KILL

"What is so powerful it can drag eight hundred to twelve hundred pounds of beef away?" Lagash asked. "A bear?"

"It would have to be a mighty big bear," Borros said, then squatted down and felt the blood on the grass. "It's dried. So this must have happened a few hours ago. And right under our noses."

If Winwalom's eyesight was so good, he should have seen it. Ferran glanced at him, but Winwalom said, "I wonder if it happened before Ranoc called the alarm."

"That makes more sense," Borros said and stood.

"The trail should be easy to follow," Lagash said.

Borros nodded, then motioned at the boys. "Form a line on either side of me and bring your spears to the ready."

Ferran gulped.

"Don't crowd each other. Give yourselves a full arm's length between you and the next man."

Ferran moved to join the line that was forming and found himself pushed to the end on the right, Winwalom on one side of him, Itch on the other, his mottled gray coat blending with the shadows. Ferran wished he was in the line next to the big man, but it was too late now.

The boys all lowered their spears to the level. Borros held a real spear with a metal blade and hook. Lagash, who was next to Borros, had a sword belted to his waist and carried a spanned crossbow.

"Follow my lead," Borros said. "Don't get ahead of me, and don't lag behind. Those of you on the ends, watch ahead and to either side. Whatever it is, if it charges, you hold your ground. Your one task is to hold your ground, find a target, and strike. Find another target and strike. Think of nothing else. The rest of us will curl around so we can attack its flank. Now forward."

Borros began to walk forward slowly. The boys followed his lead, scanning the trees ahead. Ferran glanced to his side and saw nothing. He glanced back, but there was only the cattle in the field and the camp beyond. They proceeded into the trees, following the blood trail, every ear straining to hear the slightest rustle, every eye searching for the slightest movement ahead.

Ferran's mouth went dry, and he tried to swallow, but it didn't help. He had to walk around a tree which put him practically on his own for a few yards. He closed up the gap in the ranks again and felt a huge relief. But there were a lot of trees, and so Ferran had to keep dodging them, weaving in and out.

They went maybe thirty yards, and then caught a whiff of blood and entrails. Borros halted the line. Ferran's heart began to pound in his chest. Predators liked to defend their prey, which meant the thing was probably just ahead. Ferran searched the woods. There was nothing ahead, to the side, or behind. He looked up, but nothing was visible in the sky through the canopy of leaves.

Borros motioned them forward again. A few paces later, they passed some brush, and a clearing became visible through the trunks of the trees ahead. Something large and dark was on the ground there. It looked like a creature with its back toward them, feeding on something.

A wave of fear rushed through Ferran, and he gripped his spear tighter. Any moment now, it would notice them, and then it would surely turn and charge them with a snarl. He glanced at the others down the line, but their eyes were fixed on the dark thing. Ferran turned back. He wasn't going to be the coward in this group. He was going to hold his ground. See a target and strike, he told himself. See a target and strike.

And then he recognized a cow's leg. It was right in the middle of the back of the creature, which didn't make any sense at all. And there was a second cow's leg, and suddenly Ferran realized the mound in the clearing wasn't some creature feeding on its prey—it was a cow, lying on its side. And there were two more beyond it.

"It's the cattle," Lagash said.

The line of boys and men and spears stepped out of the woods and into the clearing and stopped. Three cattle lay dead, covered by a thin layer of grass and dirt.

"Give the area and sky a scan, boys," Borros said.

They did, but whatever had done this was nowhere to be seen, and so they moved forward to the first cow. It was a yearling. Its neck had been broken. Its belly had been torn open, and its entrails ripped out. The heart, lungs, liver, and kidneys were gone. What was left were parts of the stomachs and loops of intestines. These were scattered about the carcass. And there was blood too, lots of it, splattered and smeared all around.

The other two cattle were another yearling and a heifer, both in the same condition. And just as with the first, the ground showed the marks of large claws where the earth had been dug up to hide the cattle.

"It will be back to continue feeding," Borros said. "It ate the best parts, to begin with, but will come back to eat the muscle."

"Look at this print," Lagash said.

It was a large, long foot with four toes and claws.

"That's not the print of a lion or bear. Or Og, for that matter," Lagash said.

"There are three-toed prints here," Ranoc said.

Borros pointed at Caswal and Winwalom. "You two watch the sky and woods. The rest of you form up in pairs and look for more signs. Get moving. Quickly. We don't want to be here when it comes back."

Borros and Lagash paired up as did Krov and Ranoc, leaving Ferran with Itch. The pairs moved out and scanned the field and found more similar prints plus a large deposit of manure.

And then Ferran walked over by the stream and found a clear set of prints in the moist soil. The best yet. "Here!" he called.

The others came. The prints were large. The size of platters. The creature had obviously killed and then come to the stream to drink. There were two sets of long, four-toed prints with claws. And two three-toed prints.

"What is this?" Borros said. "What makes such prints?"

Lagash bowed his head and closed his eyes. "There's something. Something. The memory is buried, but it will come."

"Well, we're not going to wait for it here," Borros said. "It's probably going to stay with its kills for a few days. By that time, we'll be in Pencoy's lands. And when it comes again, looking for an easy meal, it will find a troop with arrows and cold steel instead."

They did not eat breakfast, but broke camp, and moved the cattle out immediately. They did not stop at the next drover's field but pushed on, watching the skies with fear. The drive was hot and dusty, but thinking about what was behind them kept them alert and moving. And even though the cattle began to protest at the distance and pace, Ferran was happy to put as much distance between him and that last campsite as possible. In the late afternoon, they reached the new site.

It was located in an area with rolling hills dotted with clumps of trees. The field itself was in a hollow between two lines of steep hills. A small stream snaked through the base and joined up with the larger stream they'd been following. At the mouth of the hollow was a rail fence. At a narrow point a few hundred yards farther there was another rail fence that blocked the cattle from moving up the hollow.

Borros stood by the gate as Ferran herded the cattle into the field. When Ferran closed the gate, Borros turned his back to the cattle and pointed at a hill to the east. "Boys, Pencoy's is just over that hill. We're at the end of this leg of the journey."

Relief flooded Ferran. Help would be here soon.

Borros directed them to make camp up against a slope of the hollow with a steep wall to protect their backs.

When they finished, he said, "I'll be back before dark. What I want you to do is practice your spears and slings. Lagash will lead you.

However, half of you will be on watch at all times, so you'll need to practice in two shifts."

"Why don't we drive the cattle right to Pencoy's manor?" Winwalom asked.

"Because we're trying to stay hidden from Osson as long as possible. They have their spies in the land."

"And because he doesn't want to pay any grazing fee," Lagash said.

"What about the creature?" Winwalom asked.

"We'll have a troop of men here this evening. So there's only a small window of risk. But there's a bigger window with Osson. Do you ever wonder why we took this road? Why we ignored every side road we passed?"

Winwalom shrugged.

"It's a backtrail. How many people have we seen these last few days?"

"Not many."

"How many villages?"

"Just a handful."

"We're miles from the coast road and the eyes of Osson, and I want to keep it that way as long as possible. We're not going anywhere close to the sea without an escort." Borros pointed north. "This road runs roughly parallel to the coast right up to the spur of the mountains that stretches out almost to the sea. The road forks there. The left fork leads into the mountains and the blight in the west, the right fork to the coast road in the east. That's where we'll turn. So there's no use going to Pencoy's and turning around and coming right back. Besides, he's not that far away. About two miles. There's a turnoff just up the road, and it leads right to him. So keep a watch and practice, and tomorrow morning, you boys will be walking home with coin."

"Not back down past that last campsite, we aren't," Caswal said.

"No," Borros agreed. "You'll probably want to take another way." And then he set out at a fast walk toward Pencoy's.

Ferran knew that Borros would head out tomorrow for the second leg of the journey. That meant he had to convince Borros to hire him today. But how would he convince him? He didn't want to do it here. It didn't feel right. He'd have to pick the perfect time because he knew he'd only have one chance.

Lagash said, "We won't drill yet. Let's get some food in you first." And then he opened a barrel, pulled out something in a waxed cloth, and unwrapped a number of dark, little bricks.

"What is that?" Ranoc asked.

"Grease cake," Lagash said. "Food for real men. For warriors. And if you keep it dry, it will last a good long time." He set one of the small bricks on the lid of a barrel, took out a knife with a fox of silver inlaid in the handle.

"That's a pretty knife," Ferran said.

"It was given to me by my father," Lagash said, "who had it from his father." He forced the blade through the brick, cutting off a thick slice. He handed the slice to Ranoc who sniffed it, then plopped it in his mouth and chewed.

"Tallow," he said around the much too big bite. "And I think I can taste a berry?"

"Tallow," Lagash confirmed, "dried beef pounded to a fine meal, and dried currants. If I have good nuts, sometimes I'll grind them and add them in as well."

That didn't sound so bad. Whatever it was, it was food, and Ferran was happy to get his little brick. He found that if he rolled a bite around in his mouth for a while, the tallow would soften up so that it wasn't like eating a candle.

After getting their little grease bricks, including one for Itch, and filling their water skins, he and Winwalom took their slings and spears and climbed with Itch to the top of one of the hills. The hill itself was mostly bare of trees and gave a good view of everything all around.

Below them lay the field in the ravine with the cattle. The ravine bent out of sight, but it looked like it continued for miles, all the way to the foothills at the base of the mountains. To the northwest, there was a gap in the mountains, and that's where the old road to Broniss ran up into the blight. Ferran could only imagine what was in there. There were so many stories surely some of them were true. Maybe theirs was another that would be added, even though Borros thought the creature had come from someplace else.

Ferran and Winwalom scanned the spur of rugged mountains to the north that Borros had talked about, and then turned east and the coast. Ferran thought he could see the faintest line of blue on the horizon. "Is that the sea?" he asked.

"I don't think so," said Winwalom. "I think it's more than thirty miles away. We'd need to be up higher to see that far. And I'm not sure I want to be higher. I feel exposed up here."

"True," Ferran said. "But I guess that means it will be easier to spot your stork."

"You like how Borros said we only have a small window of risk?"

"Yeah. I guess that means you and me are up here like two little mice waiting for the hawk to come along."

Down below, Lagash began to drill the other boys. "At least we got a bit of a rest," Winwalom said and took a drink from his water skin.

"How do we get him to hire us on?" Ferran asked.

"I don't know. He sounded pretty set in not hiring us for the second leg."

"I can knock starlings out of the sky with my sling. I could help with this thing."

"You think stones will bring down something that could haul off a cow? Besides, I bet you Pencoy's men have archers."

"There's got to be something I can offer that he'd want."

Winwalom shrugged.

"What will you do?" Ferran asked.

"I have to go on. I can just travel with them. In fact, I was thinking I could buy a few bricks of this stuff from Lagash. That should last the six or seven days we'd be on the road. I could hunt up other meat to trade if I want something more than tasty candles to eat."

"I can't believe you're leaving."

Winwalom sighed. "I know. I can't either."

"Are you going to tell me what's really going on?"

Winwalom hesitated, looked like he was about to say something, and then said, "I'm going to apprentice to a felter."

"I know something is up, Win. You've always been able to see farther than me, but I'm not blind. And nobody can see in the dark like you can now. Not without an anointing."

Winwalom's shoulders sagged. "Don't press me. It's hard enough. You think I want to go?"

Ferran could hear from the tone in his voice that he did not. "Well, I'm sure you'll have lots of new adventures."

"Maybe."

Old Blood. If that's what was going on here, Winwalom was in real danger. Legally, every person was required to report those touched by Old Blood to the authorities. But if Ferran didn't know, how could he report? Even if the blood hunters came and pressed him, what would he be able to tell them? Nothing. So maybe it was best not to know what was going on.

Ferran said. "Maybe I'll come to visit sometime."

Winwalom brightened. "I'd like that," he said. "I'd like that a lot."

They sat in silence for a while, watching the skies and the land about them. Itch took to chasing grasshoppers in the breeze, and then Lagash whistled them down to their drills.

Lagash ran them through the same drills they'd been practicing, except this time he cut the grinders and grips, saying they needed to conserve their energy. Ferran knew why—he and the others would be of no use against the creature if their arms had turned to jelly. And to confirm his guess, Lagash told them that if they saw the beast to ready their slings and first try to chase it away with rocks.

Lagash then assigned them to dig the fire hole and help him peel onions and haul water to make a porridge large enough to feed dinner to the troop of men Borros was going to bring.

An hour or so later, with the sun just about to drop behind the mountains in the west, Borros appeared on the road.

He was riding a pony he must have borrowed from Pencoy.

Alone.

There was no troop. No escort. There wasn't another man in sight.

25

THE BOYS OF BUCKLE HILL

Borros rode up to the camp and reined in his pony, his face full of frustration.

"Where are they?" Lagash asked.

"Gone," he said with irritation. And then he dismounted.

"Gone?" Lagash said in shock.

"The steward," Borros said with disdain, "said that they'd been called out to put down a disturbance at Dob's Port."

Lagash said, "On the coast? That's two days to the south."

"Exactly," Borros said.

"And when will they return?"

"The steward said to wait. Said to come back tomorrow."

Ferran and Winwalom exchanged a glance, and then Ferran kneaded the fur behind Itch's neck. This was not good news at all. Their little window of risk had now been flung wide open. A small pit of dread began to form in his stomach.

"That was three hundred coppers worth of cattle we lost last night. I don't want to lose another."

Nor did Ferran because the driving agreement stipulated their pay would be cut if they lost more than two head from neglect. Ferran couldn't see how the three cattle lost could count against them. None of the boys had neglected their duty. But who knew if Borros would see it that way?

Ferran said, "Well, now we know that it's out there, we can guard against it."

Borros and Lagash both looked down at him.

And Ferran suddenly realized this is how he could convince Borros to hire him the whole way. If they could keep the cattle secure until Pencoy's men came, surely Borros would be more inclined to extend the agreement.

"You're going to fight this thing?" Borros asked unconvinced.

"We protected the village sheep and goats from a mad pack of dogs out of Haver's Bend. We stood guard when a bear came sniffing about the village for a week until the men hunted it down. You hired us on until the cattle were delivered to Pencoy. And we mean to see our part through, don't we, Win?"

Winwalom hesitated.

"Don't we," Ferran prompted again with an elbow.

"Yes," Winwalom with a little less enthusiasm. "Of course."

"We have our slings. And spears. Whatever comes, we'll send it packing."

Borros considered him. "And the others?"

"We're from Buckle Hill," Ferran said. "We don't back down when things get tough."

Borros smiled, then nodded. "Okay then. Bring the other boys down. We're going to need to make plans."

Ferran and Winwalom walked over to the slope and began to climb.

Winwalom said, "You're going to get us killed."

"We can't lose any more cattle."

"Cattle?" Winwalom said. "How about having our bellies torn open and our livers eaten out?"

"We have our slings."

"Did you not see what that thing did to those animals?"

Ferran stopped. "I did, just like you. But I can't just go back home. I can't afford to lose one copper. I must go on to Broniss."

"Whatever did that to the cattle could eat us in one bite."

"You don't have to help."

"Well, I'm going to. I'm just saying."

Ferran blew out a great breath. "I know. I can't believe I said what I did to Borros. It was like my words just carried me away."

"You can say that again."

"But at the same time, they're true. We did send those dogs packing. And we all watched for that bear."

"From the tops of the roofs," Winwalom said.

"I know," Ferran admitted. "But I've got to earn the coin."

"Well, let's just hope we don't die doing it."

Ferran didn't have a response to that. Because whatever could drag twelve hundred pounds of beef out into the woods could surely take care of a few boys. What was needed was men in armor, not a boy in threadbare clothes that almost couldn't take one more patch or mending.

His mouth went a little dry with fear, but he started back up the slope again. When he reached the top, he told the other boys Borros wanted to see them. A few minutes later, they were all back at the camp.

Borros said, "Ferran says the lads of Buckle Hill don't back down when things get tough. Is this true?"

The other boys shrugged.

"He said you chased off a pack of feral dogs and a bear."

"That's true," Ranoc said.

"Well, here's the news. Pencoy's troop is not going to be with us tonight. But I intend to keep the cattle safe nevertheless. And if you're willing, I would like to employ your skills."

"Is that bonus pay?" Ranoc asked.

"Possibly," Borros said.

"How do we fight this thing when we don't even know what it is?" Caswal asked.

"I don't want you to fight it unless it attacks us. I want you to harry it with your stones. Just tonight, and then Pencoy's men should be here."

"And Lagash will be out there with his bow?" Krov asked.

"Yes."

"But what if it attacks us?" Caswal asked.

"That's what we need to plan," Borros said. "Long Hair and Dog Boy have already committed. What do you say?"

Krov glanced at the others.

"I'm in," Ranoc said eagerly.

Krov nodded in agreement.

Caswal looked less sure, but he could see he was the odd man out and probably didn't want to look like a coward. "Okay," he said.

Ferran felt both relief and dread. They were going to do this.

"Good," Borros said. "The first thing is we need to shrink the size of the pasture. Make the area we need to protect smaller. There's a fold in the hills right there where the creek bends. I think we can move the fence at the mouth of the hollow up and around and make an enclosure there. We don't have much light. Let's get to it."

Ferran felt a new energy, and the others must have as well, for they all worked with quick vigor to dismantle the split-rail fence stretching across the mouth of the hollow and carry the pieces to the fold in the hill. Ranoc and Borros began assembling the fence in the new place while the others continued to dismantle and carry and watch to make sure the cattle didn't mosey out of the hollow. When they were done, they moved the cattle into the smaller enclosure. By this time the sun was about to set.

Borros gathered them around. "We will have two watches tonight. The first will be me, Caswal, Krov, and Ranoc. Lagash will take the second watch with Dog Boy, Long Hair, and Itch. Two of each watch will go up to the top of the hill to be our eyes. They can use those large stones for cover."

Ferran had been up there. Those large stones weren't much cover at all.

Borros continued. "If the thing shows itself, you sound the alarm."

"I don't think whistles and shouts will carry," Winwalom said. "I mean, what if there's a wind or something? We should probably use your horn."

"That's a good idea," Borros said. "If you see it, blow the horn and immediately hightail it down the hill to join the rest of us. We'll be stationed by that thicket of trees over there where the fence meets the slope. Our job will be to harry it with arrow and stone. Aim for the head with your slings if you can hit it. If not, any hit will do. We want to convince it that this prey will be too much trouble."

"And what if instead of becoming discouraged, it gets angry and charges us?" Caswal asked.

"That's where those trees will help. I'm assuming this thing is large. So if it comes after us, we move into the thicket. The trees will restrict its movements more than ours. We'll be like rabbits in a briar there. Rabbits that can continue to shoot arrows and sling stones."

"Rabbits?" Ferran asked. That wasn't the right word.

Borros looked at him confused. "What's wrong with rabbits?"

"Well, rabbits are so weak. Cowering and quivering. It makes me feel helpless. Couldn't we be more like badgers or snakes?"

"He's got a point," Lagash said.

"You and your points," Borros replied. Then he stopped and considered. "Badgers in a briar. That is actually better. A lot better. Badgers it is."

"And what if that fails?" Caswal asked. "What's the fallback?"

"Spears," Borros said.

The boys glanced at each other.

Borros swept his arm wide at the hollow. "Do you see any defense out there? If it's bent on eating us, the very worst thing to do would be to run out into the open. We need to stay together. If you run, you'll make yourself a target. It will see you as easy pickings and come after you. So stick together. If I yell for you to form a line, you line up just as you did this morning, and we'll give it a taste of our blades and spikes."

"Yes," Ranoc said, clearly looking forward to a fight.

"That's the spirit," Borros said.

And Ranoc's enthusiasm did diminish the dread Ferran was feeling, even if it didn't drive it out altogether.

"It's probably time to finish your spears," Lagash said. "By now you know where you like to grip them. What you want to do is carve some gentle bumps in those spots to give you a better grip. Or wrap it tightly with a cord or strips of leather."

"And gather stones," Borros said. "Lots of them."

They already each had a good number of stones, but they walked out into the creek in their bare feet and searched the cold water. Caswal found a good run of gravel, and they all waded over to him and picked until just before the last light faded and Borros blew his horn to call them in.

Lagash served them extra portions of the porridge he'd cooked for Pencoy's men, and for the first time in Ferran didn't know how long he actually got full. Stuffed. Like fattening a calf for the slaughter, he thought.

They wrapped their spears. And then Ranoc and Caswal climbed the hill with the horn while the second watch made their beds and lay down.

Ferran was exhausted. Itch had played in the water while they were gathering stones, and his coat was still wet, but Ferran was so tired he didn't care and let Itch lie down next to him. Winwalom was also too tired to make a tent, so he made his bed next to Ferran's.

Ferran said, "It's probably for the best. You don't want to be trying to wriggle out of your tent if that thing comes."

"No," Winwalom said.

By this time the first stars were out, twinkling in the sky.

"It's a bit shocking," Ferran said. "This whole stork thing."

"It's a little scary," Winwalom said.

Ferran had not wanted to use that word, but that's exactly what it was.

"We're going to stick together," he said.

"Whatever comes," Winwalom agreed.

And the fact that Winwalom would be at his side gave him comfort. Ferran gazed at the starry sky, looking for the creature, but he was tired from staying up last night, and the next thing he knew, he was being awakened for the second watch.

26

NIGHT WATCH

Lagash sent Ferran, Winwalom, and Itch up to the top of the hill with the horn while he waited below with the crossbow. A crescent moon illuminated the sky and the tops of the hills and cast a shadow over half of the hollow. With such good light, Ferran figured that if they were vigilant, they would see this thing a good way off and have plenty of time to scramble back down the hill to join the others.

Winwalom suggested they face opposite directions and each watch half the sky. It was a good idea, and they watched, sometimes standing, sometimes pacing, sometimes sitting on the outcropping of rock until the sky began to lighten in the east.

They stayed there until a few hours after the sun had risen and the others had awakened. Lagash fed the others more of last night's meal, then sent Ranoc up to replace them. After breakfast, they counted the cattle and found that none were missing and checked the fence.

And then Borros told them to get some rest while he traveled back to Pencoy's.

Lagash took to his hammock. Winwalom and Ferran pulled their beds into the shade of the thicket and lay down. The other boys led the other cattle out to graze.

They rested a few hours, and then Lagash woke them. He had all the boys practice with their spears again, but this time had them do it in a line, forward and back, swinging the ends of the line around as if attacking the flank of the creature. After practice, he sent them to the creek to cool off and find more stones.

The water was cool and refreshing, and as they found better stones to replace the ones they'd hastily taken last night, Ferran's spirits rose. Last night, they'd stood guard like men. They'd done their duty. And when Borros returned in good spirits with Pencoy's men, that's when Ferran would offer his services again for the second leg of the journey.

But Borros did not return in good spirits. Early that evening, he rode into the vale empty-handed and angry.

"The steward says he sent a messenger right after we spoke yesterday," Borros said.

"That should have been enough time to ride down and back," Lagash said.

"Should have been. But who knows if the maggot actually sent them?"

"Did you tell them that we have a special situation? That maybe his lordship should muster extra men?"

"I did. But if the choice is between protecting a town that's very profitable to you or someone else's cattle, it's pretty clear what you'll do."

Lagash shook his head. "I suppose I'd do the same. We can't fault Pencoy."

"He could have sent word," Borros spat.

"So what do we do?"

"We wait until tomorrow. The steward said the rider could have been delayed."

"Tomorrow?" Caswal asked in dismay.

"One more night for the brave young men of Buckle Hill to stand watch," Borros said. "What do you say?"

"I'll throw in a raisin pie to each of you," Lagash said. "A fat one."

"What an offer," Krov said.

Lagash chuckled.

They'd dodged an arrow last night. In Ferran's mind that somehow made their odds tonight seem worse. But Ferran needed the coin.

"Raisin pie sounds delicious," Ferran said. "I'm in."

"Dog Boy comes through again," Borros said.

"Me too," Ranoc added. "And the raisin pie had better be big."

"And me," Winwalom said.

Borros looked at Krov and Caswal.

"I'll help," Krov said.

"My life for a pie," Caswal said and shook his head. "Unbelievable. Sign me up." He meant it as a joke, and they all laughed, but they were nervous laughs.

"First order," Borros said, "is for you boys to get the cattle back in the enclosure."

The boys walked out as a group into the hollow to start rounding them up. When they were out of earshot of the men, Caswal said, "Well, this is a pretty posy."

"I'm still wondering what sort of creature it is," Winwalom said.

"Whatever it is," said Ranoc, "I'm going to take out its eye. Stone or spear, I don't care which I have to use."

Ranoc's response surprised Ferran. How was it that Ranoc could be so bold?

Krov said, "I would think it would be much better to take it with a stone. Whatever this thing is, I want it as far away from me as possible."

Ferran was still thinking about Ranoc. All this time, Ferran had been thinking about protecting himself. About what he'd do if the creature attacked. But now he thought about attacking it, whatever it was. He thought of the spear work they'd done. He thought about his prowess with his sling. He thought about himself being the predator, not the prey. Suddenly the fear inside his heart lessened.

It didn't depart. But it lessened.

He said, "I bet I take the eye first."

All the other boys looked at him.

Caswal rolled his eyes and scoffed, but Ranoc grinned. "You're on, Dog Boy. How much are you willing to wager."

Ferran couldn't afford even half a birdseye, so he said, "Whoever loses, the day we get back, he has to give Mad Hilda a kiss."

"Hoo," Krov laughed.

Mad Hilda was an old granny who wasn't all there and frequently came after the boys for smootches.

"You're on," Ranoc said. "And the kiss has to be on the lips."

"Deal," Ferran said.

Krov groaned in delight. "I can't wait to see this."

"Remember," Winwalom said. "We need to fight together. If you run out on your own, then, you're, well, on your own."

"True," Ranoc said.

"Also, what if you are presented a good target," Winwalom said, "but it's not the eye? If you're so bent on getting the eye, you might fail to see a chance to strike. See a target, and strike is what we practiced. See a target, strike the target."

"Well, I guess you're right," Ranoc admitted.

"So if it comes to spears, we won't worry about the eye," Ferran said. "But while we're slinging stones, now that's another matter."

"First one that takes its eye with a stone then," said Ranoc. "But I can tell you this, if that thing comes at me, I'm going to shove my spear right down its throat."

"Please do," said Krov. "I would much prefer it dealing with your spear than mine."

"Prepare your lips for Hilda," Ranoc said.

Ferran grinned. It would not be him kissing her. That was for sure. And he realized his mood truly was lighter. He was thinking about the attack, even if a small pit of fear remained, and that was so much better than quivering.

The boys herded the cattle back into the enclosure, and then Lagash served them up another meal, this time with chunks of grease cake cooked into the porridge. And then the first watch took its positions after drinking a tea Lagash had prepared to help them stay awake, while the second watch lay down on their beds as the stars began to wink into the sky.

Ferran was awakened by Ranoc, who was holding out the small ram's horn. Ferran took it, and then he and Winwalom rose and stretched.

"You got lucky it didn't come on my watch," Ranoc said.

Ferran puckered his lips at him and made kissing sounds. "O, Hilda with the hairy face, may I squish my lips upon that place that covers your toothless gums."

Winwalom grinned in the moonlight.

"Keep dreaming, Dog Boy."

Ferran made kissing sounds again, and Ranoc rolled his eyes and retreated to the fire to get a cup of tea.

"That was pretty good," Winwalom said. "How did you come up with that?"

"My miracle brain," Ferran said. "I awoke, and the lines were just there."

"Probably because you were dreaming of Hilda yourself."

"No," Ferran said.

"O, Hilda Fair," Winwalom said, "I love the single luscious hair upon your skinnish head."

"Who was the one dreaming of grannies again?" Ferran asked.

"To tell the truth, I was dreaming of a giant stork," Winwalom said. "And it was pecking at us like we were frogs."

"Enough talk," Borros said. "Up to your station."

"Yessir," Ferran said. And the two boys and Itch climbed up the slope out of the hollow and took their positions on the bare crown of the hill. As they had the night before, each of them watched half the sky.

The stars wheeled in their courses. The moon moved across the sky. Itch explored the hilltop, then came back and lay down by Ferran. The night passed, and, eventually, a breeze began to blow toward the sea. The sky in the east began to lighten, and Ferran knew morning was not far away.

His spirits rose. They'd dodged another arrow!

But then Winwalom spoke. "What's that?"

Ferran turned. "Where?"

"Blow the horn."

"Where is it?"

"There," Winwalom said and pointed.

27

SIGHTING

Ferran looked and saw nothing. "Where?"

Winwalom got behind Ferran, set his head level with Ferran's, then brought his arm out in front and pointed. And then Ferran saw it miles to the south. Something large and dark soaring high in the night sky.

"The king's eyes," he said and thought about the gutted cattle, and his heart jumped. "Maybe it's far enough away it doesn't see us."

But then it turned and began to fly in their direction.

"Or maybe it does," Winwalom said.

Ferran turned to face the camp. He brought the ram's horn to his lips and blew a mighty squeak.

"Blow it!" Winwalom said.

Ferran firmed up his lips and blew again. This time the note sounded strong and loud and carried down into the hollow. He blew again.

"To arms!" Borros shouted below, waking the others. "To arms!"

Ferran looked back and saw the creature was flying faster than he'd originally thought. They needed to get off this hill now! He dashed to the slope. Winwalom and Itch followed, and they scrambled down to the spot where Borros and the others had gathered. A spot that was maybe twenty feet from the floor of the hollow, which allowed them a clear line of sight to the whole enclosure.

"How big is it?" Lagash said, his crossbow in hand.

"Big," Ferran said.

And then the creature wheeled overhead in the moonlight. It was black underneath and lighter on top. Its wings were twenty feet across. But this was no bird. There was no beak. Instead, its head had a muzzle. At the other end, the tail flared out at its tip in the shape of long, thin leaf.

Itch barked. A few cattle mooed.

The thing wheeled high over the hollow, silent as death, casting a large moon shadow on the ground as it went.

"Get your stones ready," Borros called, and Ferran realized he was clutching his spear in a ferocious grip. He set it down and found his hands shaking.

The thing flapped once, twice, flew over the herd and the little cluster of drovers again, and then out of sight beyond the crown of the hill.

Ferran removed his sling and put a stone in the pouch.

They waited for it to fly back over the field or into their line of vision. They waited for some time.

"Maybe it's landed up on top," Ranoc said.

"You and Caswal," Borros said. "Creep up there. Signal with a fist if it's there. If it's not, stand and wave us up."

Ranoc nodded. Caswal hesitated.

"Go," Borros said. And the two boys began quietly to make their way up the slope with their spears. They crouched low as they began to approach the top, then moved higher and disappeared from view. Borros ordered the group to move back from the slope so they could see them.

As they moved back from the hill, Ranoc and Caswal came into view. They were crouching low and creeping toward the crown of the hill. Ferran expected the beast to suddenly appear from the other side and attack the boys, but it didn't. And soon they were both standing on the crown of the hill and waving the others up.

Borros led the rest of them up the hill. It was lighter now, even though the full sunrise was still a little ways off. The land around the hill was visible, as were the mountains that ran to the south. The creature was nowhere to be seen.

"It's a korrog," Lagash said.

"I thought they were just stories," Krov said.

"They were," said Borros.

"Where would a korrog come from?" Ranoc asked.

"Somewhere remote," Lagash said. "Somewhere off the map."

"Are you sure?" Winwalom asked.

"What else could it be?" Lagash said.

There were tales of ancient heroes who had fought massive korrog. There was a tale of a fair maiden being carried away because of her beauty, and a hero going to save her, having to sneak into a lair high up in the crags of a mountain. But Ferran could not fathom how some girl's beauty could move such a beast. That was probably an embellishment. The only reason something like this would carry someone away would be the same reason an eagle carried a fish away—to go someplace where it could rend and devour its catch in peace or feed it to its hatchlings.

"The queen is going to want to know about this," Borros said.

"What are we going to do?" Caswal asked.

"Daylight is coming," Borros said. "So far the pattern of this creature has been to feed at night. So I assume, with the sun coming up, we're safe until night falls again. I'm going back to Pencoy's. And I'm going to wait for the messenger. Maybe there are other men there who can help."

They ate breakfast and tried to sleep in turns and kept a watch up on the hill. The cattle enjoyed the grass, and as the sun climbed high, they lazed in the shade of the few clumps of trees that dotted the floor of the hollow. Ferran and the other boys shared all the stories they remembered about korrog and the heroes of old.

There was the story of King Brightblade who faced one alone in a tremendous battle. There was the story of the maid of Yellow Glen who was said to have found and raised a pack of seven of the beasts, but they'd been smaller in some of the tales, the size of large dogs. And they had protected her from wolves and bears and other creatures, but, in the end, they killed the boy she loved. There was the tale of the maiden in the crag. The tale of the men of the ship Skybreath who had faced a korrog at sea. And the tale of the dark king who flew the skies by night on a beast named Malkor.

They recited all the details they could remember of those stories, which they'd heard from parents and grandparents and elders in the village and traveling bards, each boy adding details the others had forgotten.

They could not believe they had witnessed such a creature and anxiously waited for the men from Pencoy's village to bolster their numbers.

Noon came and went. The watch changed. Lagash made them practice again with their spears and slings. They watched for Borros and the villagers, but none showed. They finished their practice. The afternoon grew late, and still, they saw no one on the road.

"Surely, they'll come by dinner," Ferran said.

"I bet they're gathering a host," Winwalom said. "Armor, weapons, dogs."

But the day grew late, and no host appeared on the road. And then Ranoc spied a cart and horse and what looked like a little family coming over the hill, but they turned and disappeared up the road to the north.

Lagash started dinner and ordered the boys to move the cattle back to the enclosure, and as they did, a pit of anxiety began to grow in Ferran's gut.

"Why hasn't anybody come?" Ferran asked Lagash.

"I don't know."

"Well, what are we going to do?" asked Caswal.

"We're going to eat dinner," Lagash said.

They ate in turns so that there was always someone on guard. They watched the road. When they finished, Lagash sent Ferran, Winwalom, and Krov to fetch some water. They walked out through the grass in their bare feet, minding the scattering of cow pies. Krov carried their spears over his shoulder while Winwalom and Ferran each carried two buckets. Up on the hill, Ranoc and Caswal stood guard.

The creek snaked down through the center of hollow here. Itch splashed into it and swam about as Ferran stepped in and began to fill the buckets. He was filling the third when the sound of the ram's horn carried across the hollow.

They looked up at Ranoc and scanned the sky, but saw nothing. And so they looked to the mouth of the hollow, thinking he was announcing the arrival of Borros and the villagers. But Ranoc blew again. And again and again. He became frantic, waving his arms and pointing farther up the hollow.

And then the korrog soared into view and wheeled over the meadow.

28

TARGET

One of the korrogs in the old stories had been as blue and iridescent as a peacock. Another one had been canary yellow. Others were gray as ash.

The undersides of this one's belly and wings were dark. Dark talons. A dark snout. The sides of the creature were brindled. And running down its back was a light brown stripe.

"The king's eyes!" Krov cursed. "To the thicket!" And he and Winwalom began to dash back to the camp.

Ferran tossed his bucket up onto the bank and scrambled out of the creek and chased after them, not wanting to be a lone target.

The korrog flapped a couple of times and then landed on a jut of rocks on a hill above the fold where the cattle were.

As it did, Winwalom slowed a bit. "It's not as big as I thought."

And he was right. Last night, it had seemed much larger, but now in the light of day, it was clear the darkness had played with their estimation of its size. The wings were maybe only ten feet across. It was large, but not the monster they'd imagined.

It was built like a bat. Not squat like a bat. The korrog was slender with a long neck and tail. But like a bat, it had two hind legs and two wings that also served as a second set of legs or arms. Halfway along its wings were claws. There was some joint there that allowed the wings to fold.

The korrog landed on an outcropping of rock and folded the portion of its wings beyond the joints up and above its back. It snaked its tail around the rock, bent its neck, and eyed the cattle.

"Look at the end of its tail," Ferran said.

"It's flared out a bit," Winwalom said.

Krov slowed and then stopped. "How big do you figure it is?" he asked. "The size of a wolfhound?"

"Longer," Winwalom said. "Maybe the size of a small horse?"

Over by the thicket, Lagash and Caswal moved out to get a good view of it.

Ferran focused on its head. One brindled stripe of lighter brown ran from the top of its head down past its eye like the bright blade of a dagger.

A small, dark object flew past the korrog, and the korrog looked over at Ranoc who was at least two hundred yards away. He was winding up for another lob shot with his sling. He whipped it around and let the stone fly. The stone arched up, then down. It struck the ground a few yards away from the korrog and bounced toward the beast.

The korrog flapped and stepped sideways, and the stone sailed harmlessly by.

Ranoc slung again. This one landed much closer.

The korrog sprang from its perch to one several yards lower, one that took it out of the direct line from Ranoc.

"Thank you, Sir Korrog," Krov said, dropping the spears to the ground and unwinding his sling. "That's perfect."

And it was indeed a nice clear shot.

Ranoc slung another stone, but he was slinging blind, and the stone flew well over the korrog's head and sailed out to the pasture below.

Lagash's crossbow thwupped. His bolt sped up at the creature. The korrog jumped to a different rock, and the bolt missed, striking the rock and bouncing away.

Krov motioned at Winwalom and Ferran. "What are you two doing? Get out your slings. It's nothing more than a big bird." And then he slung. His stone sailed up but struck the slope below the thing.

It was not just a big bird, but Krov was right. Ferran had been acting like a scared child. Ranoc was moving closer to get a better shot, Caswal following with their spears. Krov and Lagash were all moving forward to get a better shot.

Ferran was not going to be the one kissing Hilda. If anyone could hit the beast at this distance, it was him. He unwound his sling, placed a stone. And because it was up on the slope and probably a hundred and fifty or so yards away, he took a few running steps, planted, and slung his stone. It whistled as it left his sling, arced high, and, on its descent, struck the creature in the side.

The korrog let out an angry, piercing cry, revealing a mouth full of sharp teeth.

Winwalom let loose a stone. It looked like it too would hit the creature, but struck a few feet to one side.

"We're going to kill us a korrog," Krov said and ran to get a closer shot.

Lagash's crossbow thwupped again. This time the bolt sped up and hit the creature in the wing. It let loose a deep, throaty cry. And then it launched itself into the air with a massive leap and began to rise with big powerful strokes of its wings. The bolt of the crossbow at first stuck out of the wing, but the second flap dislodged it, and it fell to the ground.

Ferran slung another stone and hit its leg. Winwalom slung and missed it by a hair.

The korrog cried out again, then flapped and climbed higher.

"Coward!" Krov shouted. "Running off to your mother?" He slung a stone that flew up and seemed to touch the creature, then fall away.

Ranoc lobbed another stone, but the korrog was now too high, too far out of his range.

"That's right, you cattle thief!" Krov shouted.

It turned in the sky, cried out again.

"And to think we were scared of that," Krov said.

But Ferran wondered how something that size could drag off hundreds of pounds of cattle in the night.

He was standing just a few paces away from where Krov had dropped the spears, and suddenly Itch barked and snarled. A moment later, the air split with a roar that shook Ferran's bones, and a massive shadow rolled across the meadow, blocking the sun in the west.

Ferran stumbled back and shaded his eyes. It was huge, at least four, maybe five times the size of the other beast. Its black wings blotted out the sun. Its head had ridges along the snout and two horns that flowed back. Its chest was as broad as that of a bull and muscular. Its dark brindled fur was longer at the base of the wings and bottoms of its legs, almost like a fetlock. And at the end of those legs, its talons were huge, big enough to grasp a man easily. It roared again, showing a mouth full of monstrous teeth, and Ferran's insides melted with fear. What he saw was death.

And then it wheeled in the sky and turned.

"Run!" Lagash shouted from across the meadow. "Run!"

29

PREY

Ranoc began to blow the horn.

Ferran's wits came back to him. He grabbed the spears, turned for the thicket, and ran for his life through the meadow grass. Their camp next to the thicket was a good hundred and fifty yards away. A clump of trees the cattle had lain under in the heat of the day was closer. It stood a little off to the side, but he knew that wouldn't provide any real cover. They had to make the thicket where they could stand as a group and fight. He stretched his stride, Itch running next to him, his tongue hanging out, Winwalom and Krov sprinting just a little ahead.

He lost grip on two of the spears, and they fell to the ground, but he didn't stop or even try to grab them as he raced across the meadow for safety.

The korrog was somewhere up in the sky off to their right.

Winwalom glanced that direction, and his eyes went wide. "It's diving!" he shouted. "It's diving!"

Ferran looked up to see it hurtling down at them. Panic ran through him like water. There was no way they were going to make the thicket. No way to even make the clump of trees. If they kept running, it would swoop down and grab one of them and carry him off like a mouse. The four of them were mice, running through the grass, and Ferran was the one trailing behind. The obvious choice.

The creature's shadow sped across the grass toward Ferran. It was coming at him from the right.

His heart raced. He was not going to be the mouse carried away by that thing. He'd seen mice stand up to cats and dogs before. Squeaking and piping. He'd even seen some of them make it to safety.

Better to die fighting than running, his father had always said. And so Ferran roared, his heart leaping in his throat. He then planted his foot, turned, and pointed his spear up at the thing.

The korrog held its wings close to its sides, its long neck outstretched. It was massive. Ferran had been chased by Farmer Witrun's bull before. That had been frightening, but this creature was three times the size of that bull. And had sharp teeth. And talons as long as his arm.

And he knew right then that he was dead.

There was no winning against this thing. No threatening it. But Ferran yelled anyway, his terror taking his voice into a high register, and charged.

The korrog hurtled downward at an angle toward him. It flared its wings a bit to adjust to Ferran's new direction. Its wicked head stretched out for him, and Ferran remembered Ranoc's words about shoving his spear down its throat, except Ferran figured this thing would simply swallow the spear and him whole.

It opened its massive wings to glide over the ground at him.

Holy ancestors, he thought. He was going to be that guy that got eaten in all the tales. But maybe he could do some damage. He realized he'd let his spear drop a bit. But now he brought it up, sank into a low stance, and braced himself.

A moment later and the beast was there just a little higher than the height of a man from the ground. It had slit amber eyes, a scar along its snout, and a mouth full of teeth.

And suddenly Ferran knew that now was not the time to make his last stand, but to dodge to the side. To jump and roll as Borros had taught them.

And he did. He dove to the side with his spear, rolled, came up as the wing was passing over him and saw a massive talon stretched out to take him, and dove again.

The korrog flew past, touched down for a moment, then sprang into the sky again.

Ferran surged to his feet and ran for the clump of trees where the cattle had taken shade. The clump where Krov and Winwalom were heading.

The korrog flapped once, twice. They were mighty flaps that made the sound of the wind filling a sail. It rose in the sky, then turned to come back for him.

Up ahead, Itch was snarling at the korrog and barking.

Ferran ran. He knew he'd been lucky. He'd seen mice stand up to cats, but since when had any mouse bested an owl or hawk? Never.

What he needed now was speed. Like a hare that dodged both hounds and hawks. Speed, not in a straight line, because he'd never be able to match the speed of that thing's flight, but maybe, as he'd just done, he might be able to dodge its mouth and talons until he was safe. Or relatively safe. Or maybe they wouldn't be safe, but at least he'd be with the others, and they could make a stand.

Itch continued to snarl and bark. Ferran ran past him, heading full out for the trees. Itch barked a few more times, then galloped after Ferran.

Ferran flew over the ground toward the clump of trees.

The korrog began to dive again.

Ferran poured on the speed and ran with every ounce of will he could muster. Winwalom and Krov reached the trees and glanced back. Their eyes went wide, and Ferran knew the thing must be almost upon him. But he didn't dare look. Glancing would only slow him down, maybe cause him to trip.

He ran a few more steps, dodged to the right and began to run on a line that would take him around the clump of trees, ran a few steps, then dodged back for the trees.

Ferran saw something dark in the corner of his eye—the creature's shadow. He ran with every last ounce of his speed. Ran with wild abandon.

Terror washed over Krov's and Winwalom's faces, and they turned to run from the oncoming calamity.

30

KROV

Ferran dodged left, ran, knowing he was done for, expecting the talons to pierce through his ribs and yank him up. And then he and Itch ran under the outer branches of the trees. They reached the first trunks.

Behind him, the korrog landed and lunged forward. Its jaws snapped just behind Ferran. Close enough that he smelled its foul, warm breath. He ran between the trunks of the trees.

Behind him, the korrog hissed, then leapt again and beat its massive wings, creating a wind that rustled the trees and kicked up debris.

Ahead of Ferran in the meadow, Krov and Winwalom dove for the ground. A moment later the smaller korrog swooped over them, trying to rake them with its talons. As soon as it passed, they sprinted for the thicket again. But the brief pause had allowed Ferran and Itch to catch up with them, and now the whole crew ran for the thick trees where Lagash, Caswal, and Ranoc stood with their slings and bow ready.

Ferran and Winwalom began to outpace Krov. The small korrog dove at them. They darted in different directions. Ferran ducked, and when it passed by, he ran to the thicket and safety.

"Krov!" Ranoc said.

Ferran was panting, catching his breath. He turned. Winwalom and

Itch were with them in the thicket. Krov was not. He was back out in the meadow, trying to get up.

"What happened?" Ferran cried.

"It struck him in the head with the end of its tail as it flew past," Lagash said. "Knocked him flat."

Krov rose but was staggering. His eye patch was askew. He was obviously dizzy and disoriented.

Horror clutched Ferran's heart. Up in the sky, the big one was still flapping to get some height. But the smaller one was turning, preparing to dive again. And even though it wasn't the size of the other, it was still plenty large. A ten-foot wingspan. A body as big as a wolfhound's with a mouth full of teeth. It had more than enough heft to knock Krov flat again and pierce him with those talons and tear his throat with those jaws.

"Krov!" Ranoc yelled, but Krov didn't seem to hear him.

"He's going to get eaten," Caswal said.

"No!" Ferran said.

"Hold on," Lagash warned.

But Ferran knew there was no time. And he charged back out onto the field, yelling an incoherent war cry.

A few moments later Ranoc and Winwalom charged out after him.

"Fools!" Lagash cried, but he too moved out from the thicket with his crossbow.

The wolfhound in the sky turned, flapped a couple of times to speed itself downward and pulled its wings in a dive.

Krov was blinking and looking around.

"No!" Ferran yelled and poured on the speed.

The korrog shot down like an arrow.

Krov turned and looked back at the clump of trees out in the meadow, completely lost.

The korrog was coming too fast, but Ferran picked up speed, his bare feet flying over the dry meadow grass.

And then he launched himself at Krov, tackling him to the ground a moment before the korrog reached them. It swooshed past, inches away.

Ferran kept his head low and grabbed Krov's and held it down. That wicked tail flicked past, so close it cut through the meadow grass around them.

The korrog flapped and turned to come back at them, but Winwalom and Ranoc arrived with their spears, yelling and brandishing the spiked points.

It flapped and dove again. It struck again with its tail, but the two boys were watching for it and dodged aside.

Ferran climbed to his feet and hauled Krov up.

"Your mother is very beautiful," Krov said.

"Yeah," Ferran said and put his arm around Krov. "This way."

"Do we have any honey cake?"

"Come on," Ferran said, pulling him. "Run."

"Morlo stole my honey cake."

Morlo was one of Krov's older brothers. "We'll get you a honey cake," Ferran said. "Just run!"

Krov relented and began to jog. Ferran kept his arm around him and hurried him toward the thicket. They ran past Lagash who was taking aim with his crossbow. The weapon thwanked. Ferran glanced back. The bolt struck the korrog in the side.

It cried out in pain, flapped, faltered with one of its wings, flapped, then glided to a spot father out in the meadow.

"Yes!" Winwalom cheered.

"That pig!" Ranoc said. "That greasy, goat-farting, muck-eating pig. I'm going to kill it."

Ferran hurried Krov on.

And then the sky and meadow darkened. And the monster rushed past right above their heads with nothing but a single flap of its mighty wings to warn them. Ferran ducked reflexively, but the creature hadn't targeted Ferran or Krov.

Lagash yelled, tried to dodge, but the creature reached out with one talon and grabbed him, lifting him off the ground. Lagash cried out. The crossbow dropped to the grass. And the korrog flapped those mighty wings again, then landed on a little rise in the meadow and settled down on all fours, Lagash struggling in its grip.

Ferran knew what was coming next.

The korrog looked down at Lagash. It was going to tear off a piece of him like an eagle tears at a fish.

But the korrog flinched. Then flinched again. It turned its head toward the mouth of the hollow and roared at something there.

That something beyond the korrog was Borros on his pony. With him were two other men on horses. Two archers. And they were shooting at the korrog.

The massive korrog bunched its arms and legs, then sprang away. It flapped once, twice. More arrows struck it. It flinched and released Lagash who sailed over the top of the tall grass for a distance and then tumbled to the ground.

The korrog beat its huge wings, then glided to the crown of the hill, landed, and began to pick an arrow out of its wing with its teeth.

The archers urged their horses forward, trying to get a better angle on the thing.

Out in the meadow by the clump of trees, the smaller korrog sprang into the air and flapped, trying to get to the top of a tree. But it only made it part way and landed on a smaller branch, which cracked. And the korrog dropped to the ground again.

At least that one wasn't battling them. Thank the ancestors Lagash had hit it with the crossbow.

And then an idea struck Ferran.

The crossbow.

They needed the crossbow! They needed to load it and shoot that monster on the hill.

He pushed Krov toward the thicket. "Your honey cake is in there. Go get it before Morlo eats it. Go!" Then he turned to the others. "Get his darts! Get the crossbow!"

But they were so intent on the big creature, they didn't hear him.

"The crossbow and darts!" he roared and ran to where the creature had grabbed Lagash. A few paces beyond that spot a handful of iron-tipped darts lay on the ground. Ferran gathered them up and ran to where he'd seen the crossbow fall. At first, he couldn't see it, and he wondered if he'd missed the spot, and then he spotted it by some weeds.

The two archers began to shoot again. The arrows arched up, but the korrog saw them and flapped its massive wings, sending the arrows off course. The archers shot again. And again.

And then a third korrog dove out of the sky and landed on one of the archers and his horse, bearing them both to the ground. It wasn't as big as the monster korrog, but it was significantly bigger than the small one.

The horse screamed, kicking. Man, horse, and korrog tussled, throwing up dust. They slammed into the second horse which spooked and unseated its archer.

The first horse suddenly rolled up and bolted away from the korrog and dust. The archer did not. The korrog held him fast on the ground in its talons.

The second archer scrambled to get his bow. He grabbed it, pulled an arrow out of his quiver, and turned to shoot the beast. At that range, the shaft would sink deep.

But before the man could draw his bow, the korrog reached over with its long neck and snapped at the man, totally engulfing the man's head and shoulder in its mouth. It shook the archer like a dog shakes its kill. Shook him again and dropped him.

The broken man fell to the earth and did not move. And then the korrog bent down to the archer it held in its talons and took a bite, ripping what looked like the man's arm off.

Borros's pony galloped out of the hollow, but Borros was nowhere to be seen.

The korrog on the hill trumpeted.

Ferran scanned the skies, looking for more of them, but the skies were clear. And Ferran figured this was his one opening. He could run to the thicket, or he could try to save Lagash.

Ancestors, he thought. *If ever you saw fit to give aid, now would be the time.*

31

BEAST

"Help me get Lagash!" he shouted at Ranoc and Winwalom and ran toward Lagash, Itch at his side. The other two boys followed. And Ferran wondered where Caswal was. Why wasn't he out here with them? There wasn't time to worry about Caswal right now.

The huge korrog on the hill worried another arrow out of its side. The third korrog tore at another part of the first archer's body. They were distracted, which meant Ferran and the others just might be able to get Lagash back to the thicket.

And then what?

He didn't want to think about it. He raced up to where Lagash lay and found him moving, trying to get up, blood all over his one shoulder.

Winwalom and Ranoc were coming, carrying spears. Ferran held the crossbow out to Winwalom. "Do you know how to work this thing?"

"I'll figure it out soon enough," he said and took it.

"Help me with him," Ferran said to Ranoc, and the two of them squatted to help Lagash to his feet. He rose with a grunt and gasped at the pain.

"What are you doing?" he asked.

"Saving our cook," Ferran said. "I still want my raisin pie."

"Glad to know I'm wanted," Lagash said.

"Get him to the thicket," Ferran said. And they began to move, Ferran and Ranoc helping Lagash, each of them carrying a spear. Winwalom finished spanning the crossbow, slid a dart in, and followed, watching the korrog.

They hadn't gotten far, maybe only fifteen yards, when Winwalom shouted, "It's coming! The big one is coming!"

"We're not going to make it," Ranoc said.

And they weren't. They were still at least fifty yards from the thicket where Caswal and Krov stood.

"Drop me!" Lagash said. "Defend yourselves."

Ferran and Ranoc glanced at each other, then released Lagash. Ferran thought to use his sling, but saw he wouldn't have enough time and took a position next to Ranoc. Both of them raised their spears. It was laughable, their tiny sticks versus that monster.

"We're going to kill it!" Ranoc shouted. "We're going to rip out its eyes!"

Ranoc's fury invigorated Ferran. "Come on, you blackheart!" he shouted.

The monster swooped down the hill at them. The low sun in the west illuminated its face and wings with an orange glow and cast a huge shadow which sped across the ground behind it.

The sight of it made Ferran quiver.

Winwalom pointed the crossbow at it, took aim, and waited. The other two boys braced themselves.

"If it comes with its mouth open," Ferran said. "Stuff the spear down its gullet. If it comes with the feet—"

What would he do if it came with the feet? If he tried to strike the talon, he'd probably miss it.

The korrog flapped once and swooped across the meadow toward them. And what would they do when the third one came? It would be like a pack of gulls going after a few minnows.

"Come on, you filth!" Ferran roared.

The korrog was almost upon them, and then the crossbow thwupped, and the bolt shot out, but it was almost as if the korrog was expecting it, for it turned so the bolt hit its wing instead of its body. It growled. Passed ten feet over their heads. And then Ferran remembered the tail.

"Get down!" he shouted. "Get down!"

The tail flicked down and struck Ranoc's spear out of his hands and sent it flying. And then the creature made a quick turn and landed to face them not more than thirty feet away. It looked at them and roared.

The sound hammered through Ferran's body, loosening his joints. He gulped and brought his spear up. Beside him, Ranoc was fumbling, trying to unloop his sling.

The korrog hunched as if to pounce on them, and then Krov was suddenly running across the meadow, charging the korrog and yelling. The korrog and boys all turned to look at him. He had no bow, no spear, no sling. He was running with a three-foot log hoisted up over his head.

He continued to charge, yelling at the top of his lungs. And then, while he was still a number of yards away, he planted his foot and hurled the log at the creature. The log arched up, then down, then thudded into the ground about three feet from the korrog.

The korrog looked at the log, lying there on the ground, snorted in disdain, then turned and hissed at Krov.

Krov's eyes went wide, and he backed up and stumbled.

"He's not right in the head," Ranoc said.

He was korrog meat, that's what he was.

"Sling your stone!" Winwalom cried. "Hit it before it attacks him!"

Ranoc's attention snapped back to the korrog. He placed a stone in the sling's pouch, set himself, then whipped his sling around once and let the stone fly. It sailed hard and fast and struck the korrog in the neck.

The creature flinched and turned away from Krov and back to them. It bared its teeth, then crept forward, neck out, head low, rumbling a deep growl.

Winwalom put his foot in the crossbow stirrup and pulled to span it. Ranoc fumbled another stone into his sling pouch, then whipped it around and released. It was another hard throw, and the stone struck the korrog in the head.

The korrog flinched and hissed, then sprang at them, partially extending its wings.

A compulsion washed over Ferran, and he yelled and charged with his spear. Itch joined him, snarling.

Behind him, Ranoc yelled and charged as well.

And suddenly Ferran didn't know what in the world he'd been thinking. This was a creature from the tales. He might as well charge a mountain. He yelled again to shout down the fear.

The korrog opened its wings wide to grab Ferran with its talons. But then the crossbow thwupped, and the bolt struck the creature in the side. It roared in anger, landed on three feet, and swung a wing that struck Winwalom and sent him and the crossbow flying.

Ferran and Itch charged in. The closest target was its wing, and Ferran stabbed it. Itch ran past, snarling, and leapt for the trailing edge of the wing. His bite sank deep.

The korrog growled in pain and snapped at Ferran.

Ferran dodged away and rolled, coming up with his spear ready, but the korrog had followed, and it knocked him in the side with the bony, leading edge of its other wing. It was like getting clobbered with a massive bat, and Ferran went tumbling.

Itch was still hanging onto the other wing with his teeth, his feet off the ground. The korrog shook the wing to dislodge him, then brought it close to bite him off.

And then Ranoc was there. He'd somehow gotten around the creature and now launched himself onto its back and straddled it like he was riding a horse. He raised his knife, stabbed down.

The korrog cried out. Tried to reach back with one of its claws, but Ranoc ducked. It tried to bite him off, couldn't reach him, then simply rolled.

Itch lost his grip and went flying, and then the korrog rolled right over Ranok. When it righted itself, Ranoc was on the ground.

Ferran looked about for his spear, saw it a few yards away, and scrambled for it. He grabbed it and turned to face the beast.

"The king's eyes!" Krov cried, trying to get a stone into his sling and failing. "The king's eyes!" His hands were shaking.

The korrog stepped toward Ferran. Its wicked head was right there, ten feet away. It was massive, feral, with eyes and teeth full of violence.

Ferran could run, but he wouldn't get beyond the reach of those wings. He wouldn't get five steps toward the thicket.

"Aha!" Krov said.

But Ferran knew it was too late. One stone was not going to bring this beast down.

The korrog tried to knock Ferran down with its wing, but Ferran ducked and stabbed up with his spear and felt it pierce into the creature's skin.

The korrog hissed and pulled its wing back.

Ferran lunged forward, stabbed at the beast, and the creature backed up. Ferran shuffled forward as he'd been taught. Stabbed at it again.

And then the creature reached out with one claw and simply ripped the spear from Ferran's hands and tossed it.

It snapped at Ferran. He stumbled back, fumbling for his knife. And he knew he was dead. Those jaws could bite him right in half. It could swallow him whole.

And then Borros attacked from the side, shoving his spear blade into the korrog's flank. It spun to face the new threat. As it did, its wing knocked Ferran clean off off his feet and sent him flying.

He landed painfully in the dirt several yards away. The collision knocked the wind out of him, and he struggled for breath. A few moments later, he finally inhaled.

The korrog snapped at Borros, driving him back. And Ferran knew the thing was too strong. Too powerful. Yes, they'd stabbed it a couple of times, but what were a few pokes to this thing? None of them had been mortal blows.

Borros gave more ground, tried to escape, but the korrog sprang at him and cut off his retreat. It struck at him with a wing. Borros flung himself to the side.

And Ferran could see how this would play out. The creature was simply too large and fast. Once Borros was down, who was going to stand against it? It would simply slaughter them all one by one.

And then Ferran saw its eye, glittering like an amber jewel in the sun.

He grabbed his sling.

32

WOUNDS

The korrog was maybe two dozen yards away. Closer than the post that Lagash had asked them to hit to prove their marksmanship.

Ferran reached into his stone pouch. This would be an easy shot under normal circumstances. If it were merely a stationary post. Without teeth. And wings.

Borros rose to lunge at the korrog, but the beast struck him with its wing and knocked him to the ground.

Ferran slipped the stone into his sling, his hands shaking.

Borros tried to scramble away, but the korrog trapped him on the ground with one claw and held him there.

Now! Ferran thought. Now! He focused on his target. Focused on that gorgeous, terrifying, glittering eye as big as a man's head.

The korrog pulled its head back to regard Borros.

And then Ferran whipped the sling around and flung the stone with all the might and accuracy he could muster.

The stone sped across the distance. It flew straight and true. The korrog must have noticed the small missile, for it turned. And then jerked to dodge the stone, but it didn't jerk far enough, and the stone struck the corner of its eye.

Compared to the size of the beast, the stone was a small thing. Miniscule. But it broke into the eye nevertheless.

The korrog roared and flinched its head back, releasing Borros who immediately scrambled for his spear.

Ferran slipped in another stone, looked for another target. But before he could find one, Borros lunged up and buried his spear's blade deep into the creature's exposed neck, right up to the guards at the base of the blade.

The korrog flinched away. But Borros followed and sank the spear into its chest. Then again.

The korrog floundered back, then twisted and sprang away, unfolding its wings, but it could unfold only one of them fully and so leap awkwardly, flapped, and then crashed into the ground with its one wing akimbo.

It roared and turned to defend itself, twisting its head to watch Borros with its one good eye.

Ferran saw his next target. He slung again, but the korrog saw him and ducked the stone, which hit one of its horns instead. The korrog hissed, and Borros backed up to get well clear of the beast.

Ferran looked for another target.

"Stay in front of it and draw its attention," Borros ordered. "I'm going for the crossbow. Dog Boy, do you hear me?"

Ferran had, but it hadn't registered. "Yes," he shouted. And then he began to flap his arms and jump and shout. The korrog turned its one good eye on him, and Ferran saw that while the korrog was gravely injured, it was not dead. The blood was running from its wounds, but it could still charge, could still rend him with those teeth and claws. A lump of fear rose in his throat, and he stepped back a number of paces.

"Hit it with a stone," Borros ordered. "Move it from the bow."

The crossbow lay dangerously close to one side of the korrog. Ferran slung for that side of the creature. It saw the stone and moved to the side, bringing a wing up to protect itself.

And that's when Borros darted in, grabbed the crossbow and remaining bolts, and dashed back out of the korrog's reach. He spanned the weapon, placed a bolt, and skirted around the creature to find a good shot.

Itch began to bark, and the korrog turned its one good eye to see him. That gave Borros a clear shot to the creature's chest. He aimed the crossbow and pulled the trigger. The bolt buried itself deep, totally disappearing inside.

The korrog roared, spat, then and charged forward a few steps, but Borros backed out of its reach.

The korrog tried flapping its wings, but it was clear that Borros's stabs had injured the pectoral muscles on the one side, and it couldn't flap one wing properly.

Borros spanned and loaded the crossbow again. He took aim and shot another bolt into the creature's chest. It flinched, then sprang into the air and tried to fly, and Ferran thought it might escape, but the wings faltered, and it slammed into the ground in a shuddering heap.

Borros scanned the skies, then turned. "You two, get everyone back to the camp. Tend to their wounds."

"Two?" Was he talking about Ferran and Itch?

And suddenly Ferran noticed Caswal was there with his spear.

"Where have you been?" Ferran asked.

"Following orders," Caswal spat. "Unlike some of us." Then he went to help Ranoc.

Ferran whistled for Itch and then worked with Krov to help Winwalom and Lagash in.

Borros shot the korrog twice more, then came back to help tend the other's wounds.

Lagash was pierced in three spots where the korrog had grabbed him: once in the ribs, twice on the back.

Winwalom had a broken finger and several bruised ribs. He had also cut his head on something when the korrog sent him flying. Blood had soaked into his long horsetail of hair and was all down the side of his head and neck.

Krov had a massive, tender lump on the back of his head. They all thought his brains had been addled, but Ranoc held up various combinations of fingers, and Krov counted them all accurately.

Ranoc, amazingly, had only a sore knee from when the korrog had rolled over him. Ferran was bruised and cut in a few places but otherwise fine. Itch was, well, Itch, whole and sound, happily looking up at him with his patch eye.

Out in the field, the korrog rumbled. They all turned, but it wasn't charging, just clutching at a wound.

Borros made sure Lagash's shoulder was back in place, then he cleaned the wounds with vinegar, which stung, smeared them with oil, and wrapped them with a clean cloth. He gently helped Lagash into a better sling, cleaned the gash on Winwalom's head and wrapped a cloth around it, splinted his finger, and wrapped his ribs. He checked Krov over again, then ordered Caswal to get some water boiling so they could make some threshers tea to help with the pain.

Borros looked at Ferran. "Looks like you've got some bruises to go with your black eye. Anything else?"

"Just a few more tears and holes in my tunic and trousers that I'll have to mend." Then he pointed at Borros's back. "You've got blood seeping through your tunic."

Borros pulled up his tunic to reveal a nasty slice in the skin.

"You're about as patched and scarred as Ferran's pants," Winwalom said.

"Not quite," Borros said, then directed Ferran to clean it, then stitch it shut with linen thread, which Ferran did with trepidation because it was the first time he'd ever stitched a tear in skin.

By this time, the sun was just about to set, casting long shadows from the trees and bathing the rest of the hollow in a golden light. Caswal began some tea, and then there was a commotion out in the meadow.

Ferran turned to see the smallest korrog rise into the sky from the other side of the clump of trees. It flapped several times, glided, then flapped again and swooped up and out of the hollow.

"Should we go out and make sure the other monsters are dead?" Winwalom asked.

"I killed the one by the mouth of the hollow," Borros said. "And this one here, well, it's not worth the risk of getting close. If it doesn't bleed out and die in the night, then I suspect it will hobble away."

"You don't think it's going to be hungry and want to take a bite of us or some cow?" Krov asked.

"It's not going to want anything but to be away from here," Borros said. "Stay clear of it."

That order was fine with Ferran. He glanced at the others, and it was clear that was fine with them as well. None of them wanted to battle that thing again.

"Caswal, Dog Boy," Borros said. "You two come with me and help me round up the horses."

But the horses were nowhere to be seen, not even after climbing the hill. All of them were gone, including Borros's pony.

"They've probably run to Pencoy's," Borros said. "We'll get them back in the morning." And they hiked back down the slope to the camp.

When they returned, Ranoc said, "So what are we going to do?"

"It's getting dark," Borros said. "We're going to make dinner and set up our beds well inside the thicket. And if you have any ancestors with any power, you're going to pray to them to keep away any other korrogs that might be out there."

33

BORROS

They had barley and vegetable porridge again that night, which Borros, Ferran, and Caswal made. Borros added chunks of good hard cheese to it plus some grease cake and a few special spices. Then he roasted nuts with lard and honey, and while they were all sitting there eating the toasted and tasty nuts and licking their fingers, he said, "I didn't see the whole battle. We were still out on the road when I heard the horn blowing. I want to hear the whole thing from the beginning. Leave no detail out."

They told him everything. He stroked his beard and asked questions. They answered him. When they finished, he sat back and said, "You boys showed a lot of courage today."

"Manful courage," Lagash agreed.

Borros said, "It appears Krov the Log Thrower has Dog Boy to thank for his life. As do I. In fact, I think we all do. That was quite the shot. Not a better target on the beast. The distraction of that injury allowed me to get in close. But how you ever hit that target—well, that shows the value of a good slinger."

Ferran shrugged, but deep down he basked in the praise.

"Long Hair, you kept your wits about you. That's good. That shows mettle. Ranoc, I don't know whether to call you Ranoc the Reckless or

Ranoc the Ferocious, you jumping up on its back. Either way, you landed a blow."

Ranoc grinned.

"Caswal," he said and paused.

Ferran couldn't wait to hear this. The coward had left them all to fend for themselves.

Borros said, "I appreciate you wanting to follow orders. I will have more to say about that tomorrow."

What more could he say except that it's stupid to follow orders when they no longer apply.

"Itch played a part," Winwalom said.

Borros looked at Itch. "Indeed he did. Brave dog, I hope you enjoyed the taste of your enemy." And then he gave him a scratch around the head.

He motioned at the boys. "You fought with as much courage as any war band I've seen. What do you say, Master Cook?"

Lagash said, "The boys of Buckle Hill are tough. Brave. Some exceedingly so."

Krov put his huge hand on Ferran's shoulder. "Thanks," he said.

Ferran shrugged. "What else was there to do?"

"There were plenty of things you could have done," Lagash said. "But not many that were more noble."

Ferran rarely received praise from the men around the village. Never in his life had anyone suggested he was anything close to noble.

Borros nodded.

A great sensation of warm gratitude spread throughout Ferran, and he broke out in an uncontrollable, silly grin.

"How did you kill the third creature?" Ranoc asked Borros.

"It wasn't easy," he said.

The boys all waited expectantly.

"I had just kicked my mount to race to Lagash's aid when the beast dropped out of the sky. And here's an interesting thing—I've seen an eagle dive; I've heard them. It's a rush of wind as they plummet. This thing was silent. We didn't hear it until it was almost upon us."

Ferran realized he hadn't heard them much either.

"Silent as an owl," Winwalom agreed.

"Silent and deadly," Borros said. "It was on the archers before they could react. I saw the scuffle and dust flying and feared another was coming for me, so I yanked my reins to the left, then leapt from the saddle, thinking that if I presented two targets, I'd have a better chance. I rolled and came up in a crouch with my spear pointed at the sky, but there wasn't another foul creature to be seen. Then I heard the archer scream as the korrog ripped one of his arms off.

"I turned. Saw that the beast's back was to me. It was focused on the archer who, despite his pain, had pulled his knife and stabbed the thing in the leg. And so I charged. I began to fear it would see me and turn, and I'd miss this chance at a clean shot, and so instead of getting in close, I hurled the spear. The blade sank deep into the creature's back, well below the shoulder blade. I drew my sword.

"The beast spun around, snarled, then sprang at me. The king's eyes, but these things can leap like nothing I've seen. And at that moment I regretted having hurled the spear because that snarling head, half as big as a man, was coming right at me. But I charged, and when it was almost upon me, I dove to the ground below the snapping teeth, rolled, and lunged upward with my sword in a two-handed grip. I shoved for all I was worth.

"The sword punched up and in, and I felt it slide into the thing's guts. Then the beast knocked me. I think with one of its feet. Or it could have been part of the tail. That must have been where I got the gash. The blow slammed me to the dirt and rattled my jaw.

"The korrog landed a few paces away. The hilt and part of the sword were sticking out of its belly, but most of the blade was deep inside. The beast thrashed about, then used its claw to grab the sword hilt. It tried to pull it out.

"I scrambled up, pulled my knife, and realized how ridiculous I was. There was no way I was going to rush into battle against such a foe wielding a knife. But then I spotted the spear. It had come out when the thing had jumped, and was lying on the ground.

"I grabbed it. The beast thrashed again and cried out in pain and anger. Blood was pouring from its wound. And then it shuddered and dropped. But it wasn't dead yet. It was enraged and, therefore, even more dangerous than before.

"I thought about getting in close with the spear and then remembered the archers, and so I ran over to that gruesome sight. Both of the men were dead. But there was a bow and five arrows that hadn't been snapped in half. I walked back.

"The sword was still in the belly of the beast, but the creature, in its effort to yank the blade out, had somehow bent it. It has also widened the wound. I could see it was a mortal blow, but I couldn't leave the thing alive at our backs. And so I put the five arrows into it, and then turned to survey the rest of the battlefield. That's when I saw the four of you, yapping and prancing like ladies' lap dogs around a bull.

Ranoc protested. "Lapdogs?"

Borros grinned. "Okay. Terriers."

Ranoc rolled his eyes, and Borros chuckled.

Lagash said, "You were lucky that thing came after the archers instead of you."

Borros nodded. "I'm telling you, one of my mighty ancestors is watching out for me."

"Except when he's taking a nap," Lagash said.

"How do you know it's a he?" Winwalom asked.

Lagash laughed. "The Mighty She. Oh, that's a good one. He got you there."

"I'm serious," Winwalom said. "Sometimes it's the female ancestors that carry the power."

"Yeah," Borros said. "Take that, Cook, and put it in your porridge."

But Ferran looked at Winwalom and wondered. His mother had come from across the sea, and there had been rumors about her and some of her strange ways. She'd died a few years ago. Had he just let a clue slip about what was going on with him?

"Fine," Lagash said. "Perhaps you do have some ancient aunt looking over you. It would explain your campaign against the Lyrians."

"That wasn't my fault."

"No, auntie dear must have alerted them."

"The Lyrians?" Krov asked.

"Nothing," Borros said.

But then Lagash proceeded to tell them about Borros being ambushed by a petty Lyrian warlord.

"How did you get away?" Caswal asked.

Borros groaned. "Oh, here we go."

"That would have been me," Lagash said. "Saving his sorry carcass yet again."

The boys wanted more, but Borros told them it was time for half of them to retire and the others to be vigilant. And so they made their beds and followed the watch sequence. Krov woke Ferran for his turn in what seemed a kindlier way. Ferran watched the moonlit sky and cattle with Itch for an hour's turning of the stars, then woke Winwalom.

Ferran slept the rest of the night like a log and woke to the sound of Ranoc breaking branches for the cook fire. He went over and helped make the breakfast, which was more porridge and grease cake. When it was time, Lagash told Ranoc to wake the rest of the camp by banging on a pot with a spoon.

They ate, and then Borros ordered them to count the cattle. When they finished that task, Borros put on his cap with the scarlet badge and walked out into the meadow to see if the beast was dead.

34

BLACK ART

The korrog lay about forty feet from where it had been when Ferran had gone to sleep. Borros ordered Ferran and Ranoc to sling a stone at it to see if it was still alive. The stone struck it sharply in the head, but the beast did not move. He ordered them to hit it again. Again, nothing.

Borros approached the beast carefully, then relaxed. "It's dead," he said and walked right up to it and poked it with his spear.

The boys walked out to join him, and although Borros said it was dead, Ferran kept expecting it to wake suddenly. But it didn't. It was dead, surrounded by the blood that had poured out of it. Itch circled and sniffed it. The top of the body rose above Borros's waist. For Ferran, it came up to his chest.

The boys went to the head first and lay down next to it to measure its true size. It was as big around as a barrel and almost exactly as long as Krov was tall. The horns were as long as Ferran's arms and curved. The mouth itself was as long as one of Ferran's legs. They pried the jaws apart, and found it big enough to bite half a man's body off. There were many sharp teeth, the biggest of which were almost six inches long.

They examined the amber eyes which were the size of a large cabbage. They had a circular pupil like those of an eagle, hawk, or falcon. And like those birds, the eyes had a set of outer lids, plus a separate inner, mostly transparent lid that moved sideways from the front of the eye. Ferran saw where his stone had broken the one eye and bloodied it. While he was standing there, Lagash cut into the eye, retrieved the wet, bloody, and glistening stone, and held it out to Ferran. "There's your korrog killer," he said.

Ferran took it. "Technically it just blinded the eye." But it was still his stone. And it was no longer just any old stone. He was going to wash it and keep it. Or maybe he wouldn't wash it. Maybe he'd let the blood dry. Because this was a tale he would tell to his sons and daughters, and when he did, he would point and say, "And that right there is the very stone."

Winwalom drew their attention to the fur, which wasn't like any fur they'd ever seen. Instead of hairs of single strands, these hairs had other smaller hairs coming out in either side all the way to the top like a fine-toothed comb. The fur itself didn't feel like hair, but was as sleek as a feather. And the brindled coloring shone in the light of the early morning sun.

They found part of an arrow shaft in its side. It had broken part of the shaft off, but failed to pluck it out.

"Look at this," Caswal said. He had uncurled one of the three fingers at the joint in the wing that doubled as a front foot. It was as thick as a spade shaft, two hands long, and ended in a sharp, three-inch claw. Caswal and Krov took one wing and began to stretch it out to see its full length. Ranoc climbed up on its back to examine the wounds he gave it, and then got an alarmed look on his face and said, "What's this? Sir?"

Borros leaned over and looked at where he pointed and raised his eyebrows. He climbed up on the creature's back and knelt there to get a better look. "The king's eyes," he cursed.

What he was looking at was a spot on the back of the creature just below the base of the neck that was three hands wide and maybe two tall. It had been shaved. And while some of the weird korrog fur had started to grow back, a clear pattern was visible there. It looked like a mage pattern, but was rough and brutal.

"Boys," Borros said. "Check the body. Look for other spots like this."

JOHN D. BROWN

They scanned the rest of the body that was visible and pulled the wings out to examine them, but didn't find anything.

"Get your spears," Borros said, "and we'll lever it over onto its back."

They did, exposing the chest, belly, and legs. And on the legs, just above the fetlock above each of the talons, they found two more shaved spots. These were smaller, but both contained the same brutal pattern.

Borros stood back and looked at Lagash.

"There's something off about them," Lagash said.

"Wolf mage?" Borros asked.

Lagash's eyebrows went up in surprise, and then he narrowed his eyes and nodded, "Yes."

"A wolf mage?" Ferran said.

Wolf mages were renegades, traitors, treasonous, reckless, and deadly. They were those who practiced the mage arts outside of the authority and blessing of the royal houses. They were said to practice black arts. Wolf mages were named such because they were like ravening wolves, ready to destroy the flock.

"What's one doing here?" Ferran asked.

"We don't know that one is here," Borros said. "We only know his creature is here."

"Or hers," Lagash added.

"Or hers," Borros confirmed.

"Maybe it's Osson," Caswal said.

"No," Borros said. "No mage lord would allow such a thing inside the borders of his or her realm."

"What if this one wasn't from Osson's realm, but ours? Would they pay him?"

"As some sort of mercenary?" Borros asked. "I can't imagine even Osson stooping so low."

"You can't?" Lagash asked.

"All I know," Borros said, "is that these runes are not in the style of the mage house of Akken."

"Or Soros," Lagash added.

Which meant they were from some other kingdom.

"Doesn't a wolf mage need to keep close to his source of earthgrace?" Ranoc asked.

The seeps where earthgrace trickled or oozed out of the seams of rocks were precious. Kingdoms and empires were built on them. However, they weren't constant. Some seeps could exist for years and then suddenly dry up, and woe be the kingdom built on that one. New seeps were rare, but they did appear. The last one Ferran knew of was more than a hundred years ago in Sordis.

"Wolf mages sometimes have a graceseep to provide them power," Borros said. "That's how some wolf mages in the past have arisen. But not all. If some other mage is secretly supplying the wolf mage with earthmeal, then he can roam. This mage could be anywhere. A creature such as this can fly, I assume, a great distance in a night. It could have come from far out west in the deserts of the Nahav. Or even up north. It could be from anywhere."

"What would the runes be for?" Winwalom asked.

"No idea," Borros said. "But I do know this is a new threat. The queen must be informed. She needs to see these runes. We'll get a wagon from Pencoy's, then gut this thing, cut it into parts, and load it all on the wagon."

"If its prey pellet would be enough to open people's purses, this should make us a fortune," Caswal said.

Borros smiled. "You weren't listening. This one is for the queen. But maybe there is a token from the other one each of you can take to remember this battle. But before you divvy that up, we need to take care of the bodies of the archers."

That brought a somber mood back among them.

It was gruesome work gathering up all the pieces of the men and placing them together. Just as they were finishing, a rider appeared on the road from Pencoy's.

35

ESCORT

erran and the others watched him ride up. He was an older gray-haired man, and his eyes went wide in shock and horror at the sight of the creatures and then his two fellow villagers.

"What happened here?" he asked.

Borros told him, then asked, "Where's my escort?"

"That's what I've come to tell you," he said. "There will be no escort."

Borros shook his head in disgust.

"Lord Pencoy sent word that he must keep them at Dob's Port for at least two more weeks. Also, the coast road is closed. Two ships of Osson raiders have been seen in the Skal cove."

"What about the men from the village?" Borros demanded.

The man shook his head. "Two of them lie right there. Their wives and children are now bereft of their protection. The rest of the men, young and old, by Lord Pencoy's orders, must stay just in case he needs to muster them."

Borros sighed heavily but nodded. "These two fought bravely and changed the course of the battle. You must tell their children the tale of how they faced these monsters. We will leave the body of this smaller korrog to their families to cover the loss and remember their great courage."

The man nodded, and Ferran saw a tear in his eye and knew these two must have been dear to him. Borros then asked the villager to tell Pencoy's steward he needed a wagon and mule to take the other beast to the queen. The man nodded, turned his horse, then urged it into a quick trot to carry the terrible news back to the families of these men.

They gutted the larger korrog and cut it into manageable parts. Other villagers came with three wagons. The men's wives were there and wailed at the sight of their husbands. Ferran and the others helped the men load the bodies onto two of the wagons.

And then Borros and Lagash told them the tale of the battle. They did not embellish it. But they did emphasize how bravely the men of Pencoy's village had fought. And then the villagers departed, leaving the third wagon for Borros.

It was noon when they had the beast up on the wagon. Borros had cut away the sections of skin that contained the wolf mage runes on the two korrog, stretching and scraping them, hoping to preserve them from rot so the mages could read them.

When he finished, he asked the boys to gather round. "I'm going to Broniss. The queen needs these cattle. And she needs to see what has entered her realm."

"How are you going to get past the ships?" Ranoc asked.

"I'm not going that way."

"The only other way is west, through Gorland. They'll beat and rob you. They have no love for Akken."

"I'm not going through Gorland either. I'm taking them up the old road. And I'm going to need a crew to do it."

"But the old road goes through the blight," Winwalom pointed out.

"It does," Borros said. "What do the tough lads of Buckle Hill say? Are you with me?"

"Sir," Krov said. "It's forbidden to cross the blight."

"What do you think the queen wants—for you to observe a caution or deliver meat for her soldiers?"

"It's more than a caution," said Ferran.

"And the cattle will be tainted," Ranoc said. "Nobody wants blight-tainted beef."

"They won't be tainted," said Borros.

Ferran couldn't believe what he was hearing. More than anything, he wanted to drive the cattle to Broniss and earn the extra coppers. But he didn't want to walk directly into certain death.

"Boys, look," Borros said. "What was the duration of the condemnation put upon that land?"

"Twelve years," said Winwalom.

"And how long has it been?"

"Ten, almost eleven years," said Caswal.

"So the condemnation is about to expire. It's been ten years. Usually, that's the time it takes for any corruption to run its course. The queen's hunters and mages have been there. The original condemnation has not been extended. I think we're safe."

"Sir," Krov said, "but isn't it safe only when one of the queen's mages proclaims it so?"

Lagash said, "Technically, that's true. But the final years are a cushion."

Caswal said, "But things have been seen in the blight."

"Have they?" asked Borros.

"You don't believe the reports?"

Borros shrugged his massive shoulders.

It was shocking how nonchalant he was about this. This was a *blight*. Wild magic could do anything to them. Kill them. Twist them. Turn them into some horror that was half man and half vegetable. Or it might have already done that to other things, and those things would surely think cattle and boys would make a tasty treat.

Lagash said, "We talked to one who knows about this blight."

"A mage?" Ferran asked.

"One of the queen's grimsmen," said Lagash. "One of Borros's old friends."

A grimsman was one of those that hunted dangerous abominations.

Grimsmen were deadly. Some were mages. Some were simply anointed. Their feats and adventures were a staple that the bards and traveling troupes sang about.

"You know a grimsman?" Ranoc asked Borros.

Lagash said, "He used to be one."

Fear, awe, and shock tumbled through Ferran. All the boys looked at Borros in amazement. Borros had been a real-life grimsman? It was too good to be true.

And then Ferran realized maybe it was indeed too good to be true. He looked doubtfully at Lagash.

Borros waved his hand in dismissal at Lagash. "A few hunts," he said. "Many years ago."

"So," Lagash said, "Borros knows what it means to go into a blight. He knows about wild magic. And we have the report of a current grimsman who said that the blight has been clean for a number of years. It was never the plan to go in. After all, we arranged for an escort, and we were willing to pay a pretty penny for it. But things change."

"You don't think there's still a risk?" asked Krov.

"Of course there's still a risk," said Borros. "But there's a greater risk if we take the coast road. And there's a risk going back. After all, that third korrog is out there. Who knows where it went and if there are others. Everything you do in life is a risk."

"But some risks are bigger than others," said Caswal.

"Could we take the cattle to Lord Pencoy's and wait?" asked Winwalom.

Borros said, "His fighting men are out, and there's no more protection there than there is here. Believe me, I checked. Plus, we'd be closer to the coast and the Osson raiders. More importantly, that would delay supplies for the army and news of the threat to the queen."

"What is so important about getting these cattle to the army now?" Ferran asked.

"The questions!" Borros said and rolled his eyes. "They're worse than an examiner."

"The queen does not make her plans known to us," Lagash said. "But her agent was very clear on the urgency that we meet the date. My guess is she's going to start an offensive. Or she might have news of some attack. Either way, when the queen requests, you do not treat it casually."

Borros said, "We must go. And of the three routes, the old road is the one with the least risk."

Ferran was still having a hard time believing Borros was a grimsman. "Is that what your anointing was for?"

Borros said, "Among other things."

Other things? Like what? It was almost unbelievable that he was a grimsman, yet he did have the anointing, so maybe it was possible. Ferran looked around the group, and they seemed as shocked and dubious as he was. And then Ferran thought of something else.

A man or woman may be anointed, but that anointing simply gave them the ability to channel the earthgrace. To channel the power, they had to partake of the essences the mages prepared—blackmeal, iron-meal, redmeal, and so forth. A grimsman was anointed to wield great power, but without the earthgrace, he was nothing.

Ferran asked, "And do you carry the grace of the earth with you?"

"If I did, I wouldn't be revealing that to the likes of you," Borros said.

Which was true. Such substances were of great value and would be the target of thieves. "I understand," Ferran said, "but it would help us have some confidence."

"That I'm going to protect you?" Borros asked. "I'm hiring you for your slings and spears as well as your legs. If anyone is going to be protecting, it had better be you, Dog Boy."

"Yes sir," Ferran said.

"Now," Borros continued. "You have a choice. You can extend your contract and help me deliver these cattle to the queen, may the ancestors save her, so that she can protect your village and all the others from Osson, or you can return to your mothers and fathers and hope things go well. That's your choice."

Caswal said, "And how much will you pay us?"

"Four coppers per day."

Four coppers was a terrific wage.

"Four and a half," Caswal said. "Just like you promised the men."

"Four and a half," Borros agreed.

Caswal nodded, "I'll go."

"I'm going as well," Ranoc said.

"I'm in," Winwalom said.

Ferran couldn't believe he was about to agree to go into a blight, but he'd become convinced he couldn't go back with less than what was owed. It would mean certain slavery, and it would put his mother and sister at a disadvantage because they'd have one fewer family member to help pay the rent. Ferran would rather face a possible danger in the blight than the certain consequences of not paying the debt and putting them in such straits. "Itch and I are in too."

Borros turned to Krov. "What does the log thrower say?"

Krov blew out a breath. "The blight," he said and shook his head.

"Think of the tales you can tell that girl," Ranoc said.

Krov narrowed his eyes.

"Women love men who are willing to face danger," Lagash added. "It's intoxicating to them. Better even than poetry. Although if you combine the two, she will surely swoon at the sight of you."

"Really?" Krov asked.

"Oh, most assuredly."

He stood a bit straighter, thinking about that. Then he began to nod in agreement. "If that's the case, I'm in."

Lagash grinned.

Borros said, "Well, we know what coin this one falls for." He looked at the boys. "You've made a good choice. Now let's get this herd moving."

"We need to send word back," Ferran said. "Let our families know we've been hired for the full trip."

Borros nodded. "I'll tell Pencoy's people to get the message to them."

"You'll need to pay someone," Lagash said.

Borros nodded. "I'll take care of it. The rest of you get ready to move."

The boys began to break camp. Ferran and Winwalom headed over to pack up their bags. On the way, Ferran said, "You seemed eager. I'm a little alarmed, ex-grimsman or not."

"I'm not eager," said Winwalom. His hair had come loose. He undid the strap of cloth that bound it, then gathered and tied his hair tighter. "I just have to go."

"To that apprenticeship that's not an apprenticeship."

"Oh, it's an apprenticeship," Winwalom said. "You can be sure of that. Just not the kind you're thinking of."

Lords, that sounded ominous. Ferran waited for Winwalom to go on, but he just picked up his browse bag and said, "You realize you'll have enough coin to pay the debt and get new vessels for your mother?"

Ferran did some quick calculations in his head and then had to do them again because they were just too large. But his sums were correct. Not only would he be able to buy the vessels, but also a milk cow. Plus have some left over. It would change their fortunes completely. They would eat and prosper. And Farmer Hellum could go hang.

"Queen be blessed," he said, his excitement rising. "It will buy more than the vessels. This will make it possible to put everything right again."

And that is what he dreamed about as he and the other boys pushed the cattle out onto the road in their bare feet, Itch barking, and headed for the blight.

DEAR READER

I hope you enjoyed the beginning of the tale of Ferran, Winwalom, Borros, and the others.

If you did, please leave a review on Amazon.

Even if it's only a line or two, a hearty huzzah not only helps your fellow readers, it also helps ye doughty author bring you more books.

Turn the page for a sneak peak of The Drovers, Book 2: Outlaws!

SNEAK PEEK OF OUTLAWS

PROLOGUE

The guard pegged the three men as problems as soon as they rode up. The first was a big man with a full beard. The next was bald and skinny. The third had outlined his eyes with kohl. It was a fashion in the south to do that. And the guard supposed there was nothing wrong with it, but what was a Southerner doing way up here?

The tailor's son stood next to the guard. He was one of six that had been assigned to protect the money that was being collected. Everyone wanted to see the body of the korrog and hear the tale of the battle that had taken place just a few days ago on this very field. And they could for a price.

"Would you look at that," the tailor's son said. "A Southerner. They've come a long way. I told you didn't I? They're going to come from all over."

"He didn't come from the South," the guard said.

"But—"

"It's only been a few days," the guard said. "Not enough time for the news to travel that far. Certainly not enough time for anyone there to make the ride."

"They could have come by boat."

"Maybe. But if they did, they'd have to be fools. Who would risk the Osson ships raiding off the coast?"

And if they were seamen, where did they get the horses? And what kind of seaman went touring around the countryside and left his ship unguarded against an attack? No, these weren't seamen. They were trouble.

The three men tied their horses to the split-rail fence post and walked over to the greeter's wagon. The woman there welcomed them and give them a cup of sweet well water from the water barrel and directed them to the food tables. The girls at the tables pulled off the cloths protecting meat pies, cheese, and honey cakes from the flies. There were also roasted nuts there and fresh apricots. The woman at the cook fire next to the table took the lid off the pottage to show how deliciously thick it was.

The men surveyed all that was displayed, and the guard watched them closely to make sure they didn't filch a crumb, for that food had been earning them all a lot of copper. It seemed the thrill of hearing the tale and seeing the beast produced large appetites and loose purses.

And it appeared that was no different with these three, for after a bit of haggling, the man with kohl eyes bought cheese and meat pies and divvied them up with his companions. And then they sauntered over to where a guide was waiting.

Kohl Eyes pointed out into the field behind the guard. "That's the beast right there, is it?"

The guide, an older man who carved fabulous toys, said, "Oh, yes indeed. A beast most fearsome. You can see its wicked teeth, the size of which will astound you. And then there are the talons and claws. The terrible eyes. You will see its very blood on the grass round about."

"How do we know it isn't pig's blood?" the big hairy one asked.

"Oh, no, there were no pigs here. No, you'll see it is quite authentic."

"How much?" Kohl eye asked.

"How much blood?" the woodcarver asked. "Plenty, I can assure you. Why, the ground is black with it."

"No, how much for the tour?"

The woodcarver smiled at his mistake. "Oh dear. How silly of me. I see now. I see. It's one birdseye to see the sight of a lifetime. A monster from legend. But not only that. I will tell you the tale of the battle. I will walk you to the camp where you will see one of the spears that was snapped in the fight. You'll hike up to the hill where you can see one of the arrows that struck the largest beast. You'll see exactly where it fell when the creature ripped it out of its wing. It will be as if you were there with the roaring and trumpeting splitting the sky and the drover and his little band scurrying about and fighting for their lives. And then you will come down from the hill and view the beast up close. Everyone who comes is amazed. And it costs one mere birdseye per person."

Two other guides were here. Both were out with other groups. One was on the hill talking to three families from Woodstrife. The other was leading a man and his three daughters to the beast. And it was true that all who came were amazed. The guard himself was still amazed even after hearing the tale and seeing the sights multiple times.

Kohl Eye bit into his meat pie and chewed. "And this was two days ago?"

"Two days ago, just as the sun was sinking in the west, the first of the creatures appeared. I will show you the very rock upon which it landed and the scratch marks it left there."

"There was more than one beast?"

"Indeed, indeed. There were three. And as your guide, I will tell you about each one of them."

"When did the drover leave?" Kohl Eye asked.

The woodcarver smiled. "Oh, immediately after the battle, good sir. We gave him a wagon and mule. And a good sturdy pony."

"We heard he was traveling north."

"They headed for the coast, to join up with an escort that would lead them safely to Broniss and the Queen."

It was a lie, of course. The drover had not gone to the coast. Two crews of Osson scum had landed and made a camp up one of the inlets along the coast road. Reports claimed they were around a hundred or hundred and fifty strong. That was a nice-sized war band, and the fact that they were there had everyone on edge, for it meant Gallas the Bloody, king of Osson, was truly coming to bring their blessed Corwenna, mage queen of Akken, to heel. He was coming to slaughter her and all who supported her. If the drover went that way, he'd be killed and his cattle stolen.

So he'd taken the road west toward Gorland, which was madness if you asked the guard. The wildmen of Gorland were no friends of Akken. Plus a stretch of that road ran close to the blight. Nobody in their right mind would go that way, but the drover had insisted.

There had been brutal-looking runes on the largest korrog. Marks of a wolf mage. Marks that would give any man the shivers. It was probably some filth cooked up by Osson wizards. News of such black arts had to be taken to the mage queen. And quickly. And so the drover had left to do just that.

He'd asked the villagers to tell everyone he took the coast road. He was worried that brigands might steal the carcass of the korrog he took with him, for the body of such a creature could bring profit just as the one here did. Great profits. He'd also been worried about his cattle. And so the villagers had agreed. Although the guard didn't know how long the secret could be kept.

"How many men were with the drover?" the bald skinny one asked.

The guard narrowed his eyes, becoming wary of their intentions.

"Well, that is the thing," the woodcarver said. "That's part of what makes the events here so miraculous. There were five boys, although one was bigger than most men. Five boys, one dog, a cook, and the head man. You will thrill when you hear about their courage. And you will feel sorrow, for two of our number came to help and met a terrible end. The money we collect here goes to support their families who, as you can imagine, are disconsolate with grief."

"To the coast, you say?" Kohl Eye asked. "But Osson has taken the coast road. And Pencoy's down in Dob's Port, so who was their escort?"

These three were asking a lot of questions about the drover. The guard's suspicions rose.

The woodcarver smiled. "Oh, I don't know those details. Although I did hear Lord Pencoy arranged for the cattle to be pastured by one of the villages between here and Larkin on the coast, so they could be there."

That was another lie.

"Maybe we'll just go talk to them," the big hairy one said. "Hear the story right from the source."

"You may indeed," the woodcarver said. "You may indeed. But I say, why not do both? There's nothing to compare to hearing the story at the very site of the battle. There's nothing like seeing the creature where it fell."

The woodcarver was smooth as butter, but the guard wanted to steer the conversation away from the drover. His little band had no escort but one cattle dog. And if the wrong sort went after them, well, that drover might find himself hard pressed indeed.

Of course, that crew of men and boys had killed two korrogs and driven off a third, so maybe they could take care of themselves. It wasn't any of the guard's business. And it certainly wasn't the business of these three louts. Besides, there were others coming down the road to hear the tale, and he didn't want these three souring their experience.

The guard said, "So do you three want to see the sights and hear the tale, or would you like to move along?"

"Oh, we'll see it," said Kohl Eye and held three birdseyes out to the tailor's son. "We wouldn't miss this for the world."

"You won't regret it," the woodcarver said. "I promise you. Now, come with me to see where they made their camp. They told us they had seen something three times on three different nights in the sky. They thought it merely a fancy. But on the morning before they arrived here, they awoke to find that something had dragged a heifer and two yearlings out of the large paddock next to where they had camped. Right from under their noses.

"Can you imagine? What power must a creature possess to do that? Well, they followed the blood trail and found that not only had it killed the cattle and eaten their choicest parts, but it had also scuffed grass and dirt onto them. You know what that means, of course. You can imagine the shock and horror the little band must have felt upon seeing such a sight, knowing the creature could, at any moment, return to its kills. They immediately broke camp and hurried the cattle here, hoping to find safety."

The woodcarver continued walking and talking. The three men ate their meat pies and followed him out into the field.

The guard turned to the short arrowsmith who'd brought two of his bulldogs for added security. "When those three come off the hill to go view the beast, make sure you meet them there with your dogs. Keep an eye on them. Do not let them pluck even a hair from the beast's body."

The arrowsmith patted one of the bulldog's head. "We'll be happy to keep them honest, we will."

The guard nodded and thought about sending someone to go with the woodcarver. The woodcarver was smooth, but he also liked to talk. And talking sometimes led even the most circumspect to blab about things they shouldn't.

He was about to send someone when then the tailor's son spoke up. "Now, look at that crew!"

The guard looked down the road. There was crowd of at least thirty people walking along the road to come see the spectacle—men, women, children, and a few dogs.

"Did I tell you?" the tailor's son asked.

The guard rolled his eyes. "Are you going to say that for every donkey, dog, and rat?"

"I'm just saying."

This crowd looked friendly, but there were a few young boys among them. Odds were some of them would be tempted to filch some food off the tables. And maybe some of the others would try to sneak in without paying.

The guard looked out at the woodcarver and the three men. They were almost halfway to the campsite. Surely, the woodcarver wouldn't let anything slip. And it didn't matter anyway—with such a crowd, the guard needed all eyes and hands here.

Read THE DROVERS, BOOK TWO: OUTLAWS now.
Available in Kindle Unlimited.

READ MORE BY JOHN D. BROWN

More action-packed stories with characters you want to cheer for.

For epic fantasy lovers
The Drovers Series
The Dark God Series

For those who enjoy thrillers
The Frank Shaw Series

Go to www.johndbrown.com to see all of John's books.

While you're there, join John's newsletter to keep up-to-date on all of his releases and receive exclusive bonus content.

ACKNOWLEDGEMENTS

I want to thank the following individuals. **Lilia Brown** for her early read and priming the creative pump with the idea of a magic system based on goblin farts. For an accurate reports of their beta reads: **Alexandria Wall, Dave Ramey, Eadie Ogilvie, Eric Allen, Gary Ogilvie, Jared Johnson, Justin Wall, Kassandra Brown, Kami Monson, Kristin Westergard, Nellie Brown, Rick Hellewell**, and **Torie Cooper**. The report each of you shared helped me make this tale better. **Leslie Lytle** for the chat that helped convince me to write this series. A big thanks goes to **Dixon Leavitt** for all his help on the cover, **Shawn T. King** for his design of the series logo, and **Spenser Farnes** for an excellent map. And a special nod goes to the movie *The Cowboys*, starring John Wayne, which filled a young boy's mind full of terrific adventure so many years ago.

ABOUT THE AUTHOR

John D. Brown is the bestselling author of the The Drovers series, The Dark God series, and Frank Shaw series. He loves loading his stories with action, adventure, suspense, and characters you want to cheer for. He lives in the hinterlands of Utah where there's lots of fresh air, many good-hearted ranchers, and a red tailed hawk that likes to occasionally dive bomb him on his hikes.

Learn more about John at www.johndbrown.com.

If you liked this book, please take a minute to leave a review. A hearty huzzah will help the author bring you more books.